# *JENNA JEANS!*

"As a consequence," Jenna Jones continued, flushed with excitement at the idea, "there will be a complete shift in the fashion world. Women will wear what they like, not what Seventh Avenue designers tell them is 'in.' Femininity will be back, but most of these girls, who'll be in their late twenties by then, will want to wear something to remind them of the freedom they experienced when they were young. Do you know what that will be?"

"No." Milton was mystified.

"Jeans. Expensive jeans. Designer jeans. They'll wear them with silk blouses, jewelry, high boots or heels. It will be a phenomenon like you've never seen before. And every designer will get in on the act."

"Well, we had World War I and World War II—so now we'll get ready for the Jean War," Milton quipped.

"Yes, get ready," Jenna said, her eyes glittering with anticipation, "because it's coming."

*Also by Diane Masters Watson:*

**MAGAZINE    (Tower 51662)**

We will send you a free catalog on request. Any titles not in your local book store can be purchased by mail. Send the price of the book plus 50¢ shipping charge to Tower Books, P.O. Box 270, Norwalk, Connecticut 06852.

Titles currently in print are available for industrial and sales promotion at reduced rates. Address inquiries to Tower Publications, Inc., Two Park Avenue, New York, New York 10016, Attention: Premium Sales Department.

# THE
# *JENNA LOOK*

**Diane Masters Watson**

TOWER BOOKS  NEW YORK CITY

*For Stephanie*

A TOWER BOOK

Published by

Tower Publications, Inc.
Two Park Avenue
New York, N.Y. 10016

Copyright © 1981 by Diane Masters Watson

All rights reserved
Printed in the United States

## Prologue

The cold March wind engulfed the small solemn group gathered together to pay their last respects to Catherine Markham. "She was so young," Jenna heard someone say. "It's a shame," another voice echoed. Jenna pulled her black coat tighter around her thin frame. She was chilled to the bone. She felt herself shivering again. Jenna looked up from the mahogany box which mesmerized her and stared at Allison. Her husband's arm was wrapped around her, his large black umbrella protecting Allison from the light drizzle. *How loving they look*, Jenna thought. *So warm and cozy*. But the years had taken their toll on them. It was ironic how Catherine's death brought them close together again. Jenna stood alone. Three unsuccessful marriages and numerous lovers had not changed her. Alone, defiant and successful. *Damn Catherine! Why had she killed herself? Why had Catherine pushed her to the limit? At the height of her career, she didn't need to suffer the torment she now felt. But it was her fault, she knew it, and everyone gathered there knew it too.*

The minister finished his sermon and everyone bowed their heads in silent prayer.

"Jenna doesn't look well," Allison commented to her husband.

"I think the strain of the past few days has gotten to her," he replied. "She'll be okay, I'm sure of it."

"I'm not so sure," Allison went on. "She was closer to Catherine than we were. I can't understand it. Catherine was doing so well. She had everything she wanted. Why would she kill herself?" Allison asked.

"I don't know," Michael said. "But I'm sure there's more to it than meets the eye."

"She was under a great deal of pressure these last few months. Something was eating her up alive. She'd never talk about it, and she would go into awful states of depression for days. We knew her for years, but, then again, I don't think we ever knew her at all," Allison said.

"I know what you mean. She was unpredictable even in college. I wish we had taken the time to find out what was wrong."

"I know, I've been thinking the very same thing. The night she died . . ." Allison paused, "she called me." Michael looked at her with surprise.

"I didn't know that."

"I've been tempted to say something to you, but I know what you would have told me—stop thinking I may have been able to save her life or talk her out of killing herself."

"Of course you couldn't. Even if she hadn't done it that night, she would have done it another time. Catherine was doomed from the beginning."

"I wish I didn't feel so damned guilty. I was more concerned about working things out between us—that was more important to me than anything or anyone else. But, I should have gone over to see her. Talked to her. Maybe she would have told me what was wrong."

"Stop tormenting yourself, Allison. It's done, and

maybe Catherine is at peace at last," he said. His large brown eyes looked lovingly at his wife. *How beautiful she still is*, he thought. The years had been kind to her. She had become quite an outstanding woman, so unlike the tall, slim, beautiful girl he met in college. She was straightforward then, compassionate; her warmth attracted him more than her large blue eyes and dark thick hair, her high cheekbones and full mouth. The envy of every girl in her class. He wondered, if he hadn't pressed her into an early marriage, how different their life might have been. She might have become a top model. Lived out her own goals, instead of sacrificing what she wanted so he could finish law school. He realized now that he had forced her into the work relationship with Jenna, and for this he was sorry. For twenty years she helped Jenna build her empire. Three girls, all different, each talented in their own way, meshing together to form *Jenna Jeans*.


Michael tightened his grip on his wife, rubbing his hand up and down Allison's arm to keep her warm. He looked over at Jenna again, with sadness. The cold one. The icy green eyes that could melt you in one straight glance weren't so icy today. They were filled with remorse and sadness. How would Jenna go on without Catherine? No, he didn't know all the facts about Catherine's death and maybe he never would, but he had an inkling and it disgusted him. Jenna, the core and the power, manipulating everyone, especially Catherine.

"I'll never let anyone own me," she had told him, one spring day at school. "I'll never give myself entirely to one man. And children . . . what a bore." She smiled, her thick auburn hair glistening in the warm sun. He was taken with her at first glance, but her charm didn't keep his interest for long. Even her lovemaking was selfish and self-satisfying. She was a taker, never learning how to give anything, but, like Catherine, Jenna could keep secrets. Never, in all the years of their friendship and working relationship, had Jenna ever mentioned her one-night stand with Michael to anyone.

*Oh, Catherine, why did I ask you to leave my office the other night? Why was I so hard on you? I knew you couldn't take it. I knew you had to be treated with care. We were so different, yet we needed each other's strength.* Jenna went over the night of Catherine's death as she had more than a hundred times in the last few days.

Jenna was working late in her office, as she had been for months. The company was consuming her, swallowing her whole. She was fighting bitterly with the competition to stay on top. It was she who created the Jean market and it was she who was going to be the biggest and best. She would not be copied. Not if she could help it.

Catherine walked sheepishly into her office, her fine blonde hair wisped around her ears, making her face look thinner than usual. Her brown eyes looked sunken and swollen; the dark rings around them screamed from lack of sleep.

"What is it now, Catherine?" Jenna asked sharply.

"I . . . I just wanted to talk to you . . . I mean, I didn't want to bother you, but it's important."

"Catherine, I hate it when you beat around the bush. If you want to tell me something, talk."

"I can't just blurt things out the way you do. I mean . . . Jenna, you frighten me when you look at me like that."

"Like what?" Jenna was getting impatient. "And take your hair out from behind your ears. You know I hate it when you look raggedy." Catherine quickly did as she was told. "Now, you were saying . . ."

"I . . . need to talk to you. I need to see you. I haven't been able to sleep since Jon left. I can't just talk to anyone. Jenna, you know how it is. I've tried to . . ."

"Tried to what?"

"Tried to make it in the straight world, like you."

"You've never really tried. You always pick men who are bad for you. I think you do it on purpose so that you can come crawling back to me and make me feel sorry for you. I'm tired of that act. Try something different." Jenna was shouting.

"I did. I really loved Jon. I did, but I couldn't take the humiliation. He wanted me to do things sexually with him that I just didn't like," Catherine went on, turning crimson at the thought of Jon, and having to bare her soul to Jenna.

"Well be strong. You think men haven't asked me to do things against my grain? I just tell them to go to hell. They take me as I am or get out."

"But I couldn't say that. I was afraid he'd leave. I'm not you, Jenna. I'm not as beautiful as you. I can't. . . ," she started to cry.

"Stop it! I won't allow you to cry in my office. Not over a man. You are a self-supporting, successful female, and you don't need a man at all if you don't want one. You're too old to be carrying on like a school girl. Grow up."

"You stop it, Jenna," she shouted. "I won't have you talking to me like that. I can't be you. I know you've tried to make me into your alter ego, but it's impossible. Even you have failed at something. You even failed at trying to be a bit like me. Why else would you have to have Jon? He told me all about your love affair. And don't think I don't remember your trying to take Michael away from Allison. That failed too. With all you have, you're still jealous of the bit of happiness Allison and I might keep from you. I don't know why I still love you. How I can still look at your face," Catherine went on. "I only wanted you in my life. I was content the way things used to be. I didn't mind playing second fiddle to the garment industry and to the self-serving husbands. But I'm getting old. We're drifting apart, and I'm scared," Catherine said, sitting down in the large white chair across from Jenna, sobbing, her face in her hands.

The black and white office was dimly lit now by a black sculptured lamp on top of Jenna's large, glass desk. The chairs sinking into the deep white carpeting, and the large black Chinese furniture had been chosen for their intimidating elegance. "It will keep people from overstaying their welcome," Jenna had said.

Jenna got up from behind the desk. Not knowing what to say, she said nothing. She walked over to the windows and closed the white curtains. She was tempted to walk over to Catherine and console her, take her in her arms, as she had before, and give her the strength she was looking for. But Jenna decided against this. It hadn't worked in the past, and it wouldn't work tonight. It was time Catherine learned how to stand on her own two feet. If Jenna could give her anything, she'd like to give her independence.

"Catherine, why don't you go away for a while. I'm sure we could do without you for a week or two."

"You're sending me away," she stared in disbelief.

"No, I'm not sending you away. I think it would be

best. I think with Jon and being overworked here, you just need some time for yourself. It will be good for you."

"I don't want to go away . . ."

"Then don't," Jenna was exasperated.

"I don't want to leave you. I don't want to leave my friends."

"I said *don't*. It was only a suggestion. I think you'd better go home then and get a good night's sleep. You look god awful."

"Jenna, please come home with me. I don't want to face my empty apartment again. I need you tonight. I promise if you do, I'll stay out of your way . . . please."

"I can't. I have to finish this report . . ."

"Then we'll have dinner together. I can order something sent up," Catherine said moving to the phone.

"I've already eaten."

"Then take a break and have a drink with me."

"I said no! I have to finish this tonight and I don't want to leave here at two in the morning. Now be a big girl and go home. You have to face your apartment sooner or later, and sooner is better."

"I don't want to go. Maybe if I sit here quietly . . . I'll wait until you finish," Catherine went on.

"No. I'm not going to make love to you tonight or any other night, Catherine. We're over and done with. I can't take your whining and crying any longer. You're making me conspicuous, and I don't like it. My competitors would love to get something on me. And you're not what I want them to find out about."

"To hell with your competitors. I don't give a damn what they think. We're talking about human beings here, their lives and their feelings. I don't believe for one moment you can throw me away like I never existed. We've been together now for almost twenty-five years. Jenna, doesn't it mean anything to you?"

"It did, but my love for you died years ago. I kept you around because I felt sorry for you. I didn't want to hurt you. And when you finally moved in with Jon, I was glad . . . no, relieved is a better word. I thought it was finally over. You were happy, and I was happy for you. But more importantly, I was happy for myself. I thought there wouldn't be any more scenes. No more crying sessions and calls in the middle of the night. But you blew that relationship as soon as it looked serious. You're self-destructive. You may destroy yourself, but you won't take me with you." Jenna was vicious.

Catherine rose slowly from the chair, staring at Jenna in disbelief. She couldn't, or wouldn't believe what she was hearing. How could you think you knew someone for so many years and not know them at all? Jenna wasn't anything but a cruel selfish woman. A user. And Catherine was being disposed of, like the men, and the personnel over the years. How dumb she felt, how humiliated, how naive. She'd watched Jenna do this before, never thinking that it might happen to her. But why not? Had she loved her so much that she had transformed her lover into a fantasy woman? Catherine knew at that moment life was over for her. She didn't want to grow old alone. All the plans and all the dreams of the both of them retiring together in Europe had come to an end. She would grow old alone. And Catherine was afraid of old age, afraid of being alone. The wasted years. It was all too much for her to bear.

"I'll ruin you," Catherine shouted, not knowing why she said it. "I'll go to work for one of your competitors, and tell them all about you and all about the winter line.

I'll shout it from the rooftops." Catherine started to laugh.

"Stop it. You're hysterical. If someone else had said that to me, I'd be frightened, but not from you. You're too weak to hurt me. You'd never have the nerve to call anyone," Jenna went on as if to goad her. "I know you all too well." Jenna hoped that maybe even in an act of defiance, in the hopes of ruining Jenna, Catherine would become stronger. It was a fleeting thought. From the expression on Catherine's face, Jenna knew she was defeated. She wouldn't have the nerve to hurt her lover, nor try to ruin her in any way. For a moment Jenna felt remorse for talking to Catherine the way she had, but it was too late, Catherine had fled Jenna's office. Jenna ran to the door and shouted out Catherine's name but Catherine was gone. She'll be all right, Jenna told herself. She'd talk to Catherine in the morning. It would be fine. Catherine would have one bad night, and things would be back to normal in the morning.

Jenna didn't sleep well at all that night. She got up several times, stared at the telephone, wanting to dial Catherine's number to see if she was all right. But then she thought, *That's what Catherine's hoping I'll do. That's exactly what Catherine wants*. How in the world was she ever going to get Catherine to stand on her own two feet? She indeed spoke the truth to Catherine in her office. She couldn't be seen with her any longer. She couldn't afford the gossip. But they could be friends. They could enjoy one another's company. After all, Catherine was the only friend Jenna really had. She had many acquaintances during her years in the industry, but the garment people she knew would slit her throat, steal her secrets and still be able to look her in the eye in the morning. No, Catherine was a real friend—loyal, hardworking and devoted. When Catherine got over Jon, she'd see it Jenna's way. She'd understand. But there was a tiny flaw in their otherwise perfect affair. Catherine held the reins too tightly. Their secret was leaking out.

Jenna went to the office early. Allison was already in.

"Where's Catherine?" Jenna asked.

"I don't know. She hasn't called, and she hasn't been in yet. She called me last night around midnight. She wanted to talk, but I was too busy talking things out with Michael to stay on the phone long. Did she call you?"

"No, she worked late, and went home. She left here around nine," Jenna said, starting to worry. She busied herself with last minute changes in the report and looked at her watch—10:30—no sign of Catherine.

Jenna picked up the phone and dialed the familiar number. No answer. *She must be on her way*, Jenna thought with a sigh of relief, but another half an hour went by and Catherine was still not at her desk. *She's trying to make me worry. She's being dramatic again.* She got up and buzzed her secretary.

"I'm leaving the office for an hour or so. If anyone calls take messages or give the calls to Allison," she said, slipping on her coat and leaving her office through the back door. Jenna hailed a taxi on Broadway. The large garment trucks blocked most of the intersections and her taxi crawled along, unnerving Jenna.

"Can't you take another street?"

"I wish I could, lady, but we're stuck between two intersections. It's always busy here. I wish half you people would move your offices uptown or something. I should know better than to pick up a fare around this area at this time of the day," the driver grumbled.

"Just get to Park Avenue as fast as you can," Jenna told him, panic in her voice. She felt something was wrong, she knew it. If she'd get to the apartment and find Catherine sitting there sulking after taking her away from one of the busiest mornings she'd had in years, she'd fire her on the spot.

The ten minute ride took Jenna almost twenty-five minutes in the traffic. Jenna paid the driver, rushed out of the taxi, and caught the elevator just as the doors were closing. Jenna pushed the button and sighed with disgust. She opened her purse seeking the extra key Catherine had given her, and had it in her hand when the elevator doors opened on the tenth floor. Jenna placed the key in the lock, opened the door quickly and shouted Catherine's name. No answer. Maybe she did take her advice after all and decided at the last minute to take a trip. Jenna walked through the large spacious living room, tripping over the grey cat buried in the thick grey carpeting. He screeched and ran across the room. Jenna continued to shout Catherine's name, until she noticed the door to her bedroom was closed. She knocked and then turned the doorknob, letting herself in.

Catherine was asleep under the covers. Jenna, relieved, thought about letting her sleep. She needed it, but decided that since she'd come across town they might as well talk and have a cup of coffee together.

Jenna walked over to the bed, sat down and shook Catherine gently. The fear returned, the cold still body didn't move. Jenna was petrified, motionless, rooted to her small spot on the bed. Catherine wasn't sleeping, she was dead! Jenna's eyes scanned the room, noticing the empty bottle of sleeping pills and glass of water that stood on top of Catherine's night stand.

Jenna forced herself to stand up and walk over to the phone. She dialed the police.


Everyone started walking to their cars after the service. Allison and Michael walked over to Jenna, Allison embracing her gently. "Are you ready to go?"

"No, I'd like to stay here for a while alone," Jenna said. "I'll be along shortly."

# 1

September was warmer than usual. Memories of the hot summer months lingered in Allison McWilliams' mind as she entered the dormitory of Carnegie Tech. She had looked forward to this day during her whole senior year of high school—the beginning of a new life without rules and regulations. Living away from home for the first time in her life meant freedom. The perky brunette made her way through the crowds of young girls saying good-bye to their parents, brothers, sisters and other members of their families; Allison, being smarter, had said her good-byes that morning before boarding the train. Her trunks and memorabilia were sent on ahead days earlier. Room 2211. She eagerly looked for the number on the door of each room. Her heart sunk when she opened the door and, much to her dismay, saw a dingy small room, curtainless, two beds, two dressers and two plain desks. The walls were empty. She had hoped that in a school where artists and creative people made their lives the dorm rooms would be filled with untold stories and a character all their own.

"Dreadful, isn't it?" a soft voice commented from behind the closet door.

"You're right. It isn't at all what I had expected," Allison replied.

"My name is Catherine Markham. I guess we're going to be sharing the cell this year."

"I'm Allison McWilliams, and maybe this isn't so bad. You know, if we can decorate a bit, it might be livable."

"Sure, we could always make our way downtown, it isn't so far, and buy a few things. Curtains, maybe matching bedspreads, posters or something for the walls," Catherine started. "I'm going to be an interior designer and this is my first project."

"Well, if you can turn this room into a cozy, homey place, you'll be a great success."

"Ah, a challenge! You with me?" Catherine asked. "I don't know about you, but I can't create anything without feeling my surroundings are comfortable. And, besides, I know just how to do it without spending too much money."

"Oh, I don't care what it costs. I'll send the bills home to my father. Just let's get this show on the road. How long have you been here, Catherine?"

"Since yesterday. I took an early bus. I was kind of anxious to get here and get started."

"I know what you mean," Allison responded.

"But I thought better about doing something with the room until I met my roommate. Who knows? I could have gotten some nut who likes simplicity and stark surroundings."

"Well, that isn't me," Allison laughed. "Come on. Let's get going before the stores close. I couldn't sleep a wink in this room tonight the way it is. Lead the way," Allison said, as she followed the slim blonde out the door.

Catherine told Allison a little about her background.

She was from a small upstate New York town, had two sisters, older than herself, and was raised by her mother after her father left when she was an infant. They struggled to make ends meet, and Catherine was at Carnegie Tech because of a scholarship which met her school expenses; she would work for the other necessary expenses.

Allison didn't have that problem. Her father had always earned enough money for the family to live comfortably, and he would continue to do so until Allison and her brother were out of college.

The two girls rushed through the busy streets, running into one store after another, buying printed curtains, bedspreads, throw pillows, odd lithographs for the walls, and a few plants for an added touch.

By the time they returned to the dormitory, they had answered all of one another's questions, and were loaded down with bags and ideas.

Allison's trunks were in the room awaiting her, but she decided to leave the unpacking until another time. It was *operation home* first.

"Have you met any of the other girls in the dorm yet?" Allison asked, taking a five-minute break.

"A few. They seem nice enough, but I was never a social butterfly. I kind of like to keep to myself. I don't know, I feel a little uneasy here, being poor and all. I'm not in the other girls' league."

"That's silly. We're all here for the same reason—to enhance our capabilities, ready ourselves for the dark cruel world and learn how to earn a living. I mean, it doesn't matter what your father did or your grandfather for that matter. It all has to do with how you are as a person," Allison told her.

"I wish I could feel that way, but I don't. But I liked

you the minute you walked through the door. I knew you wouldn't look down on me, or anything. I guess all I want is to do a good job here and keep my scholarship."

"Me, I'm different. All I ever wanted to do was model and get married," Allison told her. "But my father is much too practical. He feels a woman should have a skill, be independent, never rely on a man to make her daily bread. He felt if I went right to New York City, I'd fall into the clutches of some sex maniac who would make me a hooker, not a model. Besides, what would I do when my looks faded, he'd ask me. So I'm here to find myself a husband, my second life's ambition."

"You're crazy. You don't go shopping for a husband the way we went shopping for the curtains."

"You think not? I'll show you," Allison laughed. "I'm not cut out to work day in and day out just to have my own apartment and my own life. I'd rather someone else supported me."

"Like your father did this afternoon when you were writing out checks like money was water," Catherine said.

"That's it. But who knows? I may change my mind. I have a few years to think things through. That is if nothing better comes along," Allison said, getting up from the chair, her eyes scanning the room with approval. "Now this is more like it." The brown and blue print they had chosen worked well, giving the room a warmth neither of them expected.

"It hardly looks like the same place," Catherine said with pride.

"Hardly. I like it. What time is it anyway?"

"Oh my God! It's nearly midnight. We've got to get

up early for orientation, and I haven't even finished unpacking."

"I haven't started." Allison's radiant smile flashed toward Catherine, making her a little envious of the girl's knowledgeable attitude. Catherine always wanted to be more like an Allison and hoped their year together would rub off on her.

The bedroom door opened and a whisper shot across the room.

"Hey, Catherine. She's coming tomorrow."

"Who?" Allison asked.

"The girl with the private room across from ours," Catherine asnwered.

"Well, who is she?"

"Jenna Jones," the young pudgy girl responded. Her hair was in pincurls, a pink net holding them together.

"Jenna Jones . . . Oh, you mean the heiress who was kidnapped by her father when she was a little girl? That's who will be living across the way?"

"You got it," the girl said. "I'm Rita, two doors down."

"Allison. I arrived this afternoon. Are you sure she'll be coming to Carnegie?"

"Very sure. The staff is beside themselves in preparation. You'd think she was the queen of Sheba or something. But I have to admit, I'm looking forward to meeting her myself. I wonder if she's a regular person like the rest of us."

"I'm sure she is. If we don't all make fools of ourselves and make too big a deal about her," Allison said. "Why don't we all play it down and let the girl alone? Give her a chance to make friends."

"I think Allison's right," Catherine said. "I think we should all leave her alone and let her find her way around first before we all barge into her room trying to become her best friend."

"Are you implying I'm pushy?" Rita said.

"No. But a little over-anxious. After all, Jenna might be just as frightened about meeting us as we are excited about meeting her. Let's remember she's a person, first and a celebrity, second."

"Well, I'll stay out of her room as long as the both of you do," Rita said, closing the door behind her.

Allison started laughing. "I can't believe it. The poor girl's been tortured her whole life, and she can't even come to school without everyone making a big deal about it. Well, I, for one, am not going to get pushy . . . although confidentially, I'd love to see what she looks like in person. I've seen photographs of her, and she's beautiful. I used to spend hours in front of my mirror trying to imitate her sultry look when I did a little modeling. She's been dressed by the best designers in the world all her life. I wonder if we wear the same size? She must have a great wardrobe," Allison rambled.

"Allison!" Catherine exclaimed.

"I'm only kidding," Allison smiled. "Well . . . half kidding."

"You're impossible. I don't know about you, but I'm going to bed. Some of us have to work tomorrow," Catherine said.

"Me, for the next few weeks, I'm going to soak in the atmosphere, and do a little searching for my prince charming."

"You're impossible. A one-track mind."

"Maybe yes, maybe no. But I'm going to have fun looking and trying out a few. You're only young once. And I want to experience everything."

"I bet you will. But do me a favor. Don't flunk out of

school. I might not get another roommate who likes this color scheme," Catherine smiled.

"See, I've only been with you one day, and you're already making jokes. There's hope for you yet, Catherine Markham," Allison said, falling asleep as soon as her head hit the pillow.

The two girls got up early, had breakfast, and followed the tour around Carnegie. They met their teachers, classmates, and did a little shuffling around of schedules to be in the same classes. By lunch time, they were already making plans and deciding on projects for each class. Catherine had never dreamed that, beneath Allison's *blasé* exterior was a very talented artist and organizer. She would get through all her classes without any trouble. Catherine wondered if Allison was putting on an act yesterday in order to make her feel less insecure and more like one of the girls. Allison was a more complex individual than she had expected, a girl with warmth and understanding far beyond her years.

As they walked around together soaking up the local color, all eyes were on Allison. Every man would look up, smile, wink, or try to get her attention, but Allison ignored them all, keeping up her conversation with Catherine and Rita.

Catherine took another look at herself in the long mirror in their room. She wished that she could do something with her fine wispy hair and thought how different clothes might enhance her painfully thin body. Maybe some make-up would bring out her blonde, fine eyelashes and eyebrows. It was as if she were an albino—no features to distinguish her face. The drab colors of her skirts and sweaters melted in with her complexion. Catherine felt like a mess and was tempted to ask Allison to help her, but to what purpose? She had neither the money nor the resources to buy anything new. She promised herself that she wouldn't care what anyone thought. She had come to Carnegie to get an education, to better herself, and to leave home, never to return. But wasn't her appearance part of her new education?

The doorway across the hall was stacked with trunks and suitcases when Catherine and Allison returned to their room after dinner. Jenna's door was an open invitation to curious eyes. Even Catherine sneaked a peek. Her eyes met the icy cold ones of Jenna. Yes, she was beautiful, tall, with thick auburn hair, but those piercing green eyes daunted Catherine. Catherine wasn't too sure she wanted to meet Miss Jones. Or had she been too hasty? Had Jenna felt an invasion of privacy as she and her maid were busy unpacking? Catherine gave her a quick smile and ran into her own room.

"God, she scares me," Catherine said.

"Why?"

"I don't know. I just think she's going to be trouble. I don't care if I ever meet her."

"Stop it, Catherine. I told you last night, she's just like the rest of us. Right now *she* feels like the outcast. We've all been here and made our friends, and she now has to make her place in the school. After a few days, I'm sure you'll change your mind."

"I don't think so," Catherine said, taking another long look at herself in the mirror, then closing the closet door.

As if Allison could read her mind, she quickly

brought out a red and blue scarf and placed it around Catherine's neck. "I think a little color would help, don't you?"

"Yes, it's very pretty, but I don't want to borrow it. I'm afraid something might happen to it."

"Then it's yours," Allison said. "That way if you lose it, you don't have to worry."

"Oh, that's very nice, but I don't think I can take it."

"Sure you can. And I'll take one of yours in exchange," Allison walked over to Catherine's closet, took the drabbest scarf Catherine had and placed it around her neck. "See? We're even," Allison said quickly before Catherine had a chance to say anything.

"Now, what I think we should do is go have a little fun tonight. We'll change our clothes and go dancing. I've heard there's a great place that all the college kids go to downtown, Charley's. What do you say?"

"I don't know, I don't think I want to go out. I want to get everything ready for class."

"Catherine, we have a few days before serious class work starts, so why not have some fun. It might be our last time for a while. This place is going to be a lot more difficult than I thought."

"I wouldn't worry if I were you. I saw some of your sketches and you are good."

"Fair, I'll never be great. What do you say?"

"Just this once. I'm on a tight budget, remember."

"Don't worry, I don't believe in Dutch treat. I'm sure we can get some *fellas* to buy us girls a few drinks."

"I'm sure you could, but what about me?"

"Your problem is in the fixing. A change in the hair style, a little make-up and you can be very striking. Your problem is that you lack self-confidence. Some of the ugliest girls I went to school with went out with some of the best-looking guys. You know why?"

"They gave them what they wanted?"

"No, there you go again. They acted as if they were beautiful and that's exactly what they projected. Sure, some women were born with physical beauty, but others have to make the best of what they have. And you have loads of great features. We're going to bring them out. And most of all, your attitude has to change. People reflect what they think they are, and the rest of the world follows in their thinking. Sex appeal, that's what you're lacking."

"And I'll continue to lack it. I'd like to be pretty but I refuse to be sexy. No, never," Catherine said.

"What's wrong with being sexy?"

"Everything. I'm not that way and I don't want to project it. Please, I think I'd rather stay home."

"Okay, okay, we'll work on the bone structure and forget about the sex appeal," Allison begged off, wondering what nerve she had just struck but deciding to drop the subject.

The door across the hall kept opening and closing. Allison could hear voices but couldn't make out what was being said. Her thoughts were on her young frightened roommate . . . and the mysterious girl across the hall.


Jenna Jones continued to yell at her maid. "I told you not to pack these clothes. They're too sophisticated for school. I want to blend in with everyone else. Why don't you ever listen to me when I speak to you."

"Sorry, madam, but I thought that these dresses were so beautiful you'd want them."

"No. It took me all summer to talk grandmother into

letting me go to college, something every young girl does at my age, and I don't want to make the wrong impression. I want to start fresh here. Now, please, telephone the house and have my other trunk sent down to me right away. I think I can get away with some of these things for a few days. It's very important to me,'' Jenna screamed again, rushing the maid right out of her room.

She sat down on her bed and looked at the piles of clothing her grandmother had sent. *All wrong,* she thought. *I want to be the rule rather than the exception for a change. I want to lead a normal existence. I'm not vacationing in Newport or on the Riviera. Oh, grandmother, I know you meant well, but please leave me alone this once. I know what I'm doing. I know the kind of life I want to lead. And you've interfered enough. I want to make it on my own.*

Jenna walked over to the large windows which overlooked the campus below. She envied the groups of girls she saw walking and talking together in little cliques as if they didn't have a care in the world. Would she ever be a part of their group, would they accept her and want to take her into their confidence? She had so few friends growing up, and the ones she did have were very much like her—lonely, bored and overindulged. The upper class seemed to be untouched by the problems of everyday life, held sacred and protected from the working class as if it were diseased. It took every bit of her energy and charm to get her grandmother to agree to send her away to school where there would be a mix. Here, she would be able to express her artistic talents and concentrate on designing. She had been taught the right way to talk, walk, set the table, make conversation, wear the right clothes, how to conduct herself in mixed company, but never had she been allowed to express her feelings. She was told it was unhealthy, and, each time she did, she was accused of being like her father—the man her mother had the *misfortune* of falling in love and running away with. Their marriage was quickly annulled but not quickly enough to annul Jenna. She spent one brief week with her father, and that was all. He was becoming a blur in her memory. It bothered Jenna sometimes at night that she couldn't see her father's face when she closed her eyes. She'd have to outline it feature by feature, and each night it was becoming harder. At twenty-one she'd be free and would feel no sorrow if she were never to see her Grandmother Jones again. She would never forgive her for taking her father away and sending her mother to an early grave. She knew now that her mother stopped living the day the marriage was annulled. If it was possible to wish yourself dead, her mother did just that. But Jenna had to make sure she'd rid herself of any of her mother's weaknesses. No man would ever possess her entirely, and she'd guard her emotions with the utmost care. Jenna was free at last. Ready for the next stage of her life, her real learning process, she would become a sponge, watching, listening, reserving judgment, taking in what she needed and discarding the things she didn't. Emma, her maid, returned with the news that her trunk was already on its way and would be in her room by eight in the morning.

Allison finished making up Catherine. For the first time in her life she was thrilled with the reflection in the mirror. Allison had not marred the original. Her makeup techniques were thorough but minimal, enhancing the large brown eyes and high cheekbones. Catherine knew she'd never be a knockout, but she was pleased at what changes had taken place.

"Now, if you take off that beige sweater and put on a red one, you'll look fine," Allison told her.

"You're really enjoying doing me over, aren't you?"

"Yes, I like seeing people at their best. It's been a hobby of mine since I was a little girl. All my friends used to sit in my bedroom and do one another up. We'd exchange clothing and make-up. It was fun. And it doesn't take a lot of money. It's all in the planning."

"Plus knowing what will look best on yourself. I guess I never cared much about clothes when I was growing up. I think I didn't want anyone to really notice me."

"Anyone or boys?" Allison asked.

"Both, I guess," Catherine confided. "I was too busy drawing to think about anything else. I didn't care much for boys and their silly games."

"Too bad. I think you missed out on a lot. I guess all of us missed out on something, but we have a great deal of time to make up for it. How about starting now?"

"No time like the present," Catherine said, "but I don't want you to expect too much. I know myself. I won't be able to change overnight. And to tell you the truth, I don't know how much I am willing to change. But I do know that I want something different."

"Let's go," Allison said. "Maybe we can catch another look at Miss Jones across the hall."

"No thanks, she looks carnivorous."

"I bet she's not. Frightened people do a lot of strange things."

"How do you know so much?" Catherine asked as they left the room.

"I don't know, but I like people and I've studied them

enough to know there's more to some people than meets the eye. And if there's not, to hell with them. Besides, I'm too excited and happy tonight to let anyone bother me. We're on our first adventure."

"Second," Catherine corrected her. "Our first adventure was fighting the crowds downtown, yesterday," she laughed.

"You look so much more alive and so much prettier when you smile. I wish you would more often. You don't have the whole world on your shoulders just yet," Allison told her, putting her arm through Catherine's as they rushed to catch the bus.

Jenna changed into her burgundy satin robe and propped herself up in the large velvet chair by the window. She listened to the giggling voices of the girls as they ran from one room to another. Yet she sat alone on her first night away at school with no one and nothing to do. She tried picking up a book but couldn't get past the first paragraph. She was bored already. How fast did she think things would change? After all, she hadn't even had the chance to meet anyone, except for the fair-haired girl across the hall whom she was sure she had scared away. Jenna made a mental note to knock on the door in the morning and apologize. She didn't want to get off on the wrong foot. But if she was anxious for some company, why not knock on the door right now. They were sure to let her in. Jenna confidently unlocked the door to her room, walked across the hallway, and knocked on the door. She tried again but no one answered. They must be in someone else's room. *I'll have to give it a try again in the morning*, she thought, disappointed. *I'll have to try and get to bed early and sleep. At least time will go faster that way.* Jenna tossed and turned for nearly an hour but the sounds of laughter kept her awake. She got up and tried her book again but to no avail. She decided to put on a pair of slacks and a sweater and take a walk. Maybe the fresh air would tire her out enough to sleep. She ran a comb through the thick shoulder-length hair, put on a dab of lipstick, and she was ready. For what, she wasn't quite sure, but anything had to be better than sitting alone in her room at ten o'clock at night.


"Hi there, beautiful. Can I buy you a drink?" Allison heard from across the crowded bar, spotting the good-looking face that went with the deep voice.

"I don't think so," Allison said coyly.

"A girl turning down a free drink. Unheard of."

"Oh,, I didn't say that eventually you couldn't buy me a drink. I just wanted a more original delivery."

"Oh okay then. Let me see. . . ," the young man smiled. "Can I buy a drink for the lady with the warm smile and twinkling eyes," he said.

"You're getting better. At least you've directed your delivery a little closer to me instead of every other female in the place."

"No, there isn't any other female like you in this place. My name is Michael Fenway, and you are?"

"Allison McWilliams, and this is my roommate, Catherine Markham."

"Is your roommate interested in meeting my roommate? We'll make it a foursome."

"Fine," Allison said too quickly without consulting Catherine. Michael walked away to get his friend.

"I don't know if I want to meet his friend. I'll be

happy to leave the two of you alone if you'd like."

"Don't be silly. It isn't like you're going on a date. We're just four people having a drink. Stop being a party pooper. Relax and enjoy the scenery."

"But what if I don't like the guy?"

"Then we'll excuse ourselves and go home. No commitments, no problems. But don't you think Michael is very good-looking?"

"Yes, he seems very nice."

"Yes, I think I'd like to pursue this a bit further, but we'll see," Allison said, cutting the conversation short as Michael and his friend drew closer to their table.

"Catherine, Don—Don, Catherine, and this is Allison, but she's for me. I saw her first," Michael said, moving his chair closer to Allison's. Don and Catherine smiled awkwardly at one another.

"What are you drinking?"

"I'm having a whiskey sour and Catherine . . ."

"Nothing for me. I'm still sipping the drink I ordered."

"Freshmen?" Michael asked.

"How can you tell? Do I look as if I'm new around here?"

"No, you look exactly as if you've been here all your life, but I've never seen you here before, so you must be new."

"Do you pride yourself on knowing all the new girls, or just all the girls."

"I'm not what you'd call a womanizer, but I do have an eye for the ladies, and lady, I know I haven't seen you before."

Allison looked over at Catherine who was trying desperately to make conversation with Don—a short, pudgy boy who seemed harmless enough. But even from across the table, Allison could feel Catherine's uneasiness which acted as a damper on some of Allison's fun.

"What is Don like?" Allison asked, changing the subject.

"Why, are you attracted to him?"

"No, for my friend. I mean she's a little shy. I wouldn't want the guy to pounce on her."

"He won't. He's shy himself, but let's not worry about them. I want to concentrate on us. What are you doing Saturday night?"

"You certainly work fast."

"Why not. I see what I like and that's that. Why beat around the bush. I'd like to take you out for a night on the town. Any objections?"

"No, you seem harmless enough," Allison said. "And since I am new around here, I'm eager to see the sights. Where do you go to school?"

"University of Pittsburgh. I'm working at becoming a lawyer. I don't know if I'll make it, but I'm giving it one hell of a try. You?"

"Freshman at Carnegie. Art student. I might change, I don't know yet."

"Let's dance," Michael said, not waiting for an answer, taking her hand and leading her to the small crowded dance floor. The rustic old bar enchanted Allison. The checkered tablecloths and worn-out dance floor only added to the character of the place. She wondered how many relationships started and ended in this college hangout.

Michael moved Allison toward the center of the floor, holding her firmly against him. Allison liked the feel of his tall lanky frame and loved the scent of him. She couldn't even hear the music above the roar of the laughing crowd but she didn't care. Michael was leading and she was following his movements. They remained there for almost three numbers, laughing and enjoying one another. When they finally returned to the table, Don was sitting there alone. Catherine had excused herself and had gone back to the dorm.

"I'd better go on after her," Allison said quickly. "She isn't familiar with this place any better than I am."

"I'll take you home," Michael said quickly, placing money on the table for the drinks, and following Allison out the door. "Hey, wait a minute. I have a car, and I'm told these days it's much faster than the bus. If we rush, we'll be home before Catherine."

"I was hoping I'd catch her at the bus stop, but I don't see her."

"Are you her mother confessor?"

"No, but I forced her into coming out tonight. I guess it's foolish but I feel responsible."

"I have a suggestion. This Saturday night we'll leave Catherine home."

"I hadn't planned on taking her," Allison smiled. "Besides, I haven't even said yes to going out with you."

"But you will."

"But I will," Allison smiled as Michael opened the door to his old Chevy convertible. "I'm used to better."

"I'm sure you are, but with me, this is all you'll get," Michael came back quickly.

Allison liked him. She'd met her match. Michael wasn't any ordinary man. She wouldn't get her way at all times with him, and she admired that. She was also feeling angry at Catherine. The girl could have at least waited until she got back to the table before she left. She had cut the evening short, and Allison didn't like that at all.

Michael drove the four miles to Carnegie in ten minutes. Allison jumped out of the car and told him to wait. She wanted to see if Catherine was in the room safe and sound. She wasn't.

"Why don't we wait here out front for her. There isn't any way she can walk past us without us seeing her," Michael said.

"You're right. I wonder where she is?"

"Will you stop worrying. She's a big girl. I'm sure she just went for a walk or something."

"I'm sure you're right," Allison said. "Now tell me a little about you. It seems half the night we've been talking about Catherine."

"Me. There's not much to tell. I'm from a long line of lawyers. My great-grandfather, grandfather, father and now me. I don't think I ever considered being anything else."

"Why not shock them and become something else?"

"Never thought about it. I guess it's because I know nothing else. Besides, I like school. I really enjoy what I'm doing."

"Well, that's all that counts. Enjoying what you do. I wish I was as sure of myself. I dabble in art. I'm good, but not great. I'll never be great. I think I'm passing time."

"Wasn't there anything you fantasized about? Something you really wanted to do with your life."

"Sure. I wanted to be a model. I always thought it was an easy way to make a lot of money until I tried it last summer. I worked nearly twelve hours a day. Someone was pulling at my hair, someone else was tearing my face apart, applying mountains of make-up. I stood in the same position for what seemed like hours. My feet hurt and my back ached. It's not what it's cracked up to be. And the rejection. God, that's something else. You think you're right for the ad, and the agency thinks you're all wrong. The people don't even say no in a nice way. Sometimes they just scream that I'm all wrong, and how could she have sent me to them? It doesn't do great things for my ego. But to tell you the truth, I'd do it again if I had the chance. Maybe when I'm finished with school. My modeling agency said they'd take me back."

"I don't see how anyone could tell you that you weren't right. And why anyone would want to cover your beautiful face with make-up . . . how about the photographers? Did they make passes at you?"

"No, not the way you think. To them I was a living prop. A dress sitting on a body instead of a wooden hanger. I was there to show off the product, not my body," Allison smiled.

"What's so funny?"

"You know who made passes? The manufacturers. They are the dirty old men, and ugly. Usually about five feet four with pot bellies and bald, they thought they were God's gift to women. If you didn't screw them, you didn't get the job."

"Did you?"

"No, but I won't say I didn't give them a hint of a promise, just to get them off my back. But usually that happened when I was working runways."

"So, are you trying to tell me, Miss McWilliams, that you're a tease?"

"Only if you're old, bald, and fat. You don't have that problem," she smiled.

"How do you know. In thirty years I may be."

"Not if I have anything to do with it," Allison slipped.

"Are you planning a future for us in that pretty little

head of yours?"

"No, I'm telling you that I don't like men who let themselves go. Take that as you will," Allison said, placing her hand on the door handle, getting ready to leave.

"What time should I pick you up Saturday."

'It's up to you and what you have planned for us."

"How about ten?"

"At night?"

"In the morning. We'll make a day of it," Michael said. "After that, I'll let you know if we can plan a future together."

Allison smiled to herself. He was a man who knew what he wanted, and she was certainly attracted to him. But she wondered why he hadn't even made a move to kiss her. Maybe he was waiting for her to make the first move.

"Well goodnight, I'll pick you up Saturday, right here. That okay with you?"

"Fine, goodnight," Allison said, letting herself out of the car and waiting for him to drive away. She hadn't seen Catherine come home but she didn't care.

The room was still empty when she got upstairs. Allison was getting ready for bed when she heard her name being paged for the phone. Her heart pounded a mile a minute as she rushed to the house phone. Maybe it was Catherine in trouble. When she reached the phone breathless, Michael was on the other end.

"Thought I'd say goodnight one last time." And then he hung up.

Catherine came in right before the midnight curfew.

"Where the hell have you been? I've been worried half out of my mind."

"I'm sorry. I was having such a good time. I forgot

about the time. I took the bus here and started walking around the campus, trying to think of something to say to you about the way I acted tonight . . . you know, running out on you the way I did, and then I saw Jenna sitting by herself under the large elm tree. She remembered seeing me in the hall this afternoon and called after me. She wanted to apologize for her behavior. It seemed all the wrong trunks were sent, and she didn't have anything to wear. So we sat and talked for hours. She's really very nice,'' Catherine rambled on nervously.

"I'm glad. You'll have to introduce her to me when you get a chance."

"Oh I will. We're sitting together at breakfast in the morning. I know you'll like her."

"What did the two of you talk about for nearly two hours?"

"I don't know . . . everything and nothing. Mostly her trips to Europe. She's been everywhere. I felt so dumb. I've never left New York, except for coming here. Jenna seems so much older than the rest of us. But what's so great, Allison, is that she wants to fit in. You were right about her. She's frightened that the girls won't like her and she really would like to lead a normal life for a change. You know her name's been in the papers for years. Jenna was even married to a prince once. It's remarkable how much she's done."

Allison was half listening and half jealous of the hold Jenna seemed to have on Catherine. It was as if Jenna was pushing her out of the picture, but that could be convenient. Let Jenna play mother hen for a while. Allison was more interested in spending her free time with Michael. That is if everything went well with them on Saturday.

"Oh, I've been rambling on so much about Jenna . . . what happened with that guy you met?"

"He drove me home as soon as we found you had gone, and we sat in front of the building for almost an hour waiting for you. We're seeing each other again Saturday."

"Do you like him? Is he your prince charming?"

"I like him, but I'm not so sure yet. I'll let you know when I am. I'm feeling very tired now. I have to turn out the light and go to sleep."


Allison had every intention of hating Jenna the next day when they met, but when Jenna extended her hand toward Allison in friendship, looking at her straight in the eye, everything Allison felt melted away. They quickly said their hello's and sat down to their meal. Allison was sure Jenna could manipulate anyone into doing exactly what she wanted. The two gabbed away during mealtime as if they were long lost friends, leaving Catherine to sit and listen. She felt no jealousy, only gratitude that her first two friends also had become friends. Some of the other girls passed by quickly, taking a quick glance, while others offered their hands in friendship. Jenna flashed her staged smile at all of them but fixed her attention on Allison all morning. The two had some of the same classes and continued their conversation during lunch and breaks. Allison watched Jenna eat her way through the morning and afternoon with more enthusiasm than anyone she'd ever met. She ate mountains of food and probably would never gain an ounce unlike Allison who had to diet constantly in order to stay slim.

Allison looked through Jenna's sketches a few days later. She had a style all her own—flamboyant and free. She turned the pages until she was mesmerized by the clothing and pattern designs she saw.

"What are these?"

"I'm going to start my own design studio when I leave here. I've been dressed by the top designers all my life and I know I can do it better. Women have no sense of style of their own. I mean, most women, with you as an exception, Allison, don't know what suits them best or how to hide their flaws. I can do it for them. And I think you can help me."

"Me! Jenna, I don't have any real desire to go out to work when I leave here."

"I know, like most of the girls here, you've come husband-hunting. You may find a husband, but you will work too. I know you will. You're not going to waste all your God-given talent. Not while I'm around."

"It's funny. You're the second person I've met who has tried to plan my future for me. Well, so to speak. He doesn't really know it yet."

"He? You've found someone already. No . . . No . . . You must do more looking. I didn't take you for someone who settles on the first man, or the first anything you see. You must be more selective."

"You haven't met him yet. He's a law student."

"You could do worse. But you must do something with your talent. You also have that marvelous kind of personality that encourages people to talk to you and to listen to you. I need that kind of expertise. And I trust you implicitly."

"You're amazing, Jenna. You think you can snap your fingers and I'm going to change my way of life."

"Maybe not now, but you will. You'd never be happy

as just a housewife. Make sure you marry someone who won't stand in the way of your career."

"I'm a very old-fashioned girl. I feel women belong either in the home or in the business world. I don't think the two mix well. Somewhere along the line something will break down."

"Not for you Allison. You can do both. You'll just have to get someone in to help take care of your husband and the children. You'll be earning a good enough living to afford that."

"Well now that you have my youth tied up, what am I going to do when I retire?"

"You won't. You'll be like me. You'll work all your life and love it."

"I knew you spent a lot of time in Europe, but I didn't know you were a Gypsy reader in your soul," Allison laughed, but half-heartedly. She was afraid Jenna was dead serious.

"No, I spent too much time wasting away. I have so much to do. And I know you feel the same way. My words will ring true someday. You'll see," she said, closing the door to her room. Allison went back to her own room, bewildered.

"When Jenna has her hooks into you, you don't get off with just a smile and a friendly handshake. She wants your heart and soul too. She's crazy."

"I know what you mean," Catherine said. "She's hypnotic. She makes you feel as though you can't say no. I've never met anyone like her."

"Well, she's dead wrong about me. I'm not going off on some crazy career move. I like life simple. I'll draw when I feel like it and when I have time. If I knew I had to do it every day of the week, it wouldn't be fun anymore."

"But doesn't her company sound ideal? I mean, to be part of the beginning and build up to something. I'd never thought of that before. I just hoped I'd get a job somewhere and that was that."

"She'd like you to work for her too?"

"Yes, but she didn't offer me half of what she offered you. I mean, you could run the place if you wanted. I'm not the type."

"And she's not the type to let anyone run her. She'll always be the boss and don't you forget it. Jenna will die reminding you that she made you and what you've become."

"Maybe, but it's exciting."

"Sure and graduation is a long time off. She might offer the same deal to two other girls next year."

"Oh. . . . " Catherine said, disenchanted. "I never thought of that."

"Well think about it. If she still feels the same way about me a few years from now, then I'll think about it. Now what am I going to wear when I see Michael tomorrow?"

"You look good in anything you put on," Catherine said.

"I know, but tomorrow I just don't want to look good, I want to look like a knockout."


Allison awoke earlier than Catherine. It was a glorious fall day. The sun was shining, the sky clear and blue, and the air had the scent of fall in it. Cool, crisp and inviting. She took a long hot bath, washed her hair, and wondered what Michael had planned for them. When he called the night before to confirm their date, he wouldn't tell her what he had in mind. He just told her to dress casually and he'd be by to pick her up on schedule. Allison thought about Jenna's proposal. *What gall and conceit! She thinks she can snap her fingers and we'll all come to her beck and call. Well, lady, you've met the first person who'll say no to you* . . . Allison towel-dried her hair. It's natural wave and fullness made her long hair easy to care for.

"What do you plan to do today?" Allison called to Catherine.

"I have to work this afternoon in the office, then I think I'll stay in and work on some sketches."

"Why don't you invite Jenna to a movie or something?"

"I don't feel much like going out."

"Why? When you and I went to Charley's the other night, you seemed so uneasy. Didn't you ever go to a bar before?"

"Yes, and I didn't like any of them any better than Charley's. I guess I'm not a bar person. I don't know. I feel more comfortable around the girls than the boys. I guess I think they want something I can't give."

"Like what?"

"I don't know. I'm scared they'll make a pass or something."

"Well, if a guy makes a pass, it's up to you to accept or decline. It isn't difficult. You'll have to learn how to say no nicely. Guys don't get offended, not really. And maybe you'll meet the right man and you won't want to say no."

"I don't think so, but maybe," Catherine responded quickly. "Jenna feels the same way I do."

"Jenna? I don't believe it. She could say no to a man and still have him eating out of the palm of her hand. I can't picture her uneasy around anyone."

"I think you're giving her too much credit. She was a very sheltered child."

"True, but beneath that sheltered exterior is a real killer. Don't get me wrong. I like her, but I wouldn't want to get on the wrong side of her. And, Catherine, don't let her get to you either. Spend the evening with Rita or Amy, or one of the girls down the hall. Seeing too much of one person isn't healthy. I mean, I keep getting the feeling Jenna wants to drain people of all they have to give. As if she's living her life through ours. Do you know what I mean?"

"No. I think she's nice and could be very helpful to someone like me."

"Well, I'm not going to mother you for the rest of your life, but when she hurts you, don't come running. I warned you."

"It's on record. We'll see which one of us is right."

"I hope for your sake, it's you," Allison said. Taking one last look at herself in the mirror, she rushed out the door. "Have a good day."

Michael was waiting for her when she reached the front of the building. He was leaning against his car, and in a dead-pan voice, "Right on time. I like a woman who's prompt," he said, opening the car door.

"Where to?"

"Are you hungry?"

"Sure."

"I know a great little Italian restaurant. The best fresh-baked Italian bread, buns, and black coffee in town."

"You know the way," Allison was flip.

Jenna sat in her room sketching new ideas for fabrics

that she had thought about the night before. She loved simplicity, durability, and femininity. Women were meant to be pampered and to feel pampered, even if they were the ones doing the pampering. The courses she was taking were only the means to the end, and she hated the thought of waiting so long to get her ideas off the ground. But, either way, she'd have to wait until she was twenty-one for her inheritance which would start her company. She'd even thought about asking grandmother to give her money to start her off in a small summer research endeavor where she could utilize Catherine's and Allison's talents. She knew for sure that she had Catherine, but Allison was another matter. Her headstrong personality would clash with Jenna's if pushed too hard.

Jenna absent-mindedly was even designing her own logo—*JJ* and a small butterfly after her favorite opera, *Madame Butterfly*. Two more long years—how she wished they'd fly by. If only she could sit back and enjoy school, feel free, express herself, let her hair down and have fun.

It seemed as though she was always wishing time would fly. When she was twelve she couldn't wait until she was eighteen and able to go away to school. Even the private boarding schools she was sent to were either half or partly-funded by grandmother. She was always the *little darling* carefully watched and allowed special privileges when the other girls were not. After all, whatever Jenna wanted, Jenna got. If any one dared to insult her, maybe grandmother's checks wouldn't be so large. All she ever wanted was to be left alone and treated like the other children, away from grandmother's watchful eyes. It was as if she was under a microscope, grandmother waiting to see if the headstrong behavior of her mother would show up in her. Another disastrous marriage would kill the old girl. The Jones family was a long-established dynasty. They married the right people, mostly for convenience rather than love, and they did the right things, travelled with their own circle of friends, and worked very hard at having fun. The women lunched, planned menus, shopped, had their hair done, and, if the situation was right, took a lover in order to fill their monotonous schedule. They had children cared for by maids or governesses. Jenna wondered why these people had children at all. Her only memory of love came from the week she spent with her father when he sneaked her away from her nanny in the park. He was so sweet. He played with her, dressed her, bathed her, and spent hours combing her long hair. They'd talk and walk together, eat together, and she felt an intimacy she had never known before. Even the running away was an adventure. They were together and she didn't care where they went as long as he was with her. Daddy was charming and very handsome, and he wanted her, he wanted to raise her himself. But grandmother would never hear of it. He didn't have any money and, instead of trying to help them out so they could be together, she took her back. Daddy tried for years to fight her in court, but he couldn't compete with the lawyers that grandmother could afford to hire. Jenna was heartbroken, crying herself to sleep night after night, wanting him to hold her and tell her a story instead of some strange lady.

She remembered running into her grandmother's bedroom one morning and begging to see her father. "Please, grandma, please. I want to see him one more time. I promise I'll come back. I promise I'll never ask you for another favor as long as I live." Jenna was seven years old at the time and it was the height of the court battle.

"Jenna dear, someday when you have the world at your feet, you'll thank me for not letting your father raise you. What can he offer you? He can't even send you to a good school. You'll become a nothing. No, I'm doing the best for you. I know in my heart I'm right. Your mother would never forgive me. She'd turn over in her grave if I sent you back to him."

"But she loved him, grandmother. She'd want me to see my father. I know she would."

"Stop it, right now, Jenna. Jones people don't cry. We're strong and take each day in our stride. You're young now and don't know your own mind. Wait and see." And wait Jenna did. But her father lost. She wasn't sure what grandmother did or said to keep him away from her, but her father never made an attempt to see her again.

Jenna wondered where he might be now. Even if he was still alive. If she were to look for him, she didn't know where to start. All records of her birth were changed, and she didn't even have a picture of him. But sometime, when she had enough money of her own, she'd start her search, she'd find him, even if it were to see him only one more time. But then the old familiar doubts and fears would return. What if he had remarried and had another family? Would he want her to barge in on him? Hadn't he long ago put her out of his mind? But how could he? He fought so hard to keep her. She'd have to know the answers to her questions, someday. Jenna could never rest if she didn't.

She threw the sketching pad on the floor and lit a cigarette. Maybe Allison had the right idea. Get involved with a man, a plaything to pass the time, and, during Christmas recess, she'd fly to Palm Beach, spend the holidays with Grandmother, maybe try to get a small firm going before school finished. She'd tell Grandmother that it would be good experience, something to get out of her system so that when she did finish school she would be ready to settle down to a *proper* life.


Breakfast was delicious, a treat Allison was enjoying thoroughly. And Michael was even more charming than she had imagined. A wit and warmth she loved and could easily fall in love with.

"Now that you're full and contented, why don't we go for a drive. I'll show you the more picturesque parts of Pittsburgh," Michael said, taking a look at the shoes Allison wore. "A girl after my own heart. Practical. How did you know I planned a lot of walking today?"

"Second-guessed you, I imagine."

"Good. I brought a picnic lunch, blanket, wine and you can supply the music."

"I'm game if you are," Allison said, taking Michael's arm as they walked out of the restaurant.

Michael drove around for over an hour trying to find just the right place for their picnic. He wanted to have privacy, snuggle up to Allison and make love to her. He knew he might blow it by rushing but he couldn't keep his hands off of her one more minute. He wanted her and that's all he could think about. He was sure even as early as this morning, he would spend the rest of his life with this girl. She was everything he ever dreamed of and more.

They walked about a mile before Michael put the

blanket and picnic basket down.

"It's about time. I was wondering when we were going to stop."

"Are you tired?"

"No, curious." Allison wouldn't give him the satisfaction.

"Hungry yet?"

"No, I'm still full from breakfast. But I will be in a little while. The fresh air is so exhilarating. I feel so peaceful and contented," Allison said, resting her head on his thighs. Michael placed his hands through her thick hair.

"Don't ever cut it," he said.

"I don't plan to," she said, looking up at him. He bent down and gave her a soft kiss on the lips.

"I was wondering when you were going to get around to kissing me," she smiled.

"I didn't want to rush you," he smiled.

"You aren't," she said, pulling him down again and giving him another kiss, longer and more passionate than the first.

"Allison . . . Allison, you scare me. I want you so much."

"I feel the same way," she said, turning around and lying next to him.


Jenna knocked on Catherine's door and found her friend working at her desk.

"Allison still out?"

"I guess so. She's amazing. Sees what she likes and goes right after it. I wish I could do the same thing, but then I start fumbling. I guess I'm not what you would call the girl most likely to succeed. In the male department anyway."

"It doesn't really seem to bother you. If it did, you'd do something about it."

"No. I'm happy the way things are. The guys in this school are such babies."

"I know what you mean. I haven't seen one yet I'd like to get to know better. But I can't say the same about some of the teachers."

"Jenna, would you really consider going after an instructor?"

"Why not? They're human. Have to have their kicks, too. I'm not here to get serious, but to have a little something on the side, that could be fun," Jenna smiled.

"Do you have someone in particular in mind?"

"Yes. Jeff Conroy. Now he's a sophisticated good-looking older man. I like his style. I'd go to bed with him in a minute if I could get him alone sometime."

"I bet you would."

"Are you willing to help me along?"

"What can I do?" Catherine asked.

"Well, I have a plan. Jeff usually spends his evenings over at the Canteen. He enjoys talking to the students, hearing their ideas. And I'd like to go over there tonight. Come with me."

"I don't think so. I have too much work to do."

"Come on, take a break. As soon as I know I can score, I'll give you a wink and you can come back here. Maybe there will be someone there you'll like."

"Oh, no. I tried going out with Allison, remember. I was much too uncomfortable, but if you think I can help you, I'll go for a while."

"Thanks. I'll be ready in a minute. Comb your hair, and get ready," Jenna said, dashing from Catherine's room to her own.

Jenna primped in front of the mirror, put on lipstick, her favorite perfume, and polished her claws. She was out for the kill.

Jenna spotted Jeff as soon as the girls entered the Canteen. He was sitting with a group of seniors, and Jenna forced ahead through the crowd, making her way toward him. Catherine followed behind.

"Now remember what I told you," Jenna started. "Introduce yourself, and then me."

Catherine felt shaky but did what she was told. When she felt a lull in the conversation, she cleared her voice and started talking, "Mr. Conroy, I'm Catherine Markham. I have you for fundamental design, and this is Jenna Jones. She'll be transferring into your class on Monday."

"Good to see you both. Sit down, join in. I always like to see my students outside class. I learn so much more about their goals this way. Jenna Jones . . . *the* Jenna Jones," he said.

"Yes, but let's not be formal. I'd like you to think of me as you would any other student. I'm here to learn as the rest," Jenna said, extending her long, slim hand. He took it, and pulled out a chair for her. He flashed his boyish smile. Jenna eyed him carefully. The lines around his eyes were more pronounced, his face more intense. His salt and pepper hair blended with his grey tweed jacket and black slacks. His light blue shirt enhanced the left-over tan from the summer months. Jenna sat, legs crossed, her skirt riding up her shapely legs. Catherine sat beside her, trying to catch the conversation between the other students.

Jeff turned away from the others and focused his attention on Jenna.

"What brings you to Carnegie?"

"I want to be a designer. The best in the world. And I think I've chosen the right school to help me reach my goal. I feel the faculty is the finest in the country. Don't you agree?"

"Yes," he smiled, his even white teeth glowing. "But I'd be foolish to say anything else. I must say though, you've chosen a most difficult undertaking. You want to be the best. The competition is stiff out there, don't you think?"

"Yes. But I'm confident that I can do a better job. I have my eye on Catherine. I think she would be a fabulous asset to me. She's one of the best illustrators I've seen. Makes my work look second rate."

"Oh, no, Mr. Conroy. Jenna is much too modest. Her work is terrific," Catherine said, blushing from Jenna's generous compliment.

"I'd like to see it sometime. Do you have a portfolio?"

"Many. May I be so bold as to bring them one day after class?" Jenna started. "And do be critical. I'm here to learn."

"Oh, I will be, Miss Jones. Don't you worry."

"Well, speaking of work, I must be getting back to mine," Catherine said.

"I'd like to stay a little longer and talk, if you don't mind, Catherine," Jenna stated.

"No. Go right ahead. I'll see you tomorrow," Catherine said, her job done.

Jenna sat back in her chair and sipped her wine, watching Jeff, his movements and his interaction with the others. She was making him feel a bit uneasy, and she liked it.

As the kids started drifting away, Jeff looked up at

Jenna again.

"Think you'll be happy here?"

"Very. Are you?"

"Yes. But I'm a lot older than you. I've rid myself of the idealism of the young, and you, I think, you're the most idealistic girl I've met. You've been spoiled all your life and you think the world is at your feet. If you want to be the best, you will be. True, Miss Jones, you may have a great many friends, and be very talented, and full of ideas, but life out in the world is different. The establishment doesn't open its doors readily to a newcomer. There are many years of hard work, rejection, playing second fiddle to others more experienced . . . thievery . . . it's all more than you expected," he went on, not knowing why he thought he had to burst her bubble.

"Don't you think I know that. First of all, Mr. Conroy, I don't intend to work for anyone when I leave here. I plan to start a small design studio of my own and let it grow. I'm not working for just money. I really don't have to work at all if I don't want to, but I feel the need to prove who I am and what I can do. I think it's time a Jones got up off her *derriée* and did something."

"Very commendable. And I honestly hope you succeed. Maybe in twenty years we'll meet again, and you can tell me to go to hell—you made it in spite of all my warnings."

"Why wait twenty years?" Jenna said, moving closer to him. "I hope we'll become good friends, and I can call on you for advice if I need it. Which I'm sure I will," Jenna shifted, not wanting him to feel threatened.

"I hope we will become friends, Jenna. I like being friends with all my students."

"I see. Well, I have to be getting back to the old grindstone. Can I drop you off on the way?"

"No. I'll drop you off. I have to pass the dorm on the way home," he said, escorting her out of the Canteen.

"Do you live far from here?"

"No, about a block or so from you," he said hesitantly, "in the small group of faculty houses owned by the school. Mine is the smallest white one." Jeff stopped in front of the dormitory. "I'll see you in class Monday," he said.

"Good night, professor," Jenna said, giving him a kiss on the lips. He grabbed her before she could step out of the car.

"Miss Jones, I don't play with my students. It's one rule I've been able to stick to since I came here ten years ago. Although, I have to admit, you are hard to resist."

"Then don't resist me. I'm not a child, Mr. Conroy. I'm very much a woman."

"I'm sure you are. But there are rules," he stated.

"What fun are rules if they can't be broken, and I'm the silent type. I never kiss and tell," she said, looking straight into his eyes.

Jeff wanted to send her away but he was overwhelmed by her beauty and determination. He knew Jenna wouldn't give up on him easily. She saw what she wanted and took it. And she wanted him. He felt his body tightening, crying to touch her, to make love to her, and he knew he'd eventually give in.

"Go upstairs, collect your portfolios and bring them to my house in fifteen minutes. If we get caught, at least we'll have an half-hearted excuse. And Jenna, use the back door."

"I'll be right over," she smiled, thrilled at the thought of staying with him.

Jenna rushed to her room, grabbed her three black portfolios and composed herself. She closed her door quietly and rushed down the stairs.

Jeff had the lights turned off, the house in total darkness. Jenna tripped three times trying to make her way up the back stairs.

"Shhh . . . you can't be seen by anyone," she heard him say.

"I may not have been seen, but I'm going to be heard if you don't come out here and help me to the door. I can't see where I'm going."

"Okay," he whispered. "There are only three more steps."

Jenna entered the darkened house. Jeff had two candles burning in the living room.

"I brought my portfolios, but I don't think you'll be able to see my work by candlelight."

"I had no intention of looking through them tonight. We're here for other amusements," he smiled, pulling her toward him and kissing her.

"You taste good."

"So do you," Jenna said, pulling him down on the couch.

His hands searched for the zipper on her dress. Pulling it down, he unsnapped her bra. Her skin felt soft and warm.

"Take your clothes off," she whispered. "I want to feel your body beside me."

Jeff got up and led Jenna to his bedroom. He undressed himself first, then undressed her. They stood in the darkened room, lit only by the moonlight, kissing, touching, and exploring one another. Her shoulders stood even with his, and Jenna moaned with each caress, bending her head back so Jeff could devour her neck. Jeff kissed her shoulders, and worked his way to her breasts. He picked her up and carried her to the double bed. Jenna reached up for him, pulling him down on top of her.

She was ready for him, wanted him, and dug her nails deep into his back when they reached their climax together. Jeff held her close, "I'm glad I took the chance. You are worth it."

"What time is it?"

"Almost eleven-thirty," Jeff answered.

"I have to go soon. I don't want to be grounded," Jenna whispered.

"I wish you could stay the night. I'd like to make love to you again."

"I'm going to be here for a while. We can see each other again."

"How about breakfast tomorrow?" he smiled.

"What time?"

"Seven-thirty," he laughed. "I don't know if I can last any longer."

"You'll have to. I don't get up until ten. How about brunch instead. Do I have to use the back stairs."

"Not in the morning. We'll go over your sketches. I want to see if you're as good an illustrator as you are a lover."

"Better," she smiled, searching on the floor for her clothes.

Jeff didn't make a move to get up. He lay there smoking a cigarette, watching her every movement.

Jenna reached over and took a puff. "I like my coffee black and my bacon crisp," she ordered, walking to the bedroom door. "I'm sure we'll have a very comfortable year together. I enjoy being with you," Jenna told him, leaving the room.

Jenna's step quickened. She always felt light and

exhilarated after sex. Nothing satisfied her more, not drink, conversation or parties. Nothing got her as high as making love. It gave her unlimited energy. She felt like going back to her room and sketching a new batch of fabric designs. She was much too excited to sleep.

Catherine didn't feel as happy. She sat alone in her room, wondering when Allison was going to return. She knew Jenna would be triumphant with Mr. Conroy and she envied her. Yet her own gnawing secret remained inside. She wished she could see a man, want him, and have him. But whenever a man looked at her, she turned into jelly, her body broke out in a cold sweat, her knees knocked and her heart pounded. The old fears and hurts returned. When was she ever going to get over it? It had been almost five years since that awful night. Five long years of fear, loneliness, disgust and shame. She told no one. Maybe if she verbalized her fears, they would vanish.

Catherine heard the sound of Jenna's key in her door. The door closed swiftly and quietly. One down, and one to go. If Allison didn't hurry, she'd be late and lose her privileges for the rest of the semester.

At one minute to twelve, Allison ran into the room, her eyes red from crying.

"What's wrong? What happened?" Catherine asked, jumping out of bed.

"Oh, Catherine. I like Michael, I think I might even love him. But I know we have to cool things down a bit. I almost let my emotions carry me away today. I mean, I almost let him make love to me."

"Would that have been so terrible?"

"Yes. I'm not ready. I keep thinking about my parents and how disappointed they'd be in me if I got pregnant."

"Allison, you know better than I that you don't have

to get pregnant if you're careful."

"Well that's not all. I'm still afraid that if I give in too soon, I'll lose Michael. And I don't want to."

"What does he think?"

"He wants me to make love to him, but he understands how I feel. I know we'll still see one another, but what if he finds someone else who'll give him what he wants?"

"Then he really doesn't love you and he was worth losing. That's what my mother used to say. It's hard to swallow at the time, though," Catherine told her.

"I know. The part that scares me is that I want him as much as he wants me. I wanted to make love to him so much this afternoon. I could die."

"Well, how did you leave it?"

"He's coming by tomorrow night."

"Good. Then why are you crying?"

"I'm over-reacting. I know it. And the next time we're alone, I'm going to let him make love to me. I've decided and that's that. I'm old enough to make my own decisions, and live my life my way."

"Are you trying to convince yourself or me?" Catherine said.

"I'm not sure. All I know is that I love him, and I want us to be together. I'm scared . . . I've never felt this way before. I don't want to lose him."

"I don't think you will, Allison. Michael is a nice guy, and I have a feeling you'll be together for a long time. You've found the man you will marry."

"I think so too," Allison said. "But so fast. I can't believe it happened so soon."

"Love doesn't have any time limit."

"If everything works out, I'm going to ask Michael to come home with me during Thanksgiving."

"I'm going to stay here."

"Why?"

"I don't want to go home."

"Then you'll come back with us, too. None of my friends are going to spend a holiday alone."

"What about Jenna?" Catherine asked.

"I think she's going to fly to New York City and spend the holiday with her grandmother. She said it's the only holiday they spend in New York. Christmas is in Palm Beach."

"Well!" Catherine laughed. "The rest of us peasants will be freezing our buns off in the cold weather."

"If you're good, Catherine, she may ask you along. After all, she does want you to work for her," Allison imitated Jenna.

"Don't be foolish. I'd never fit in with the Palm Beach crowd."

"Sure you can. Markham . . . say you're one of the *Chicago* Markhams. I'll bet those snobs would never know the difference. They'd be too embarrassed to ask questions."

"I can see it all now. Hick from the country dining with the elite. What a let down."

"Let's plan it. I'm sure you'll have a good time. You can borrow some of my clothes, learn to hold your head up, and I know you'll get through it like a charm," Allison told her.

"I'd like to, but how are we going to convince Jenna?"

"Leave that to me," Allison said, washing the make-up off her face. "That's the easy part."


For the next month, the girls got into a regular

routine of classwork, dating, and studying. Allison saw a lot of Michael and, although she was prepared to sleep with him, Michael made sure their dates consisted of movies and crowded places. He'd park in front of the dormitory after bringing her home and kiss her until it was time to go in. Their affection grew with each date. They spent most of their free time on the phone, and Michael agreed to go home with her during the Thanksgiving holiday.

Jenna saw Jeff every weekend, spending Saturday nights at his house. Their lovemaking was becoming routine, and Jenna was beginning to look elsewhere. Catherine continued to work and kept up her marks. She had become closer to Jenna than to Allison; she became Jenna's confidant, lying for her, making excuses to the house mother if Jenna was a few minutes late, handing messages to Jeff, but she didn't mind. It was as though Catherine was having her own adventure through Jenna. Allison and Michael would occasionally take Catherine with them to a movie or out for dinner. Each time Michael would suggest Catherine double date with them, Catherine found some excuse to beg off. She avoided any unnecessary contact with men except for Arnie. Arnie was in her figure-drawing class. A quiet boy, well mannered and nervous. He felt comfortable with Catherine because she posed no threat to him. They'd occasionally lunch together and were thought of as the two odd ducks. Some of the boys just felt sorry for her, the plain girl living with two beauties. It was enough to make anyone feel insecure. Each was happy in her own way—learning, living and finding herself. No complaints, no tears.

Jeff was the fly in the ointment for Jenna. He was in love and obsessed with her. He spent more time on her work than any of his other students. In his own way, he was helping her achieve her goal—pushing her, giving her extra work, developing the discipline she always lacked, and for this she was grateful.

Catherine and Allison planned to drive to Philadelphia in Michael's car for Thanksgiving. Everyone in the girls' dorm was getting anxious for the break. Michael called home, explained why he wasn't coming home for the holiday, and promised he'd bring Allison with him during Christmas. After a long crying session with his mother and a lecture from his father, Michael started packing for the trip.

Jenna left earlier than the others. Her last class was Jeff's and he gave her the morning off. She flew home determined to talk her grandmother into giving her money to start her summer project.

"Michael's waiting downstairs, Catherine. Hurry up," Allison said, picking up her suitcase.

"I'm almost ready. I keep thinking I've forgotten something."

"If you did, I'll lend it to you, whatever it is. I can't wait to get home."

"Anxious to see your family? Or to have your family meet Michael?"

"Both. I just know they'll love one another. I wrote my parents lengthy letters about him. I think they know everything there is to know about him already. Meeting is just a formality."

"Are you sure I won't be in the way?"

"Of course not, silly. Now come on," Allison pulled her out the door.

"I feel like I'm leaving home. I've gotten so used to this room. Let's see if we can get it next year."

"I hope so, after all the redecorating. We'll talk to

Mrs. Koch about it when we get back."

Jenna was met at the door by Mrs. Hudson, her grandmother's secretary. "Mrs. Jones is napping, and doesn't want to be disturbed until after two," she told her. Jenna went up to her room, changed her clothes, and called Jeff.

Jenna and Grandmother dined alone. The conversation was limited. Jenna talked about school, some of the friends she met, and then Jenna cleared her throat for the big moment. She told her grandmother what she wanted to do with her fabric designs. "I want to open my own firm after graduation and I need time to try out some designs and fabrics. I'd like to work this summer with two friends. A bit of research now could save us a great deal of money later."

Grandmother sat a moment in silence.

"I think it is a very wise move. You have talent, I always knew it. It isn't shameful for a woman to work these days. And I'd rather you had a place of your own than slaving under someone else."

Jenna couldn't believe it. The old girl was actually on her side.

"I'm so glad you think that way. I was almost afraid to tell you," Jenna confided.

"Jenna, whatever is on your mind tell me. We'll talk it out. If I think it's wrong, I'll tell you and, as in this case, if I think it's a good idea, you'll have my total support. What do you think you'll need?"

"Well, the three of us will have to have a small place to work out of. Catherine and Allison will need a place to stay. I would say we'd need about five thousand dollars. And it's only a loan. We'll pay you back with whatever money we make," Jenna said enthusiastically.

"Jenna, that's very commendable. I don't expect you to pay me back. Any money you make should go right back into the business. But I do wish you'd make an appointment to see David White before you go any further. He'll advise you about leases and probably put you in touch with some of the manufacturers in town. Promise me you'll do that."

"I promise. I'll call him first thing in the morning. I'll ask Allison and Catherine to come into town during Christmas to look around at some locations. Thank you," Jenna said, kissing her grandmother for the first time in years.

Jenna rushed upstairs and called Allison's house. Everyone was sitting in the living room when the call came through. Jenna asked to speak with Catherine. She knew that between now and Christmas she would have to work extra hard on Allison, even if she had to break up the relationship with Michael. Jenna needed her to make her venture successful.

"Who was that on the telephone?" Allison asked.

"Jenna, she spoke to her grandmother and everything is all set for the summer. Isn't that exciting?"

"What's all set?" Mrs. McWilliams asked.

"Oh, Jenna Jones, you remember I wrote you about her. She has this plan about opening a design company of her own and she'd like Catherine and me to work for her this summer. Sort of on-the-job advance training."

"I think that's a wonderful idea," her mother said.

"It doesn't sound bad to me. You'll be starting at the top," her father put in.

"How come you've never mentioned this to me before?" Michael said.

"Because I've never taken her seriously before. I

don't know if I want to work for Jenna. She can be a real slave driver. She envisions herself as the great lady of Seventh Avenue."

"If anyone can do it, she can," her mother told her. "The family is rich enough to get her the best clients in town. You know dear, the rich do stick together. They'll probably support Jenna until she gets established on her own."

"Maybe so, but if you don't mind, I'd rather not talk about it now," Allison said. "Catherine can do as she pleases, but I need more time to think this whole idea out."

"Speaking of time," Catherine said. "I'd like to say goodnight to everyone and go to bed."

"Sure, go on up. We won't be long. I'll be up in a minute," Allison said.

"She's very nice, and so is Michael," Mrs. McWilliams told her daughter in the kitchen. "Do you think things are very serious between Michael and you?"

"I think so, but he hasn't asked me to marry him or anything. Remember I have to finish school yet," Allison said. "Besides I'm afraid to think ahead. Something might happen. I'm getting superstitious in my old age."

"He's very much in love with you, Allison. I can tell," her mother said.

"Thanks, mom. And thank you for having my friends here. It was very nice of Dad and you."

"Any friend of yours is welcome in this house. You know that. And I've missed having you around so much, it's good to see you home and happy."

"I've missed you, too," Allison said, kissing her mother. "I think Mike and I are going to go for a walk before we turn in. Do you mind?"

"No, go on."


Catherine sat in Allison's room. It was the kind of bedroom she'd always dreamed about. Yellow and white ruffled bedspreads and curtains, delicate furniture, high school pennants and books. Allison must have had a wonderful childhood. And her parents were the nicest people Catherine had ever met. Mrs. McWilliams was an older version of Allison—warm, pretty, exquisitely dressed, soft-spoken and maternal. Mr. McWilliams was very polished and handsome for his fifty years and devoted to his family. He was every bit the gentleman, making Catherine feel very much at home the moment she walked into the house. She knew her Chrstimas vacation wouldn't have the same warmth and congeniality.


"I like them," Mike said. "Now I know why you're such an extraordinary girl."

"I like them too," Allison said, walking arm in arm with Michael. "Although I wanted to go away to school, you know, to get away from the restrictions, I do have some great memories. My parents are the most understanding people I've ever met. They supported me in every endeavor. I couldn't ask for better."

"You know we've never talked about this since our first date, but I'd like to bring it up now," Michael started. "I'm sort of glad you put me in my place. I just wouldn't have wanted to face your father knowing I'd slept with his daughter. It sounds odd, but I'd feel uncomfortable around him."

"Michael, I'm so glad you said that. I've been afraid to talk about it too. It's almost as if you've been afraid to be alone with me ever since that night."

"I have. I know I'd want you, so why frustrate myself? It's hard enough now to say goodbye to you each night after some heavy kissing. I've taken more cold showers this year than ever before," he kidded.

"Me, too."

"You?" Michael looked surprised.

"Sure, girls get turned on, too, or hadn't you noticed."

"How are we going to go on for another three years?" he asked.

"We don't have to. I think if we both have a mature outlook, and we know we want to marry one another, then we should make love."

"We should?" Michael looked startled. "I don't know."

"Michael, do you think we can go out night after night for the next three years and just kiss?"

"No. And I know I want to marry you. And, believe it or not, I'm not interested in seeing anyone else, even for sex. So the answer is impossible. When do you want to do it?" Michael smiled.

"Sometime before the end of our education."

"You mean between now and three years," he laughed. "I'm ready whenever you are."

"I know we're both kidding now, but I do want to make love to you. But promise me we'll be careful."

"Very. I don't want to ever hurt you," he said, kissing her. She pressed hard against him. "I love you, Allison."

"I love you too," she said. "Maybe if I were to work with Jenna, I'd have a place of my own in the City. You can work there, too, and we'd be together next summer."

"I'd like that. I know my father would let me work in the office. I can use the experience. I'd have to live at home, but I don't have any restrictions."

"Then it's all settled. We'll spend the summer together, and spend the summer nights at my place. I'll let Jenna talk me into it when we get back," she smiled.

Jenna and her grandmother spent a quiet Thanksgiving together, the dinner lavish enough to feed an army—all seven courses. They talked about her plans for the summer and her phone conversation with David White. He promised to look around for a small loft in the garment district. All three could share an apartment in the East Village, giving them almost five months to show their work around town. Jenna was chock full of ideas and spent the rest of the weekend doodling and walking around the fabric district, checking out material. Jenna thought their first project should be designing new sheets and bedwear, coordinates to warm the cosiest room in the house. They could continue to work during the school year if they had to. Although Jenna was glad she had some schooling, she knew she didn't need much more to take her where she wanted to go. Jenna was certain she could talk Catherine into quitting early, but Allison would be a problem. She was still stuck on her middle-class ideals.

Thanksgiving at the McWilliams' was much different. Mr. McWilliams said grace, carved the turkey, and everyone chatted around the table, stuffing themselves like they hadn't eaten for months. Catherine even enjoyed the preparation. Everyone got up early, helped

Allison's parents with the salad, stuffing, vegetables and appetizers. Mrs. McWilliams invited all the relatives which made twenty-four for dinner. They were a happy family. Uncle Harvey told jokes. Aunt Miriam played the piano while everyone gathered around and sang along with her. The day went on forever. Every time Catherine turned around there was more food on the table. There were four different kinds of pies, cakes, pudding, coffee, and then a huge assortment of fruits and nuts. If she ate another morsel, she'd explode. The whole family made a fuss over Michael, opening their arms and hearts to him, making him feel like one of the family already.

Even Catherine was made to feel like one of them today. She wished she was an orphan and could be adopted by these wonderful people. Maybe if her father had stayed home, things might have been different. Instead, everyone seemed to go their own way, rarely together. Her sisters were always running off to meet their friends or boyfriends. Mother used to work two shifts sometimes in the hospital to make ends meet. When she came home she was usually too tired to think about anything else but sleep. But Catherine couldn't blame what she had become on her mother. It wasn't her fault. She did the best she could, kept food on the table, a roof over their heads, and clothes on their backs. It wasn't easy supporting a family on her own. Catherine wished her mother would have had the time to talk to her sometimes, see her fears and talk her out of them. She needed the love and affection of a family. Sometimes, what you never had is not missed, but, when you see what life could have been, it's agonizing. Catherine was beside herself with grief the morning they packed the car to go back to school. She wished she could hide away in one of the closets and never go back. Stay there and become the second daughter Mrs. McWilliams never had. Catherine ran to her and gave her a hug and kiss before she left.

"I hope we see you again, dear," she said.

"I'll write and be back whenever I'm invited," Catherine said.

"It's a standing invitation. Whenever you'd like to come, do. Even if Allison isn't around. Maybe some weekend the two of you can take the train in. We'll go shopping," she said.

"That sounds like fun," Catherine answered. "If Allison doesn't want to come, I'll come alone."

"You do that," she said, giving Catherine another hug, understanding her loneliness.

"Bye, Mom, and thanks for being so good to Catherine. She can use a friend like you. Confidentially, mom, I think it would be nice if she came down here alone one weekend. There are some things that are bothering Catherine and she won't talk to me about them. Maybe she'll talk to you."

"Just tell her to give me a call. Any weekend is fine. Take care of yourself and write," her mother said. "Drive carefully, Michael."

"I will. See you at Christmas," he shouted as they drove away.


The second semester flew by faster than the first. Catherine, Allison and Jenna took a few weekends off from school and traveled to New York City to look for a unique work location. With David's help, they were able to find a large, sunny loft in the Murray Hill Section of the City. It was large enough for them to both work and live in. The apartment was owned by an artist at one time and was sectioned off ideally. Each of the girls had a room of her own, leaving a large sunny section for work space. Mr. White arranged for art tables to be brought in, supplies, light boxes, and racks made for sample fabrics. As skeptical as Allison was, even she was caught up in the excitement of their new venture. And much to their surprise, Grandmother Jones gave the loft to Jenna as a Christmas present, leaving them enough money out of the original five thousand dollars to eat regularly and pay their bills. The girls returned to school with a new excitement and loaded down with ideas for their summer break.

Michael spent Christmas with both Allison and his family, while Catherine went off to Palm Beach with Jenna. As Allison told her, it was easy for her to make the adjustment. She was wined and dined in luxury, unlike her Thanksgiving vacation. The atmosphere was sterile but educational, leaving Catherine with many new ideas about dressing the affluent. Catherine found herself wandering off on long walks, sketching isolated beaches and large estates. In spite of the warm weather, Grandmother had prepared a lavish Christmas Eve party with a twenty-foot tree trimmed in antique decorations from France and Germany. It was at this time that she gave Jenna the deed to the loft. It was theirs to do with as they pleased, and a place to go to during summer and vacations. Catherine and Jenna couldn't be happier. They toasted their new venture together that night, forming a new and unique bond between them.

Michael's and Allison's Christmas was quieter. She

went off to New York to spend a few days with his family, his father loving her as much as Michael. And she becoming very fond of Michael's father and grandfather. His mother was a different matter. She seemed somewhat distant, as if Allison was taking her son away. Her jealousy was almost the cause of a disastrous New Year's Eve.

Michael and Allison had stayed behind at the house after everyone left. Allison was in Mike's room talking to him as he dressed. The situation was very innocent. Mrs. Fenway came back to the house, feigning a headache, walked into Michael's room and found the two. She dashed out of the room, screaming for Michael to ask Allison to leave her house. She didn't want him dating a girl who'd give herself so easily. It took hours to convince her nothing was going on—that they were just talking. If anyone was at fault it was himself. Allison had rebuffed all of Michael's sexual advances, and she would remain pure until they married. It wasn't until Michael told his mother that he would never talk to her again, that she agreed to apologize to Allison for her behavior. She was insincere, but it was a step in the right direction.

Michael and Allison left the Fenway home the next morning two days ahead of schedule. Allison vowed never to return, and Michael tried to soothe away the hurt. The two hardly said anything to one another the whole trip back.

Allison first spoke when she was getting her suitcase out of the car. "I don't think we should see so much of each other this semester."

"What are you saying?" Michael said, surprised.

"I think your mother was right. We are going a little too fast. I mean, since I got here, I haven't even dated anyone else."

"Do you want to?"

"I don't know. But I think if we are meant to be together, we will be. This is sort of a test. Please understand. I love you, Michael, but I have to think things out," Allison told him, running up to the dormitory, leaving him standing alone watching her. He called her as soon as he got back to school. Allison had Catherine answer the phone to tell him she wasn't ready to talk. Jenna, though, trying to comfort her best friend, was relieved the whole relationship was over. Michael was out of the way, and now they could continue to plan their future together.


Allison threw herself into her school work. She desperately wanted to pick up the telephone and call Michael, but she had to let it rest, had to give him time to decide whether he wanted to spend the rest of his life in a constant running battle with his mother over her. It was a pity Mrs. Fenway didn't have any other children. Michael was her whole life. In a way, Allison felt sorry for her.

Jenna called Michael occasionally to report on Allison, how she was doing and what she was doing. Her life with Jeff was becoming monotonous and she could use a fresh body. Michael, in his weakened condition, would be an easy catch. She called him one afternoon when Catherine and Allison were out.

"Michael, can we get together and talk? I have a few things on my mind, and you're the first person I thought of. And besides, I do have some news about Allison."

"Allison, what about her?"

"Can we get together later?"

"Sure, I'll pick you up after dinner. Is that all right?"

"Fine. I'll see you around seven," Jenna said, hanging up. She went back to her room, opened the window, letting in the cool spring air. She'd have to call Jeff and cancel their date, but he wouldn't be a problem. Jeff was always understanding.

Michael was waiting outside at seven as promised. Jenna dressed in a cool green skirt and blouse which brought out the green in her eyes even more. She walked casually to the car, enjoying watching Michael appraising her. She got in.

"Where do you want to go?" he asked.

"Can we go back to your place? We'll have more privacy there. I hate trying to talk over crowds of people."

"Sure! Whatever! I don't feel up to seeing a lot of people myself."

"Still pining away for Allison?"

"I wouldn't call it pining. I love her, Jenna, and I want to spend the rest of my life with her. Can you understand that in your calculating heart."

"Michael, you don't have to yell at me. I have feelings, too. It's just that I never had a chance to let them out. I never shared anyone or anything in my life. I never had to. Please be patient with me," Jenna said, putting on her most feminine pleading look.

"I guess so. I'm sorry. I didn't mean to bite your head off. I feel miserable tonight."

"I'm sort of feeling down myself," Jenna told him.

"What's wrong?"

"I need a man to talk to. I think all the girls in the dorm are getting to me. They're always pulling at me, asking me to talk about my childhood, travels, looking through my clothes. If you can understand, I just want to be left alone."

"I guess it isn't easy for you. I know, I for one have been too hard on you."

"You have," she agreed.

"Let's make a deal. Let's be friends and try to help one another. I know I need someone to talk to sometimes myself. And the guys aren't the right medicine either."

"You've got a deal. I'm feeling better already. You'll become the brother I never had."

"Well, sis, do you want to pick up a bottle of something to drink, while we pine away," he smiled.

"Sounds good to me. And you're much better looking when you're not frowning. You have a dashing smile," Jenna flattered him.

"What are you drinking?" Jenna asked, when Michael got back into the car.

"Bourbon."

"My favorite," Jenna said, hating the stuff.

"You know, you'll be good for my reputation. If anyone sees you coming into my room, they'll know I'm still human."

"Still a red-blooded American man with feelings."

"Can't hurt. Maybe everyone will get off my back."

"Anything I can do to help, please let me," Jenna told him, moving closer to him. Michael didn't object. He seemed to be in better spirits than when he picked her up. Much to Jenna's surprise, she was enjoying being with him more than she had realized.

"So how's Allison?" he asked.

"I'm worried about her. She doesn't seem to leave her room anymore except for class. Does that answer your question?" Jenna said.

"What are you driving at?" Michael asked.

"She's not dating anyone else. She still loves you.

Feel better?"

"Then why won't she talk to me?"

"She wants to make sure you know what you're doing. Girls learn early how to fight the competition, but when the competition is one's prospective mother-in-law, then the rules are very different. It seems no matter what Allison does, you'll be the loser in the long run. You know you may feel now she's more important than anything in this world, but don't you think eventually you'll feel guilty for hurting your mother?"

"That's silly. It will never come to that. Mother was a little jealous. Allison's the first girl I've ever been serious about. Mother was bound to have some reservations. I'm sure when the two of them get to know one another better, they'll like each other," Michael said.

"Then maybe you should talk to your mother. Have her write to Allison or something. It could help."

"That's a wonderful idea. I know Allison is very family oriented and she wouldn't do anything that would hurt anyone. If I could work things out between the two of them, Allison and I would be fine. Thanks, Jenna, I feel better already."

"You look better," she said, giving him a quick kiss on the cheek.

"What was that for?"

"Nothing. I felt like it. I think you're terribly sweet."

"I like you, too. Here we are," Michael said, parking the car. "I have to warn you. It isn't much, but then us guys were never one for cleaning up and redecorating."

"I promise not to notice."

"I'm sure you will, but what the hell," Mike said, feeling his oats again. Michael escorted Jenna upstairs and, as luck would have it, no one saw them. Michael climbed the two flights of stairs to his room, Jenna beside him. He opened the door, pulled some clothes off a chair and asked her to sit down.

"Have you ever been in love, Jenna?"

"Not really. I've had crushes, but I made a promise to myself never to give all of me to one person. I never wanted to become like my mother. She let the love of a man kill her. It isn't worth it."

"Maybe not. But I'm sure she was happy when she was with your father. Probably happier than she ever was in her life. It might have been worth it."

"Then why did she give in? Why did she let my grandmother take him away? I would have run away . . . done anything to be with the man I loved. She was weak," Jenna said.

"You are a romantic," Michael said, surprised to see another side of Jenna, one well hidden.

"No. Not anymore. Not since I was an adolescent. I'd rather live alone."

"No one can be happy living life alone. We all need someone. And I don't feel it's a sign of weakness to admit it," he said, handing her a drink.

"I don't know. Maybe I haven't met the right man yet. I guess I'm afraid," Jenna told him, being more honest than even she expected.

"Love doesn't have to be disastrous all the time."

"Look at Allison and you. Two people who love one another. Look at the hurt you're both feeling now."

"Sure, we're hurt now. But it will work out. And when it does, our love will be stronger than ever."

"I hope so. Oh, Michael, now you're making me feel depressed again. I wish someone loved me the way you love Allison," Jenna said. Michael walked over to Jenna and put his arms around her.

"I know if you let yourself go, someone will.

Probably many will."

"I don't want many. One will do," she said, holding him tighter. "Pretend I'm Allison tonight. Love me the way you love her," Jenna said, meaning it.

Michael looked at her for a moment. He was taken by her vulnerability and honesty. But most of all, he wanted her. He hadn't made love to anyone since before he met Allison.

Michael moved his hands up toward Jenna's face, touching her cheeks lightly. Her eyes never moved from his. He bent down and kissed her softly. She reached up, holding him tightly and returned his kiss with more passion than Jenna was even aware she had. She wanted him, not only physically, she wanted all of him. Jenna could feel his excitement. He was young and vibrant, hungry, different from Jeff—less experienced, yet eager. He wanted to please her. She led and he followed. Touching, kissing, willing to give everything. Jenna eased him inside her, moving with him, biting his ear as he moaned in release. Michael turned over and fell asleep next to her, in peace.

Jenna spent the night, never anticipating Michael's change of mood the next morning. He was distant, almost sorry he had given in to his emotions. Feeling his mood, Jenna made the first attempt at conversation.

"If you're afraid I may tell Allison what happened last night, don't be."

"Thanks, Jenna. I . . . I'm sorry. I shouldn't have used you the way I did."

"Michael, please don't. We both needed one another. I'm not sorry it happened."

"But it won't ever happen again. I have to get over to Allison's. I have to talk to her and make everything right between us. Please understand."

"I do," Jenna said, feeling sorry for herself.

"I meant everything I said last night. I do want to be your friend and help you out or talk whenever you want. I like you."

"I'm glad. Now I think you'd better drop me off downtown. I have to do some shopping. I wouldn't want anyone around the campus to see us pulling in together."

"You're right. Thanks for understanding and for helping me last night. I owe you one," Michael said.

"Thank you. You're really something special. You are worth waiting for," Jenna told him and meant it.

"I hope Allison feels the same way."

"I know she will. Are you ready?"

"As ready as I'll ever be," he said. "Let's go."

Michael dropped Jenna off downtown and headed back to the school. He decided to be forceful. Do all the talking. Not let Allison say anything until he was finished. She'd have to see it his way. Michael didn't bother to call when he got to school. He by-passed Mrs. Koch and ran up the steps to Allison's room. He found her sitting on her bed, still in her bathrobe. She was shocked to see him there, and closed the door immediately behind him.

"I know I shouldn't be here. But I'm not going to leave until you promise to let me have my say."

"Okay . . . but hurry."

"I love you, and that's that. Any problems we may have can and will be worked out. I don't want to spend anymore time without you. Not one more minute. These have been the worst three month's of my life."

"Mine too. . . ," she interrupted, running to him. "Please, let's not let anyone come between us again."

"We won't," Michael said, holding her, hoping

Jenna wouldn't be the someone she was talking about. His happiness was in her hands.


"I'd like to propose a toast," Jeff addressed Allison, Catherine, Jenna, and Michael. "Since this is our last night together until school starts again next fall. I'd like to wish all you young ladies a happy and prosperous summer."

"Hear! Hear!" Michael returned.

"I have to say that I was very skeptical of Jenna's idea about starting her own company. But, I think the steps she is taking now to find the right niche for herself by doing research in the field are definitely the right move."

"And I might add," Michael started. "I think she's picked the best two partners in the school. What a gorgeous trio."

"They can't miss," Jeff said. "What they lack in skill, they'll make up for in charm. Who could resist the requests of such lovely ladies."

"Well, thank you gentlemen," Allison said. "But I have to admit, as anxious as I am to get started, I'm going to miss this place. Charley's has become like a second home to me. I'm really looking forward to returning this fall."

"I'm glad you said that. Many young people think with a limited education and a few bucks in their pockets, they can conquer the world. I'm so thankful to hear you will be coming back to finish."

"We will be. I want to add some retailing courses to my schedule. I think everything we learn will be useful to us. Plus we'll be working the better part of our lives. Why miss out on the fun of our youth?" Catherine said.

"Commendable, but not really what I wanted to hear. But, in any case, whatever motives you have for coming back, I'm glad you are," Jeff said. "Now anyone for another round of drinks?"

"Sure. Let's make a night of it," Jenna said. "We're all packed and ready to leave in the morning."

"Are you all set to get your room back next year?" Allison asked.

"Yes, both of you?"

"We made our requests last November. We believe in thinking ahead," Allison told her.

"Good. Now, if you don't think I'm terribly rude, I'd like to spend the rest of the evening alone with Jeff," Jenna whispered to Allison.

"Not at all. Did he say he was coming to New York to visit this summer?"

"Yes. He'd move in if I'd let him. He's asked me to marry him, you know."

"I didn't. Are you going to?"

"Maybe. It might be fun for awhile. My family would die."

"Jenna, do you love him? Never mind the waves it would make."

"I love him as much as I'm capable of loving anyone. I think he'd be good for me. He has a way of pushing me to my limit in terms of my work. He's a perfectionist. And he's very good to me. I've learned a great deal from him this year."

"Jenna, then do it. I mean, if you think it's best. I wish I could marry Michael, but it wouldn't be practical right now."

"Or wise. You haven't even slept with him yet."

"I'm a slow starter. We'll get there. Probably this summer, when we have more time to ourselves. Will you tell your grandmother about your plans?"

"No. If I marry him, I'll just do it. Will you and Michael stand up for us?"

"We'd love to. This is really exciting. Can I say something to Michael?"

"No. I'll tell everyone," Jenna said, standing up.

"I'd like to call everyone to attention here at this table," Jenna said, enthusiastically. "Jeff has asked me to marry him. I haven't given him an answer yet. But I'm about to. I *am* going to marry him," she said, looking at him. "As soon as we can."

"Jenna. I can't believe it," Jeff said, getting up and kissing her in front of everyone. Catherine stared in total dismay while Michael hugged Allison.

"Did you know anything about this?"

"She told me a minute ago. She asked us to stand up for her."

"I'm really happy for you, Jenna. I told you once that everything would work out." Michael's slip went unnoticed with the excitement. "Allison and I will be there."

"When do you want to get married?" Jeff asked.

"Tonight, no time like the present."

"Right now? I mean we have to make preparations," Jeff said.

"Why? We're all here. The car's parked outside. Everyone's packed. Why not leave and get started. We'll go back to New York in the morning."

"You're crazy, but that's one of the reasons I love you," Jeff told her beaming.

"I'd like to wish you all the luck in the world, Jenna," Catherine said, tears in her eyes. If there was ever a moment in her life that she felt totally alone, it was now. Everyone seemed to have someone but her.

Now she was losing her best friend to a man. Things would never be the same again. Even the summer seemed dismal to her at this moment. Everyone got up excited, still talking about how things worked out, and Catherine trailed along in a daze. She picked up her suitcases in her room and followed everyone into the car. Jenna and Jeff rode in his car, and the others got in with Michael. They would drive to Maryland and get married in the morning. Catherine rode in silence. Her mind traveled back to the turning point in her life a few short weeks before.

She was working late at the drafting table. Allison was home for the weekend with Michael. They were to return the next day. Jenna was over at Jeff's. Suddenly she heard a knock on her door. Jenna was back early. She had decided not to spend the night with Jeff.

"Come in. I have some coffee on. Help yourself to a cup."

"I feel like something stronger. Do you mind if I bring in my bottle of vodka?"

"No, go ahead. You can fix me one if you'd like. I'm almost through with what I'm doing. You look down. Do you want to talk about it?" Catherine asked.

"Yes," Jenna told her, closing the door to Catherine's room. "I'm sick and tired of this affair. I don't know; Jeff doesn't satisfy me any longer."

"So don't see him anymore," Catherine said.

"I can't. I need his help. He's a very good teacher. He's helped me more than anyone else in this school. Oh . . . and I know myself. If I stop seeing him, in a few days I'll miss him and go back. I guess I feel like an old married lady. I can't live with him or without him. But you seem to be all right without male attraction. How do you do it?"

"I put my work first," Catherine lied.

"I don't believe you. Something had to have happened. You must have a deep dark secret you're not telling me," Jenna coaxed. "Or are you secretly sleeping with Arnie?"

"Are you crazy? Arnie's never tried to touch me. I have more to think about than sex. You and Allison are different from me, that's all."

"Catherine, you're not being honest with your best friend. Don't I always tell you everything?"

"Oh, Jenna, I wish I could talk about it. But it's too painful."

"Come on, Catherine. Let it out. It might not be so terrible. Maybe it will make you feel better," Jenna begged, dying to know what made Catherine tick.

"Maybe you're right. I'll take it slow. Be patient," Catherine said, taking a deep breath.

"I will. Take your time. Here, have some of this," Jenna handed her another drink, and poured one for herself.

"About six years ago, back at home, I was about as shy as I am now. I used to stay after school and use some of the art supplies. The teacher said I could. And really there was no reason to go home. My mother was always working. So this one night, it was getting dark, I seemed to have lost track of the time, and . . ."

"Go on," Jenna said.

"And . . . it was almost seven when I put away the art supplies. I heard a noise coming from the hallway. I wasn't frightened at first. I thought it was the janitor or something. So I put on my coat, and started to go. I saw one of my classmates, Leo Sturges, coming down the hall. He wouldn't let me pass. You know what I mean, I'd go to the right and so would he . . . and so on. I was getting scared. I didn't say anything to him at first, and he continued. I got away from him somehow and got out the door. Well, waiting outside were three of his friends. All fellow classmates. They stopped me . . . pushed me back and forth among them. They were laughing and yelling . . . Then Leo came out. He smiled at me; sort of a sick smile, and looked up at the rest of the boys. It was almost as if it was some kind of a signal."

Jenna moved closer to her, almost knowing what Catherine was going to say. "Go on, Catherine. Let it out."

"Well, they grabbed me, and dragged me to the back of the school. I . . . I wanted to scream but nothing came out. I was so frightened. One of the boys put his hands around my mouth, while someone else pulled up my dress and ripped my panties off. I was frozen, I don't remember feeling anything. They took me one at a time. All of them laughing. I couldn't see anything but the cold piercing eyes . . ." She stopped and took another sip of her drink. "Then one of the boys heard someone coming, yelled to the others to let me go, and they all ran away. Leo came back and told me if I ever mentioned this to anyone, I'd get more of the same, but I wouldn't be so lucky as to walk away next time."

"You didn't listen to him, did you?" Jenna asked.

"Yes. I tried to pull myself together and started walking. Fortunately, no one was home when I got there. I was able to go upstairs, take off my clothes and soak in a hot tub for hours. I didn't ever want to get out of that tub. I kept washing myself until my skin was raw. It was almost as if I was trying to wash away the memory of the night. I ran into my room afterward and lay on my bed, staring at the ceiling."

"You mean that you never told your mother?"

"No. I told no one."

"Didn't she ever notice anything was wrong?"

"If she did, she didn't say anything to me. I know mother. She probably attributed my attitude to my period or adolescence. I was only thirteen."

"My God! You were a baby. And the boys, did they ever bother you again?"

"No. I was lucky. I guess they were afraid I'd say something. After a while, instead of staring at me, they'd just walk past me like nothing happened. I never stayed late at school again. I borrowed the art supplies and went home with everyone else. I haven't ever wanted to go near a man since then. I'm still frightened," Catherine cried.

Jenna put her arms around her friend, feeling her hurt and anxiety. "No one is ever going to hurt you like that again. I promise."

"What am I going to do?" Catherine said. "I can't go on alone for the rest of my life."

"Look, there are others who've had problems like yours. I myself was hurt by someone once," Jenna began, feeling the strength of the vodka. "When I was sixteen, I was madly in love with a dealer in Nice. I mean I followed him everywhere. I dressed up, pretending to be older so he'd notice me. And one day he did. He wasn't at all interested in having a long relationship, not as I imagined anyway. He told me to meet him at midnight when his shift was over. I did, and he took me for a ride in his sports car. I was so excited. He must have been about twenty-eight or so. A beautiful man. Tall, charming, tanned, you know, white even teeth that flashed each time he smiled. Sandy hair, dark brown eyes. I thought I'd never seen a more handsome man in my life. I was ready to lie down and die for him. Anyway, he took me for the ride, and we stopped at a very secluded spot. He took a blanket out of the car, a bottle of wine and two glasses. I felt so old and sophisticated.

"We sat on the blanket and without even asking me a question about myself, he started making love to me. I didn't know what else to do, so I let him. It was over before I knew it. All I remember is that he seemed fulfilled, and I hurt, and thought all my anticipation about sex wasn't worth it. I didn't even enjoy it. He got dressed as quickly as he could, and told me to do the same and drove me back. I couldn't believe it." Catherine was mesmerized by the story.

"I ran up to my room and cried my eyes out. Angelique, our housekeeper in France, came into my room and sat by my bed. She asked me if I wanted to talk about it. At first I didn't but, with a little coaxing from her, I told her the story. She was very sympathetic. She told me that all men weren't like Carlo, some were warmer and more in tune with pleasing their partner. But what she said that was most important was that, if a woman didn't know how to please herself, no man could ever please her. She told me to take off my nightgown. I did as I was told. She then asked me to feel my breasts and put my hands between my legs. I felt very uncomfortable doing it at first. But Angelique had a soothing voice . . . a way of relaxing you. She made me aware of all the places that were sensual to me. I closed my eyes and let my hands roam. When I opened them again, she was lying next to me naked. She helped me find myself. It was the most beautiful and fulfilling night of my life. No man has ever been able to please me the way she did," Jenna stopped and looked up at

Catherine. She knew she had hit a nerve. Catherine was turned on, yearning for Jenna to hold her the way Angelique had done.

Jenna got up and shut off the lights. She walked over to Catherine, unbuttoning her shirt. Catherine sat there limp, willing to let Jenna do anything to her. She felt her body relax to Jenna's touch. Catherine looked up and eyed Jenna's exquisite body, lean, firm, and perfectly proportioned. Jenna kissed her softly on the lips, and Catherine felt herself give way to all her deeply suppressed feelings. Jenna brought her to heights Catherine never dreamed about. She was so warm and soft that Catherine felt secure for the first time in years. She loved Jenna and knew she would continue to love her the rest of her life. Jenna was gone when Catherine woke up from a peaceful, restful sleep. She felt as though there was a void in her life. She never wanted to let go. She wanted to run into Jenna's room and stay there forever.

Now, without any notice, without a word of explanation, Jenna was getting married. She was leaving Catherine and their beautiful night was ruined. If Catherine could crawl into a hole and die, she would.

Michael and Allison were snuggled together in the front seat of the car, laughing and chatting away about the wedding. Catherine couldn't drum up any enthusiasm. Allison attributed this to the end of an era. The end of the threesome. Jenna couldn't spend as much time with her friends now that she was married, and Allison knew Catherine was closer and would miss her more.

"I wish we could find a nice guy for Catherine,"

Allison whispered. "She looks so miserable."

"She's going to have to find her own man. I've given it enough tries. Besides, when the three of you are working together this summer, she'll be all right."

"I hope so. I feel so guilty. Only Catherine is alone."

"That, my darling, is her business. You can't worry about her like a mother hen. Or was this where we came in so many months ago."

Allison smiled, remembering their first night.

"Jeff's slowing down. I think he's trying to tell us something," Michael said.

"Maybe Jenna changed her mind," were the first words Catherine had uttered in hours.

"I think they want to stop. Let's pull up next to them," Allison told them.

"What's up?"

"Jenna wants to stop and have a cup of coffee before we get to our destination. I think she wants to make last minute preparations or something," Jeff told them.

"Follow us."

Michael did just that, and both cars stopped in front of an all-night diner a half a mile down the deserted road.

Jenna jumped out of the car and ran to Catherine. "I think the two of us should have a little girl talk. You don't mind, do you Allison?"

"No, go ahead."

"Allison, Catherine looked so depressed back there. I had to stop and talk to her. I think she felt left out. I *did* tell you first."

"Sure." Allison smiled and watched the two go into the ladies room.

"I want to explain something to you, Catherine. The other night was nice, but it isn't my life. You needed a lift, and believe me you can come to me whenever you need me. Nothing is going to change between us. We're still friends. Jeff will never get in the way. Besides, I'm sure we'll be friends longer than the marriage will last."

"If you think this is a mistake, then why are you marrying him?"

"I want to. I'm never sure though what tomorrow will bring. We may last and we may not. I'm a pessimist in the romance department. This way, I'm never disappointed," Jenna went on. "I know someday you'll fall in love with someone."

"I have," Catherine interrupted. "I love you," she said, frightening Jenna.

"It's natural. But I mean you'll find someone—a man to understand you and bring you out of your shell."

"I don't want to. But don't let me dampen your day," Catherine said, fearing alienation. If she pushed Jenna too far, she might never see her again. "I promise not to cry at your wedding."

"Good. Then let's get back to the others. I want you to be as excited as I am."

"Don't worry about me. I'll be fine," Catherine said, giving Jenna a kiss.

"I know you will," Jenna told her.

Catherine and Jenna joined the others at the table.

"I'm starved. I can eat everything on this menu," Jenna said.

"I've never seen anyone eat the way you do and stay so thin," Jeff told her. "It's unbelievable."

"Some of us are lucky I guess," she smiled, hoping she had done the job on Catherine. She didn't want their little secret to slip out on the long drive to Maryland.

"How far would you say we are?" Jenna asked.

"Hour at the most," Michael answered.

"Then why don't we spend the night here, and continue on in the morning?"

"Sounds good to me," Jeff said.

"Now the girls will share one room and the guys another. Fair?"

"Hey, wait a minute. We're getting married in the morning," Jeff protested.

"Then you can do without me for one night. I must protect Allison's virtue," Jenna smiled.

"You really know how to hurt a guy," Michael told her. "But we're all old enough to make our own decisions. What do you think, Allison?"

"I think Jenna's right. All us girls should sleep in the same room. And you guys could have sort of a bachelor party," Allison joked.

"Oh good. We're really going to get a lot of sleep tonight. Michael, did you bring the cards?" Jeff asked.

"No, but we'll pick some up. I plan to spend my evening in the cold shower."

They got up and drove to the motel. Girls in the room next to the guys.

"I'm going to be the one who chaperones all of you," Catherine joined in.

"I knew we brought her along for something," Michael joked. "See you in the morning girls . . . if Jeff and I don't get any bright ideas on how to break into your room."

"I'll be up waiting for you, if you do," Catherine smiled.

Everyone fell asleep right away. They were too exhausted from the night's adventure to do anything. Catherine stayed awake the longest. She watched Jenna sleep. "She is beautiful," Catherine thought. "I'll never leave her. I'll take any piece of her life she's willing to give."

# 2.

The wedding went through on schedule. Jenna was dressed in a white Dior suit, a borrowed handkerchief of Catherine's and a blue scarf of Allison's. The boys looked so handsome in their suits, so solemn. It was more like they were going to a funeral than a wedding. The ceremony only lasted five minutes then it was over.

"Now for the hard part," Jenna said. "I have to call home."

Mrs. Jones didn't take the news as hard as Jenna thought. She knew it was a ploy of Jenna's to see how far she could get. Jenna would live with this man, have her fun, and get rid of him when she was through. It was nothing like her daughter's marriage. Mrs. Jones had promised herself when her daughter died never to interfere in her grandchild's relationships. Had she not pressed her own daughter so hard, she might be alive today. No, if Jenna was trying to hurt her, she failed. Grandmother knew there was a strong element missing in Jenna's character . . . compassion . . . she loved herself more than she could ever love anyone else.

Two days later, for appearances, Mrs. Jones arranged a formal reception for the newly married couple. She invited her close friends, had a few of Jenna's friends, and stood up and toasted the bride and groom. Jenna looked at her coolly, and Grandmother knew she had done the right thing.

Allison and Catherine moved into the apartment first. Jenna had gone off to the country for a few days with Jeff. Allison explored the City with Michael while Catherine threw herself into her work, counting the days until Jenna's return.

"I wish it had been us up there getting married the other night," Michael said.

"So do I. But you still have another three years of law school, and then you have to wait to take your bar."

"I know. I hate wishing my life away, but I don't want to wait that long."

"What do you want to do?" she asked.

"I want to marry you as soon as you finish school. With your taking an accelerated course and getting out in two more years, I'll still have another year. But if we budget our money and I get a part-time job to help out, I'm sure we'll make it. Look, I know it's a lot to ask. It won't be easy. But, Allison, I want to be with you. The sooner the better. What do you think?"

"I think it's a wonderful idea. I was going to suggest it myself, but I didn't know just how you'd feel about it," she told him, giving him a hug.

"I'm so relieved. I've wanted to tell you about my plan so often. I was afraid you'd think I was crazy."

"It's fine with me. I can work with the girls until you get settled. It won't be so bad."

"What about your modeling?"

"That, my dear, was a childish dream. I'd much rather be Mrs. Fenway."

"I'd much rather that too. I love you, Allison. And to think we wasted so much time this year over nothing."

"I know. But it's better now than it ever was. It was

worth it," Allison told him. "Why don't we celebrate tomorrow night? Catherine is going out to my parents for the weekend. Jenna is still away which means I have the loft entirely to myself. Why don't I cook your dinner?"

"Why don't I devour you first, and we'll order a pizza," he smiled.

"I didn't invite you over for a seductive night. Only dinner."

"Oh yeah. I know you better. Besides we made a pact. We'd spend our summer nights together. And I'm glad our first night will have no limits," he whispered kissing her. "We'll have the whole night."

"Michael, you're turning me on. I may not be able to wait until tomorrow night."

"Good, then let's throw Catherine out early."

"Don't be mean. She's depressed enough. I feel sorry for her. She's really taking Jenna's marriage very hard."

"I know. I've tried not to notice. I can't understand it."

"That's why I'm glad she's going out to my parents. My mother has a way of cheering her up. Do you know, she hasn't been home once since school started. That's something else about Catherine that bothers me. I know they were poor and all, but not to ever want to go home again! I can't even imagine it."

"Maybe she doesn't have a mother. She's pretending."

"Michael, don't be silly. I've seen letters from her. Catherine puts them away after she reads them. She doesn't write back. It's odd."

"A woman of mystery. Do you think Jenna knows any more?"

"If she does, she's not talking. Jenna may be a lot of things, but she is very close mouthed. She'll die with a secret."

"I know," Michael confided. "I admire her for that. I wonder why she ran off and married Jeff?"

"Beats me. She must have been in a romantic mood the other night. Well, here we are. I will say goodnight to you down here, like a good girl."

"You only have one more day," Michael laughed.

"See you about six-thirty tomorrow," Allison said.

"I'll be right on time. Flowers and all. Oh, don't cook anything elaborate," Michael said as an afterthought. "I wouldn't want it to go to waste."

"I'm preparing a meal that tastes as good cold as it does warm. I may be hungry afterwards."

"You're sending out for Chinese food," he smiled.

"Maybe. See you tomorrow," Allison said, closing the door and running up the four flights to the loft, happy with the way she handled herself.


Allison helped Catherine pack for the country. She told her to take casual clothes and one long dress. Saturday night was always dinner at the club.

"Tell mother I'm sorry about not coming out this weekend, but I will be out soon."

"Sure. I think it would be better if we all had some time alone anyway. I know I need it," Catherine said.

"Do you want to talk about what's bothering you?" Allison asked, concerned.

"No. I'll be okay. The old gang is breaking up. That's all."

"We'll all be here together soon. I'm sure things won't be different. After all, Jenna spent a great deal of time with Jeff in school."

"I realize that, but he didn't live with us," Catherine said.

"He won't be living with us now, either," Allison told her. "Jenna is taking a place with him in Mid-town. It's her aunt's apartment. She gave Jenna the keys as one of her wedding presents."

"She what?"

"You didn't know," Allison said, spilling the beans.

"When did this all come about?"

"The day of the wedding . . . I told you. I think it's a much better idea, don't you?" Allison said.

"I guess so. I wish I wasn't the last to know all the arrangements."

"Catherine, it's only for the summer . . . what's the difference?"

"And what about the winter?" Catherine interrupted. "She'll be living with him in his house."

"Catherine, we don't own Jenna. I think you're overreacting," Allison said, wondering what really was going on in her friend's mind.

"You're right. I guess you're not as sentimental as I am. . . ," Catherine said, trying to cover up.

Allison didn't say anything more. She was confused about many things, but Jenna's hold on Catherine was something she dare not even try to figure out.

"You'll be all right here by yourself? What am I saying . . . the minute I'm out the door, Michael will be over," Catherine smiled, kissing her friend goodbye. "Have a good weekend."

"You, too. Give mother and father my love," Allison shouted down the stairs to Catherine.

"I will, see you Sunday."

Allison shut the door and locked it. She walked over

to the window, watching her friend walk to the bus stop. *She's a strange girl*, she thought. Allison walked around the apartment, finding herself in Catherine's room. Maybe if she sat there long enough, a clue to Catherine's behavior would come to her. Allison was tempted to go through her friend's drawers hoping to find the unanswered letters her mother wrote. Catherine kept so much bottled up inside. Allison wondered how long it would be before she exploded. And most of all, what strange hold did Jenna have over her? And she over Jenna? For a moment, Allison felt like the outsider. The two sharing a secret life she knew nothing about.

Allison walked out of the room and into the kitchen. The heat of the small kitchen overwhelmed her. She no longer felt festive. Everyone was different. In one short year, they had all grown too fast. Allison sat down in the large chair by the studio window. The cool breeze felt refreshing on her warm face. Allison thought about what the next few years would bring. Jenna would be pushing harder than ever to get the company started. Michael would be pulling at her to get married. And she'd have to work with even more ferocity to get both done. Added classes in school, long hours of work to help get Michael past the bar. Then, and only then, could she think about putting her life in proper order. Michael would have to transfer to a school in New York where they'd share a small apartment. He'd be working part-time, studying whenever he had a free moment, and she'd see little or nothing of him. Was she caught up in the festivity of Jenna's wedding and rushing her answer to Michael? Everything she dreamed about was turning around. Allison was frightened, hoping she was making the right decision. She didn't know how long she had been sitting in the chair, but she snapped back to reality when she heard the familiar knock on the door. It was Michael. Her heart leaped, nothing was ready, and she didn't know if she was ready for Michael.

Her fears disappeared the moment she opened the door and saw him standing there, a dozen yellow roses in his hand, and the soft inviting smile on his lips. He kissed her and all thoughts of life without him vanished as quickly as they came.


"This is not what I call dinner," Michael smiled. "Potato chips and three over-ripe bananas."

"Well, if you weren't in such a hurry to get me into this bedroom, I would have had time to prepare something," Allison said, snuggling up to him.

"Did I sound as if I was complaining . . . not me . . . not at all," Michael smiled, holding her in his arms. "I'd give food up for you anyday."

"It was worth waiting for?" Allison said, searching him out.

"More than worth waiting for. And we still have plenty of time," he said, turning her over, and taking her again. Feeling more confident, Allison enjoyed him more the second time, feeling no shame and no disappointment. They belonged together. They were comfortable and relaxed with one another. Even when Michael threw off the covers, appraising her long firm body, Allison felt no embarrassment. She loved Michael. Their love-making was good and fulfilling for both of them.

The next morning, Michael and Allison walked around the City together, hand in hand. They went to the zoo, fed the animals, and stopped at every hot dog vendor, ravenous from the night before. They lunched at a small coffee house in the Village, talking, looking radiant for all to see. The business, Catherine, Jenna never entered their thoughts for the two days.

"I'm stuffed," Allison said after her third pastry.

"You should be, the way you packed it away today," he said affectionately.

"Well, we can always go home and exercise," she laughed, her blue eyes twinkling like a mischievous child.

"I'm ready whenever you are," he told her. "We still have some time before our roommates come back."

"Our roommates?"

"Sure. Didn't I tell you? I've decided not to leave you, ever."

"Not even to go to work tomorrow?"

"No. I'll bring the files home."

"Fine, and I'll sketch in bed."

"Now that we have the rest of the summer worked out, let's start," he said, grabbing Allison by the hand and escorting her out of the restaurant and into a taxi. The house was empty when they returned. the two returned to bed, the cool sheets felt good against their naked bodies. They made love again, Allison the aggressor.

"Did you hear something?" Allison jumped up.

"No. What time is it? It might be Catherine."

Allison looked at the clock. It was five-thirty. "No, she isn't due until seven." Allison got up, put on her bathrobe and walked into the studio. Catherine wasn't there, but Jenna was.

"Did I frighten you?" she turned quickly, taking Allison off guard.

"A little. I thought it was Catherine, but it doesn't matter. What are you doing here?"

"I live here remember?" Jenna said, picking up her suitcases and taking them into her room.

"Jenna, where's Jeff?"

"I left him in the country."

"Did you have a fight?"

"Sort of. We'll make up. He has to think things out . . . Oh, I didn't know you were here," Jenna said, staring up at Michael. He was dressed only in his pants. "I see you have more to tell me than I do you," she smiled.

"What happened?" Michael whispered to Allison.

"I think the lovebirds had their first fight. And I also think it's time you got dressed . . ."

"And left," Michael was startled.

"No, just dressed. I'll put on some coffee. She always liked talking to you. Maybe you can find out what happened."

"He started making noises like a husband," Jenna told Michael.

"He *is* your husband," Michael started. "We were all there to see you two get married," he tried making her laugh.

"I know," she started to explain. "There we were, having a wonderful time. Dressed up, dancing by candlelight, and then Jeff says something about his being thirty-five and wanting to start a family."

"That's only natural," Michael said.

"For him, maybe, but not for me. I never want to have children. I don't want a conventional marriage, as others do . . . as Allison wants. I want him to love me. Be friends. Have other people over to our house. Go out when we feel like it. Have fun together. Be lovers forever."

"That's a tall order. But just mentioning having a

family doesn't mean the love affair is over. Children can enhance a marriage sometimes, not hurt it. But I know it's not you. But you didn't have to walk out."

"It was more than that. We started to discuss the future. Jeff wants to stay at Carnegie teaching, and I want him to come back here as soon as I can to start the company. He thought because I married him, I wanted the same type of life. His life."

"Jenna, I'm sure the two of you can work out a reasonable arrangement. Maybe you should work here and go back on weekends, vacations, summers. I know lots of men whose families are in the country and they have to stay in the City all week. It works out fine for them."

"I thought so, too, but Jeff is a bit old-fashioned. Remember, I'd be the one living in the City, and he'd be the one, the outsider. He won't go for it."

"You are saying the marriage is over?" Allison asked, horrified.

"If we can't come to any suitable arrangements."

"But, Jenna, we still have two years of school. I think you're being a big premature. Let it ride for awhile. Maybe in time both of you will have a change of heart," Allison went on.

"Look, go back to whatever you were doing. Don't let me spoil your fun. I'm sure you're right. Jeff and I will be fine. Where's Catherine?"

"At my parents for the weekend. She'll be back soon. I'm sure she'll be happy to see you. She's been in a blue mood ever since the wedding."

"Maybe I'll take her out to dinner. That will give the two of you more time together," she smiled, pushing them both back into Allison's room.

"The girl can be helpful at times," Michael smiled,

pulling Allison down on the bed.

"I can't, not right now. I'm not ready to make love to you with someone else here. Can you understand?"

"No. But I'll live. We'll just sit here and talk . . ." Michael said, reaching into her bathrobe, touching her breasts.

"You're not playing fair, Michael," Allison giggled. "I'm trying to act like a lady."

"Ladies belong in the living room not in bedrooms."

"Oh, the hell with it," she smiled, giving in.

Allison heard voices outside, then the sound of the front door closing. Catherine and Jenna were out together for the evening. Again her mind went to them, their strange relationship. She looked over at Michael sleeping, snoring softly, in deep contentment. She lay down close to him and fell asleep.

The summer flew by quickly, and the fall semester was on them before they had a chance to do half of what they planned. Catherine and Allison went back to their room. Jenna moved into the tiny house as Mrs. Conroy.

"Oh, I think it's going to be very hard to get back into a regular routine," Catherine whined. "The summer was fantastic."

"You sure changed rather quickly," Allison said. "I'm not looking forward to settling down to work either. I'm going to miss Michael."

"He's not that far away."

"Yeah, but he can't come and go the way he did this summer. Let it be semester break tomorrow," Allison sighed.

"It will be here sooner than you think."

"God, I'm not looking forward to unpacking all this

junk. I'm not in the mood to do anything but sleep. I'm too tired."

"I know. Jenna and Jeff give some crazy parties. If I averaged two hours of sleep a night in all those months, I was lucky."

"Me too. Do you want to tell me about the man who's kept you away from home the last few months?" Allison teased.

"There's nothing to tell," Catherine said nonchalantly.

"Are we ever going to meet him?"

"No. I won't be seeing him anymore," Catherine went on. Allison stared at her. She didn't see any sign of remorse or resentment. She let the subject drop.

"We're all invited to Jenna's tomorrow night for dinner. You going?"

"Sure," Allison said. "Mike is picking us up after class." She opened her trunk. "Why did I bring all this stuff?"

Catherine smiled to herself while she hung her clothes up neatly in the closet. She was proud of the way she kept her secret. As close as she was to Allison, her friend had no idea what was going on. The summer brought Allison closer to Michael, and she, closer to Jenna. How can anything start so wrong and end up so right? She should never have over-reacted to the marriage. She should have known better. Jenna had to get bored with Jeff. He could never keep her satisfied. While Allison was busy making love to Michael, Catherine and Jenna were planning their future together.

Catherine was shocked and excited to find Jenna home when she returned from the McWilliams. With a quick word and loving glance, Jenna took Catherine away from the studio and out to dinner. She explained everything to her then.

The two sat at a small table in the corner of the dimly-lit French restaurant three doors down from the studio. The place was almost empty. Everyone was still away at their weekend homes. Jenna ordered a martini and told Catherine the story.

"I married Jeff too fast. I hoped that I'd hurt my grandmother. I keep wanting to punish her, but all I do is punish myself. The old girl's too smart for me. Now I'm stuck. He's making plans for twenty years from now. Talking retirement . . . God, it scared me. I can't imagine living with anyone twenty years. Suddenly, everything came into focus. I was really married and about to set up housekeeping. How boring. I'm too young."

Catherine's heart jumped a mile. She couldn't believe what she was hearing. Jenna was back and confiding in her.

"I think you shouldn't jump out of the marriage as fast as you jumped into it. Jeff can be rather useful to you next year. Being married to him can give you certain privileges at school. You'll be part of the faculty. You'll have no restrictions or curfews. I mean you can do anything and go anywhere without the scrutiny of anyone's eye," Catherine said, placing her hand on Jenna's. Jenna did not pull her hand away.

"I see what you mean. Very true. And Jeff does spend most nights with his students, which would give me plenty of free time," Jenna's mind drifted off to some rather fun nights of sex with Catherine to cover for her. Married life was looking better. *No one knows how to play the game better than me*, she thought. *I can make Jeff believe anything I want. And when school is over, so is my marriage. We'll have a wonderful year.*

"And I can always cover for you, Jenna," Catherine said as if she was reading Jenna's mind. "I'd do anything you wanted," Catherine told her, looking lovingly into her clear green eyes.

"To us," Jenna said, lifting her glass to Catherine's, meaning one thing.

"To us," Catherine returned, feeling something else.

Catherine tiptoed into the studio first. Hearing no noise from Allison's bedroom, she went on to hers. It was the farthest down the hall. Jenna joined her a few minutes later, lights still off and locked the door. She would reward Catherine for her loyalty. It was a price she had to pay.

Jenna called Jeff the next morning, but she heard he was already on his way down to the City. She awaited his arrival, tears in her eyes and warmth in her voice. Jeff played right into her hands. They moved into her aunt's apartment that very afternoon.

She and Catherine spent their days roaming Seventh Avenue. Catherine invited herself to Jenna's apartment whenever Jeff was out. She was careful and never let Allison know where she was going. Allison assumed she had finally met someone.

Jenna pushed hard, as Allison suspected. They were invited to all the fashion shows, many private showings, and, after each show, the girls would return to the studio and sketch from memory all they had seen. Then they'd tear the new lines apart bit by bit, decide where they'd make changes, how they'd alter the accessories, use new bold colors, and then put everything away in private files for future reference.

David White was a great help to the girls. He was able to get them into the workshops of some of the most established designers on Seventh Avenue—Trigere, Orsini, Mainbocher, Adrian, and Norell.

Allison and Catherine were mesmerized by the pace and candor of the designers. They observed the in-house models parading back and forth, and Norman Norell snipping and cutting down what didn't appeal to him. His new season consisted of the chemise, a 1920's look, low-waisted dresses with hip belts and flared skirts. Piqués and silks were his fabrics. The two girls made mental notes.

The lady of their choice was Pauline Trigere. Her fashions were simple, yet elegant. Once a woman invested in a Trigere, she could wear it for life, if the hemline didn't vary too much. She was a self-made woman, very much their role-model—a teacher, a designer, and a warm, intelligent individual, who built up her dynasty from nothing. Pauline Trigere answered all their questions and took a great deal of time to explain her philosophy of the fashion industry. The girls listened and recorded what she said in their permanent memory file.

Pauline told the girls that the woman's figure is important. Women love dramatic evening clothes. For this reason she used *Peau de soie*, the fabric with superb capabilities. It's as stiff as taffeta and yet defined the figure. A woman should always feel feminine. If anything, Catherine and Allison learned that lesson. They'd keep their styles simple, accent the figure, use comfortable fabrics, and plan each design with the right jewelry in mind. But they would never forget the aura of the dramatic. Each of them wished she could afford to buy one Trigere dress for posterity. Another important aspect—their own designs must be affordable to most women.

By the end of the summer, the girls felt they knew about the heart and soul of the fashion industry. Jenna studied the retail end, while Catherine was more interested in the inception of ideas. She liked sitting at the drawing board. Allison, much to her surprise, loved what she thought was the glamor end. She found her niche in publicity and promotion. She wanted to be out there talking to the public. Allison needed to know how people felt about clothes, their needs and ideas. This would be functional in any company—filling the void, she called it—knowing what the public wants and giving it to them, of course, with some flair of her own added in. Allison learned that Jenna had been right from the beginning. People don't really know how to dress or what looks best on them. Allison decided, if she was going to join Jenna, it would be in the teaching and education of these women.

The summer, for all intents and purposes, was a success. Each girl had found her own area of potential expertise.

Jenna announced at the end of the summer that she would be spending the following summer in Europe taking a sneak peek at their designs and following through. Catherine agreed to join her, but Allison begged off. She didn't want to spend three months away from Michael and thought, for her own purposes, the American women were her game.

Each of them was set, exhausted, full of ideas, and ready to begin, once they got themselves back on schedule, for their new undertaking.

Michael entered law school, and Allison, her grades high, was able to take extra courses for early graduation. Catherine and Jenna followed suit.

The semester got off to a slow start but was full of

excitement. Jenna was the perfect hostess, wife, and student. She held all the faculty in the palm of her hand. Jeff beamed with pride at his new bride, rich, elegant, sophisticated beyond her years. He had no idea his marriage was faltering in any way. Jenna remained a perfect bed partner, but avoiding any talk of children and the future. Jeff believed that if he was patient Jenna would be ready.

Jenna socialized with Allison, Mike and Catherine, although Catherine's whining was getting to her. She cut lose when she could for one night stands and new adventures. The students at school caught a smile or a glance. She talked to them when the mood struck her fancy and quickly dismissed them when she was bored with them. For her own pleasures, Jenna kept the room across the hall from the girls. A place of her own to sit and think, she told Jeff, but Catherine knew better.

Christmas, Allison went home, then to the apartment in the City. Jenna invited Catherine to spend Christmas with her again in Palm Beach with Jeff and the family. She felt all advances from Catherine were safe there.

It was during the Christmas holidays that Jenna faced her first crisis. The first few days of vacation, Jenna was exhausted—she couldn't get out of bed for more than a few hours at a time. Everyone was worried about Jenna's health. Even her grandmother showed deep concern. She insisted Jenna be brought to the best specialist in town. It didn't take him long to find Jenna's problem. She was pregnant. The thought repulsed her. She got sick in Dr. Morley's office. Jenna put her thoughts in focus; she asked the doctor to keep her secret. She wanted to tell everyone herself. He smiled knowingly and promised he wouldn't breathe a word. Jenna rode around all day in a daze. She had to get rid of the baby before Jeff or anyone else found out. But abortion wasn't legal, and she didn't know anyone who could help her. She'd have to confide in someone, and Catherine was the only one she could trust. With a plan in mind, she asked Catherine to go for a walk with her, telling everyone else the doctor said she was just run down. Working all summer and the rough new schedule of going to school and being a married lady was taking its toll. Everyone, including Jeff, bought her story.

"I know you told me a long time ago, if there was anything you could do for me, you'd do it," Jenna started. "Now I need a very big favor."

"Anything," Catherine said. "Whatever you want, consider it done."

"I need to have an abortion, and *you* have to help me," Jenna blurted out much to Catherine's surprise.

"What happened?"

"Catherine, that doesn't matter now. We have to think. I can't disappear for a few days without someone wondering where I am."

"I know," Catherine started. "Allison thinks I'm involved with someone. I can say I'm pregnant and that will let you off the hook. We can do all the necessary planning. I will find someone who will be safe and will keep his mouth closed. After I make the arrangements, I'll ask you to come with me for emotional support. Everyone will buy the story."

"Oh, Catherine, that's a good idea. No one would ever suspect. But we'll have to wait a week or two. You know, put up a good show. I don't want anyone to put the pieces together. My being tired and the baby."

"I'll just have to throw up my breakfast for a few days. Or pretend to," Catherine smiled. "I'll make a few calls and see. I know one friend who went to Puerto

Rico. It's legal there. I'll give her a call and find out the name of her doctor."

"Thank you so much. I'll never forget you for this," Jenna was in Catherine's debt further. "If Jeff ever found out, he'd be buying cigars."

"Let's make plans to leave a few days after Christmas. This way, we'll have time to rest up before we go back to school. It will give us plenty of time."

"True, and leave Jeff to me. I'm sure he won't mind if I go with you," Jenna said, hugging her friend in relief. "I'll tell him I'm paying for everything."

Catherine played up her condition to the hilt. Allison and Michael flew down to Palm Beach to be with her. Everyone felt sorry for Catherine. Michael helped her make arrangements for the abortion. And two days after Christmas, Jenna left with Catherine for Puerto Rico.

The girls promised to call as soon as they knew where they were going to stay, and to report to everyone how everything went.

Jenna, though composed, was feeling sick. Operations and doctors frightened her. She felt no remorse about the abortion, the sooner it was over the better. Where most women start feeling maternal when they are carrying a child, Jenna felt hostility. She made up her mind on the flight that she would talk to the doctor in private, protecting herself against ever letting this happen again.

Catherine took charge, made all hotel reservations and appointments with Doctor Hernandez. Jenna sat and relaxed as if she didn't have a care in the world. Catherine loved it. She discovered that she was good at taking charge. She tapped resources she didn't know she had. She felt useful for the first time in her life, and

Jenna enjoyed the pampering.

Jenna used Catherine's name when she went to see the doctor the following morning. The abortion was scheduled for the same afternoon. Much to her surprise, the hospital was unlike what she imagined. It was a clean, sterile place, rows of clean beds and polished floors. The nurses were in clean starched white uniforms and the clinic was run with order and dignity. Doctor Hernandez believed in a woman's right to decide for herself what she wanted to do with her own child and her life. He took pride in his small clinic, and she found him neither disapproving nor contemptuous. She opened up to him right away and decided to tell him her problem.

Doctor Hernandez wasn't used to hearing a sterility request from such a young girl. As a matter of fact, in his thirty years in practice, he had never had someone as young as Jenna come to him. He sat behind his large desk for a moment pondering her request, his small dark frame twisting back and forth in the large chair.

Jenna sat tensely across from him, waiting for his answer.

"Miss Markham, I'll make this short. I don't believe in lectures. But you are a very young girl. An operation such as the one you've asked me to perform is irreversible. I have to make sure you are absolutely sure you are doing the right thing. It will affect your whole life."

"Doctor, years ago when I was a little girl, I never played with dolls or pretended they were my own children. I had illusions of becoming my own person, making my own way in this world. For obvious reasons, I may marry, but to become a mother is not in the cards for me. I have neither the desire nor the patience. I don't want to spend any more time in clinics like this one when an accident happens. I feel, in time, several abortions could be dangerous to my health," Jenna told him, straightforward and sincere.

"You put me in rather an odd position. I understand your feelings. I agree in every way that each person has the right to make up his or her own mind where their lives are concerned. If I didn't perform the operation, I'd be a hypocrite, but if I did, I'd feel I would be instrumental in helping you destroy your life."

"Doctor, you did tell me that this was the best time to have such an operation."

"Yes."

"Then perform it or I will find someone else later on who will," Jenna was determined.

"I'll have to reschedule you."

"Fine. I can stay down here as long as need be," she said.

"Tomorrow, at seven a.m. I hope you know what you're doing," he said, feeling dismayed.

"Believe me, doctor, I do. Thank you. And if it makes you feel better, I'll drop you a card in ten years, to let you know I still agree with my decision."

Doctor Hernandez didn't answer. Jenna got up and left the office. She went back to the waiting room.

"Are you all set?" Catherine asked.

"Change of plans. My blood work didn't come back in time. I'll have to come back early tomorrow for the operation."

"How about having dinner somewhere?" Catherine asked.

"Yes. Dinner, a show, and maybe a little gambling. I feel lucky tonight."

"You certainly are in good spirits."

"Whenever I make a decision and know it's for the best, I feel better. Meeting the good doctor has made me feel much better about the whole affair. To the hotel to change," she said, spirits high.

"I think we'd better call Jeff and give him the new schedule."

"Yes, that's a good idea. Tomorrow I won't be in the mood to talk to anyone. As a matter of fact, I'll call him tonight and tell him it's all over. You're doing fine and we plan to stay a few more days to rest."

Jenna was prompt. Doctor Hernandez asked her one more time if she was sure about the operation. When she insisted that she hadn't changed her mind, he gave her many forms to fill out and sign. She was very glad she had used Catherine's name since, as a single parent, she could determine her own fate. If she were married, her husband would also have to sign the papers; a married woman wasn't really in control of her own destiny at all.

Catherine paced the halls until she was allowed to visit Jenna in the recovery room. Jenna, still groggy from the anesthesia, mumbled a few words and drifted back to sleep. She continued to sleep through most of the day. Catherine walked to the beach and shopped for the next few days until Jenna was released from the hospital. Feeling weaker than she had expected, Jenna extended their stay another few days.

When the two women returned to Palm Beach, Jeff was gone. He had told Mrs. Jones that he had to return to school early to prepare for the coming semester. Jenna, relieved not to have to face him or his sexual advances, slept in peace the rest of the vacation. When she returned to school, things had definitely changed. Instead of Jeff's usual loving welcome, he was cold and uninviting. He gave her a quick peck on the cheek, excused himself and went out. He made excuses every time she'd try to make love to him and then started coming home when he was sure Jenna was asleep. Jenna went back to class, planned the season's dinner party calendar, and accompanied Jeff to other faculty members' homes. She couldn't understand his attitude, but, until he was ready to bring it up, she was happy the way things were. Jenna attempted to draw him into conversation one evening after a quiet dinner. She spoke about the European itinerary.

"When do you think we can leave?"

"You can leave anytime you want," he returned.

"Jeff, I'm talking about Europe. I have to go and I'd like to make the arrangements as soon as possible. It's getting late in the season."

"I know. You can leave whenever you see fit. I'm not going."

"Are you taking summer classes this year?"

"Yes. I'll be spending the whole summer in town. So go off whenever . . ."

"Okay, I promised myself not to press you but I think this has gone on long enough. What's wrong? You haven't touched me since I got back."

"I'll never touch you again. I thought in time my mood would change, it hasn't. I hate you more today than I did in December. I see no future for us," he went on.

"Why? Can you at least try to explain."

"Why don't *you* tell me. Catherine needed an abortion . . . Bullshit," Jeff started. Jenna stood frozen. How did he find out?

"You forgot something, my beautiful wife. Your grandmother happens to know Doctor Morley. And when he came over to congratulate me, I put all the pieces together. Why didn't you even ask me? We could have worked something out."

"I was afraid you'd try and talk me into having the baby. I know how you feel about a family. I'm not ready. I don't know if I ever will be," Jenna panicked.

"You lied to me and you brought that poor innocent girl into your plot. I don't know how she puts up with you. All I know is that I don't ever want to see you after you leave for Europe. We'll get a quiet divorce. I'll mark it off to your immaturity or something. I won't spill the beans."

"Jeff, I'm sorry. If I had any idea you'd have gone along with me, I would have told you."

"I probably wouldn't. You are the most selfish, self-centered human being I've ever had the misfortune to meet. I've put you out of my life . . . gotten you out of my system. You didn't think it was possible. You thought all you had to do was crook your little finger and I'd come running. No more. Never. I can't stand the sight of you. But I do know I have to work here. I'll keep up appearances until this semester is over. Then get out and don't you ever come near me again," he told her, disgusted, turning his back and walking out the door. She couldn't believe he could turn on her. She was sure she could convince him to stay, but not now. Jenna walked over to the phone and dialed Catherine's number.

"Will you come over?" was all she said.

Much to Jenna's dismay, Jeff didn't return that evening. She wanted to hurt him the way he hurt her, and Catherine was perfect. Let him see the two of them in bed. That would teach him. He'd never be able to look at another woman without thinking of her. But

Jenna didn't have her revenge. Not then, not ever. Jeff outsmarted her. Catherine didn't know either that she was being used for all Jenna's needs. Catherine was too busy basking in her own victory.

Jenna and Catherine made their European plans. They'd leave the day after school ended. Much to Catherine's surprise, Jenna packed all her things, shipping everything she wasn't going to need in Europe to her grandmother's house in New York. She told no one about her divorce. The papers were signed quickly and painlessly before the plane took off. Jeff sat alone in the Canteen, drinking, thinking about his own foolishness and male pride. He never saw Jenna leave.


"I can't believe we're really graduating," Allison said. "And a year ahead of everyone else. What a relief."

"I'm not going to the ceremonies," Jenna told them. "I feel like celebrating alone. What are you going to do?"

"Look for a place to live. Remember, Michael and I are getting married next month. I have a million things to do. You have to go for a fitting on your dress, Jenna," Allison said excitedly.

"I know. I'll do that next week when I'm home. Why are you and Michael looking for an apartment?"

"We have to live somewhere. I don't believe the bride and groom should live in separate houses after the wedding."

"No. I mean, you have the studio in New York. It's paid for. Why not stay there?"

"We can't, but thanks. Michael still has to finish school. He's going to need a quiet place to study. It wouldn't work."

"Okay. I hope we can make enough money to support you," she smiled at Michael.

"I'm supporting myself. I'll be working part-time. And Allison will have a job."

"True. I wish you two all the luck, or have I said that?" Jenna went on.

"You did, but it's nice to hear. How are you doing, really?" Michael asked with concern.

"Me? Fine. If you were a betting man, Michael, you should have set odds on my marriage. It could never have worked."

"I liked Jeff, he's a very nice man. I thought he'd be good for you."

"He was, for a while. But enough ancient history. Let's toast the bride and groom, maid of honor, everyone. It's graduation. We made it and you two have a tough road ahead. But I am a betting lady, and I bet you are going to have a long and happy life together."

"I'll drink to that," Michael and Allison said. "And me," Catherine added.

"Now, my present to the two of you," Jenna said. "You go home, make all your arrangements, have a happy honeymoon, and don't you dare set one foot into our office until July first. The best part is, you'll be paid in full."

"Jenna, can we afford it?"

"Sure we can. I inherited my trust fund last month. We don't have to worry about money for the next two years."

"Jenna, I don't think it's fair for you to put in all your money."

"Why not? It's my business . . . the majority anyway. But if we're successful, the small portion of stock I issue to each of you will be worth a fortune."

"*If* we're successful," Michael smiled. "Jenna, you're slipping. But thank you, it's very generous."

"It's the least I can do. After all, your girlfriend chose your company last year instead of a trip to Europe. I like to be fair."

"Well, I do appreciate it. I was wondering how I was going to manage to get everything done in time and still go to work everyday. But Michael will have to get along without me except for weekends until after the ceremony."

"I never thought of that. You'll be home and I'll be working away."

"Where are you going on your honeymoon?" Catherine asked.

"We haven't made any plans. We thought we'd get in the car and drive up to New England. Play it by ear. It's more fun," Allison said.

"Yeah, we decided not to be put in the category of newlyweds and go to one of those regular honeymoon places. As long as we're together, the rest doesn't matter."

"Michael, you're still a romantic. I think I like that best about you. You're one of a kind," Jenna said, looking enviously at Allison. "Let's get out of here; this place is giving me the willies. I planned my own marriage here not so long ago. I don't want to sound superstitious, but why chance it?" she said, leading the foursome out of Charley's. Jenna thought she saw Jeff when she left, but the man walked by too quickly. They had avoided one another as much as possible all year. Allison wanted to invite him to the wedding, being fond of Jeff and never knowing the real reason for the divorce. Jenna asked her not to, and when Allison spoke to Jeff, he agreed. He gave them a thoughtful wedding gift the last day of class. A twenty-five dollar savings bond to be put toward their first child's education. Allison sent it home with the other gifts for safekeeping. She felt sorry for Jeff, wishing that things had turned out differently for him. He seemed to be taking the divorce very hard. He aged almost ten years in one. Rumors started about his excessive drinking. But Jenna—Jenna was Jenna. Whatever she was feeling never showed. She never mentioned Jeff's name the whole year. She looked radiant, and dated frequently. She never returned to the dormitory. She rented an apartment near school and held court there every weekend. Allison and Michael frequented her apartment, and Catherine spent most of her time there. She was never alone, serving buffet luncheons, dinners, liquor, and no invitations needed. But Allison felt that she had been hurt by her divorce more than she'd ever let on.

The industry didn't open its arms to welcome *Jenna Jones Incorporated* as it had a few years earlier when the girls were doing research. It was one thing to help out school girls and another to find a potential competitor. Jenna learned fast that brains, beauty and limited money were not all it took to make a name for oneself on Seventh Avenue. Nearing the end of their second year in business, Jenna had to make a quick turn around. Her fashions were impressive on the drawing board and luscious on the models, but the chain stores were reluctant to buy them. She was too young, too untried; no one was willing to be the first to put his head on a chopping block. What she needed was massive advertising, but Jenna didn't have the millions of dollars necessary to launch her name. And grandmother was not about to have her grandchild throw away money on a media campaign. Jenna called the girls into her small office—fashions were out, accessories were in. They'd try their hand at designing sheets, towels, wallpaper. She knew that there would never be any big money in her new plan, but it was a start. If she could be tried and found true in these areas, maybe in a few years they'd be able to make their mark on the fashion industry. Catherine felt more secure. She had tried to tell Jenna during their first year in business that she was going too fast. Allison, wrapped up in getting Michael through school, cared only about making enough money to meet her expenses. So, they'd try again, a new game, hoping they wouldn't have to close their doors when Jenna's money ran out.

Jenna's next move was to put Allison in charge of sales. She needed someone out in the field to represent her, and she couldn't afford to hire a top-notch salesman. Allison had some limited experience, knew her way around the buyers, and represented Jenna with the type of sophistication needed for a Jones. Although Allison wasn't too happy with her new assignment, she was willing to give it a try, also feeling relieved to get out of the stuffy office where depression was slowly setting in.

Allison's big break came a few months later. After pounding the pavement, day after day, talking to buyers, store owners and sales people on all levels, she stopped for lunch at a chic French restaurant on 57th Street. Tired, her feet aching, and fed up with the whole business, she sat patiently at the bar waiting for a table. She felt a pair of eyes staring at her. Her first instinct was to stare back in her *screw off or I'll kill you* fashion, but thought again about it. The man returned her smile and walked over to sit on the empty bar stool next to hers. Allison tried to compose herself, putting on her best stewardess smile, and sipped her martini. The drink was having a relaxing effect on her, enough to tolerate the conversation about to be struck up.

"I see you're carrying around a sample case. What do you sell?" the amiable gentleman asked. Allison guessed he was about fifty. More than five inches shorter than she, he was very well dressed, spoke remarkably well, and seemed harmless enough.

She took another sip of her drink. "Do you really want to know or are you just making conversation?"

"No, I've been working around here for many years. I haven't seen you before. I'm really interested. It may be something I can use."

"Sure you can," Allison told herself, smiled again, and answered, "I'm representing Jenna Jones. She's presenting a new line of bedroom and bathroom accessories. And I'm very tired of getting the door shut in my face," Allison said, being more frank and honest than she should have been.

"Then I think I'd better get you a table," the man smiled, snapping his fingers for the maitre d' to take notice. "Is my table ready, Charles?"

"Yes, Mr. Wordsworth. You may come with me," he stated.

"Please set another place. This very hungry young lady is joining me for lunch."

"Oh, I couldn't. It's very nice of you . . ."

"I won't take no for an answer. I hate eating alone and, as I suggested before, you may be selling something I can use," he said, picking up her sample case and handing it to Charles.

"Bring this to our table for me, please. And order Miss . . ."

"*Mrs*. Fenway," Allison corrected him.

"Mrs. Fenway another drink. Bring it over to the table."

"Yes, sir. Right this way."

Allison got up and followed the gentleman and the maitre d' to the table, too tired to argue. *Stranger things have happened in life. Maybe he can really use Jenna's merchandise*, she thought.

"Now we haven't been formally introduced. My name is Frederick Wordsworth. And you are?"

"Allison Fenway. Thank you for inviting me to lunch. I don't usually . . ."

"Usually take strange men up on their offers for lunch," he said, completing her sentence. "Maybe you should. You know it's not what you have to offer that's important, it's who your contacts are. It can be a very cold industry when you're approaching it from your angle—knocking on doors. What you need is a recognizable name to get the doors opened."

"Don't you think Jenna Jones' name is very recognizable?"

"Yes. But it doesn't matter. People in our business don't know her. They've never seen her work. And frankly, dear, they're not going to be the first to take the chance. It's amazing how, when and if she does become famous, everyone will take the credit for giving her her first break."

"I'm beginning to wonder if that will ever happen." Allison sighed and took another sip of the drink the waiter had brought to the table.

"I started to say . . . you're going about it in the wrong way. This business is mainly a social business.

You have to meet people socially, mention what you do, then drop it. Call them a day or two later and invite them to lunch, dinner, a drink, and make your pitch. It's amazing that all buyers aren't built like Amazon Annie. It seems we do nothing else but eat and drink . . . party."

"Are you telling me very little business is conducted in the office?"

"At first. We do favors, take them, and utlize what we need. Now, a sweet girl like you poses no threat to anyone. Doesn't know the ropes and isn't about to offer anything interesting. Not because you can't, but because you don't know you have to. So why should anyone waste their time seeing you?"

"Oh boy. You are really an awful man. What do you think I am? I don't need this job badly enough to sell myself for it," Allison's dander was up.

"Don't fly off the handle. I'm not asking for anything. I'm giving you the facts of life. As hard as they are."

"So were do I go from here?" Allison asked.

"First you order lunch. We'll talk a bit about the company. What Jenna is all about. Then you can show me whatever's in that bag of yours. If I like it, I'll take it. I'm not afraid to make the first move. I have a hunch Jenna is going to be a big name in this business one day. I'd like to be the first to take a crack at her," he said.

"What do you want for that?"

"The right to have first choice at whatever she's designing. No more, no less."

"Mr. Wordsworth, I hope you like our samples because if you do, you have a deal," she beamed, gulping down the rest of her drink.

"Frederick. I hate formality."

"Frederick. I feel better already."

"I didn't see anything yet," he said.

"I know, but you aren't throwing rocks. Even if you take nothing, it's one hundred percent better treatment than I've been getting," she said in relief.

"My dear, you're learning very fast. How can I possibly say no to such a sincere, honest, and beautiful lady?" Wordsworth smiled. He had done his homework and knew that anything Jenna designed was going to be delicate, tasteful and useable in his store.

"By the way, where do you work?" Allison said, getting started on her salad.

"Bergdorf Goodman," he said nonchalantly.

"I don't believe it! I've tried my best to get an appointment with someone in that store. I can't believe it!"

"I told you, lunch more often. We don't see just anyone," he smiled, loving the game he was playing.

Allison and Wordsworth chatted away like old buddies during the rest of lunch. Time was flying by, and yet he didn't ask to see her samples. They had their coffee, Frederick ordered an after-lunch drink, and still nothing. Allison was getting nervous, wondering if he really was connected with Bergdorf's. Was he some nut who hung around restaurants picking up young girls? Just as Allison was about to bring up the subject again, he asked to see the samples.

Allison eagerly handed the case to him. He flipped through the book in seconds, making little or no comments, and closed the case. Allison's heart sank.

"I like it. I'll take five dozen of each, and keep the supply open for reorder."

"Just like that?" Allison gulped.

"Just like that. I'll even go one step more. I want a

full display of Miss Jones' merchandise in my office tomorrow morning. I'll set up a photography session and play the new line up in one of our Sunday pages of *The New York Times*."

Allison sat back in her chair, stunned. When the day she had hoped for finally happened, it was almost anticlimatic. You walk your feet off for miles, days, months. You hope someone will look at what you're selling, rant and rave about how good it is, then order up a storm. It didn't happen like that at all. One quick glance, and "I'll take five dozen." She couldn't believe it.

"Now, be in my office with the merchandise. I'll sign the order, and you should really be at the shooting. I think you have the flair for niceties."

"I'll be there. I'll even bring the samples with me. What time?" Allison babbled eagerly.

"Eleven. I never get in much before ten and I'll need some time to make arrangements. Now, although I've enjoyed myself immensely, I do have to get back to work. See you tomorrow at eleven," he said, helping her out of the chair and handing back her sample case.

Allison stood on the corner, checked the money in her purse and decided to take a taxi back to the office. She couldn't wait to tell Jenna what had happened.

On second thought, she quickly pulled out a dime, dialed Bergdorf's number and asked for Mr. Wordsworth's office. It didn't hurt to do a little checking. When the soft-spoken secretary answered the line, identifying herself as Mr. Wordsworth's secretary, Allison, not knowing what to say, hung up. Well, he was at Bergdorf's, he had a secretary, so he had to be able to order from her. What was she worrying about?

As the taxi crawled down Fifth Avenue, Allison

became impatient. She was anxious to get to the office and scream out her news. Would everyone get the hell out of her way! Didn't they know she was in a hurry.

Jenna sat at her desk in total disbelief. Catherine was speechless. All anyone could say was, "Are you sure?"

"Yes, I called the store! Now get me everything I'll need for the shooting tomorrow."

"You know the restaurant you were at today?"

"Yes," Allison said.

"Could you work that beat more often?" Jenna laughed, breaking the tension, finally letting the first sale sink in. "What a way to make a sale," she went on.

"I could get used to that," Catherine said. "Sit up at the bar, look pretty, and make money. Sounds more like the life of a hooker."

"Believe me, at first, I thought that's what he had in mind."

"Would you have?" Jenna asked mysteriously.

"Jenna, I love you dearly, and I would like nothing more than to see this business get off the ground, but not enough to put my nicely-shaped fanny on the line. I'll leave that one to you."

"Oh really," Jenna was startled.

"I mean, I'd say very sweetly, 'If you think I'm good looking, you ought to see my boss. She's a much better catch,' " Allison said, being catty.

"I bet you would. I'd have to do a little soul searching to think that one out. No, I don't. If it meant a large sale, why not go to bed with the buyer? I'm not going to shrivel up and die if I do."

"Jenna, let's drop the subject. If we have to stoop to that level, then we'd better get out of this line. We'll sell quality."

"Exactly, and quality comes very expensively. Especially since with quality we're getting quantity."

"I give up," Allison said. "And I'm going home to make dinner for my adoring husband. Have everything ready in the morning."

"We will," they both mimicked. "Isn't she sickening?"

"You're both jealous. I made the first sale and have the sexiest man in the world. What more can I ask for?"

"More sales," Jenna said, half joking.

Allison arrived at Wordsworth's office promptly at eleven. The secretary quickly ushered her into his adjoining office. He sat behind a large oak desk surrounded by floor-to-ceiling windows overlooking a spectacular view of Central Park. Off to one side, one could see the magnificent line of old buildings with a history all their own and the flavor of a long ago elegance. On the other side, the line of newly-constructed, ultra-modern highrises brought to Manhattan a new kind of wealth and distinction. Wordsworth sat between the old and new. Allison wondered which would she choose—the grandeur of the old, or the steel and glass symbol of newly-acquired money?

"First, we'll take care of the business aspect. Did you bring me the order form?"

"Yes, all neatly typed and ready for your signature," she said, handing him the paper.

He quickly glanced over it, scribbled his signature on it, and returned a copy for her own files. Allison didn't know whether to kiss it or frame it for posterity.

"I've sort of taken an interest in this account," Frederick stated. "So I'm going to accompany you to the shooting."

"Oh, I'm glad. I didn't know exactly what I'm to do," Allison said, feeling more inexperienced by the minute.

"It really isn't so hard. You hand over the merchandise to the photographer and he sets up for the shoot. You may make a few suggestions, and then it's over. It doesn't take too much skill," he told her.

"You make it sound so simple."

"On the way over, I'll tell you how to make a good impression," he said, putting on his jacket and taking the package out of her hand.

"Make suggestions. Keep the photographer on his toes. Don't let him for one minute think he can talk you into a shot you don't like. And always make sure your label is showing, the small JJ. It's the only way one will ever tell the difference between what *you* have to sell and others."

"You mean, give the people the *spiel* that if they're not sleeping on JJ sheets, they're just not sleeping in comfort and elegance."

"My, you do learn fast. I like that slogan. Remember it. It can be useful in any ad campaign you might run."

Allison liked Wordsworth. He brought out a creative side she could quickly develop. Allison felt she was better suited for promotion than sales. In time, she hoped the company could afford someone else to represent them; she'd like to stay on the creative end.

"I know I'm picking your brain, but I want to make the most of what we have. I'd like to know more about your ideas to sell Jenna Jones. I think it could be advantageous to both of us."

"More than you think," he said. "The more publicity she gets, the more people will come into the store and ask for her name brands. As it stands now, Bergdorf is selling her exclusively."

"True. I wish I could lie and say it's selling elsewhere."

"Look, when a woman comes into our store looking for Jenna Jones sheets, she's apt to buy something else before she leaves the store. It's good for you and better for us. So before the day is over, I'd like to set you up with some press people. I think we need more on Jenna in all the news media. She is available to give interviews?" he asked.

"All the time," Allison told him, totally absorbed in thought.

"Now. I want you to give Harry Tomes a call this afternoon. He's the best publicist I know. He doesn't come cheap, but the money you spend will come back triple. I don't say you have to use him forever. I'm sure a bright girl like you can learn quickly how he works, and, in time, take over from him."

"My God, Fred, what would I have done without you?" Allison joked.

"Eventually someone would have spotted the possibility in Jenna. You may have had to pound the beat for a few more months," he said. "Here we are. Now remember, don't make yourself appear as if this is your first shooting. Be aggressive. Tell the photographer what you want. He's the best and we'll all be happy with the results, I'm sure," Wordsworth said, paying the taxi driver.

The two walked up to the second floor of the large studio. Gregory Niles was waiting for them. His assistant was setting up the lights and testing them. The young man walked over to Wordsworth, hand extended.

"Gregory, I'd like you to meet Allison Fenway. She's

handling the Jenna Jones' account.''

"Good to meet you," she started. "I've heard so much about your work. I think you're one of the best photographers to come along in years," Allison lied.

"Very good," Frederick whispered, giving her a wink.

"May I see the sheets?" Greg asked.

"Oh, they're in the package," Allison stated.

"Oh no! We'll have to get someone to iron these up. They're all wrinkled. Well, don't worry. It will only take a minute," he said, sorry that he had snapped at her.

Allison walked around the studio. Several people were setting up the props, beds, chairs, curtains—everything to make one think they were photographing in someone's bedroom. The navy blue backdrop against the heavy brass headboard would definitely make the cream-colored silk embroidered sheets and pillow cases stand out. The matching quilted bedspread, folded down at one corner showed the two-tone effect, deep brown on one side, matching cream-colored silk on the other. Both had the dainty *JJ* embroidered on the corner, the butterfly symbol wrapped around the letters. Allison loved the logo.

It took everyone almost an hour to set up for the shot. She looked at Fred a moment. She really didn't have anything to add. Gregory and his staff knew exactly what they were doing. The only thing she could think of to say was, "Make sure the logo stands out."

"We will, Mrs. Fenway."

Then in one corner of the studio, Allison spotted a beautiful bouquet of flowers in a dainty cut-glass vase.

"I think this would be a nice touch on the bedstand, don't you?"

"Yes. I'd forgotten about it," Gregory said. "Thank you," and he placed it on the table, stopping to arrange the flowers for a moment.

"Now we're ready," he called. "Backlight." And before Allison knew it, a full role of film was shot. She looked over at Frederick, smiled and set her eyes again on the setting. He was finished.

"I'll have the proofs back in a few hours. Do you want me to send them to you or to Mrs. Fenway?"

"To me. Mrs. Fenway and I are having lunch, and we'll both be in my office to take a look at the proof. Thank you. We'll send a messenger back here this afternoon to pick up the merchandise," Wordsworth said. "Are you ready to eat?" he said, addressing Allison.

"Starved." She took his arm, followed him out of the studio and into a taxi.

"Oh, it went so well. I'm speechless. This is really exciting," Allison told him. "It sure beats knocking on doors."

"I told you. With a bit of polishing you would be good at this. But the best part is seeing your first ad in print."

"Are you kidding. I'm going to wallpaper my walls with it."

"Remind me to show you the copy going on the ad," he told her.

Allison read the copy at lunch and couldn't believe her eyes. "*If you're not sleeping on Jenna Jones sheets, you're not sleeping in luxury. Jenna Jones' sheets sold exclusively at Bergdorf Goodman.*"

"You used my slogan?"

"Why not? It's good, says it all," he beamed.

"What happens if someone should call us and ask if they can order the sheets?" she asked.

"Then you sell them what they want. I told you, all I wanted was first crack at her designs. We'll remove the word *exclusively* from the ad. It's simple."

"Frederick, you are my luck charm. I don't know how to thank you. I've learned so much in these two days. I don't know what to do first when I go back to the office."

"First, you call Harry Tomes. Then I'll have my secretary give you a list of buyers' names who are personal friends of mine. If you use my name after the ad comes out, you'll have no problem getting in to see them."

"I can't believe this is all happening to me."

"It is, and enjoy it. You know, Allison, it's always a vicious circle. If you've never had a job, no one wants to hire you without experience. But how does one get experience without working? Once you have some sort of track record, you haven't any problems. We took the chance on you; others will follow suit."

"But the names. That list is worth its weight in gold."

"Yes and no. People will call you after they see the ad, but I'd rather you did business with the people on my list. We all do favors for one another in this business. The results in the end will be the same as far as Jenna Jones is concerned. But you'll be dealing with a better class of people."

"You may be right. You know Jenna has no desire to stay in the linen line forever. She'd like to branch out into fashion," Allison said, talking too much.

"I know. Although this industry seems very large, it isn't. News travels fast. I heard about her half-hearted try at better dresses."

"It was awful. The line was very good but it went nowhere."

"Tell Jenna for me that she needs a great deal of backing for an endeavor that size. And if she was smart, she'd tie up with one of the larger textile mills. They have the money, and in time she will have the name and sophistication. It could be a marriage made in heaven."

"Fred, is there anything in this business you don't know?"

"No, not really. I'll tell you a secret. About thirty years ago, I wanted to own my own place. I worked twenty hours a day, saw everyone, borrowed a large amount of money until I was so in debt that I thought I'd never see the light of day. But I forged ahead, hoping, knowing that someday I'd be able to break through. I remembered the people who helped me and the people who closed their doors to me. As you figured out, I didn't make it. But I have a long memory."

"Now I see where the list of names comes in," Allison remarked.

"Exactly. One hands washes the other. I'll never forget the people who tried to help me."

"And neither will I," Allison said, picking up her martini and toasting him. And she knew she wouldn't. If there was one thing she had to remember in the jungle in which she was working, it's know your friends, be cordial to your enemies, but be loyal to those who won't stab you in the back. They may be few and far between but they were worth seeking out.

Allison and Wordsworth returned to his office about three. The proofs were waiting on his desk. Allison went through them eagerly.

"They're wonderful. I can't wait to show Jenna. She'll be thrilled."

"I'm sure she will. When am I going to meet her?" he asked.

"Anytime. I'm sure she'll want to meet you."

"I have an idea. After you talk to Harry, have him set up some kind of press party. Her name should draw everyone easily. Send me an invitation, and we'll meet."

"Don't you think we can have you down to the studio before then? I mean, we really don't need a party to have you meet Jenna," Allison told him.

"No. I'd like to see the lady in action. Watch the way she moves, talks to the press. I want to feel the full flavor of the much-publicized Miss Jones."

"Unfortunately, the press she's gotten in the past isn't exactly the kind of publicity she's after," Allison said.

"True, her marriages don't seem to last very long. Many people are jealous of the rich, and love to read of their misfortunes. And the society page is only interested in whom she's dating, and what she's wearing," Fred went on.

"Don't I know it. But fortunately, or unfortunately for us, in the last two years, she's only been seen wearing her own creations. You'd think that would help."

"No, not really. Everyone seems to think the rich are also void of talent. Why should they have to work for a living, or want to work? They feel some poor idiot is designing her clothes and she's taking the credit," Fred went on.

"It isn't true. She's very talented. Every idea is her own or her assistants," Allison said in defense.

"You don't have to sell me. I remember Jenna when her father was fighting for custody. I felt sorry for the child. One day when I was flipping through a magazine and saw Jenna about age ten playing on the beach at Newport, I stopped a moment and studied the picture, the beautiful face. But I saw more than beauty. I saw a determination in her expression that truly entranced me. I knew somehow Jenna would grow up and not be like the other children in her world. She'd become her own woman, a person of strength and power. I found myself following her life, and with each photograph I searched to see if the expression was still there. To my surprise, I found it became stronger. I knew she'd never be a follower. She'd be a leader. And I'm very happy to be in a position where I may be of some help. I also want to watch Miss Jones' progress," Wordsworth went on, completely mystifying Allison.

"You really do know her without ever having met her. She's exactly like that. When we first met at school, and she told me about her plans for the future, I thought, sure, we all have fantasies. But during the years we were together, I discovered Jenna always made her dreams come true," Allison explained.

"Then you and she have been friends for a long time?"

"Yes, almost five years now. I can't say it's been uneventful."

"I'm sure. I just wish she'd find someone who'll marry her for herself and not because they think they'll live on easy street for the rest of their lives," he said.

"Oh, that's not true. Jeff Conroy wasn't interested in her money. He would have been very happy if Jenna stayed with him in Pittsburgh. He really loved her. I think Jenna was too young to appreciate him at the time," Allison went on, not knowing why she was giving away all of Jenna's secrets.

"And Philip?" he asked.

"I didn't know him. He was a playboy of sorts. It was a whirlwind romance, marriage and divorce. She met him in Europe after her marriage to Jeff failed. It was a rebound thing I'm sure. Jenna never really talks about him," Allison went on, wishing she'd shut up. She decided to change the subject. "But anyway, I think I've taken up too much of your time. To tell you the truth, I feel a bit disloyal talking about Jenna this way. I hope you understand," Allison said.

"You didn't tell me anything, my dear, that I haven't read about in all the gossip columns. But it's good to know Jenna has such a loyal and trustworthy friend. They are hard to find."

"Thank you for everything. I'll send the proof up to you in the morning after Jenna gets a look at them."

"Fine. I'm looking forward to hearing from you. And Allison, if there's anything you need, or anyone you're having problems reaching, please call me. And let me know how you like Harry."

Wordsworth remained seated until he heard the outside door close. He reached into his jacket pocket and pulled out a key to the middle drawer of his desk. He opened the drawer and pulled out a small white envelope yellowed with age. He reached in and took out a picture of a little girl. "Jenna," he whispered, "there isn't anything I wouldn't do to help you make your dreams come true. I'll pull this town apart so that you will be the great lady you need to be."


Allison followed all the leads Wordsworth gave her. The buyers she contacted were cordial; they invited her up to their offices to see the new line, each taking a minimum order. It was a far cry from what she had experienced in the past. She felt as though she had a guardian angel in her hip pocket. She took her clients to lunch, got to know what they liked and disliked, and began a file on each one. Through Harry Tomes she was able to get tickets to hit shows and sports events, sending the tickets off to those who would appreciate them. She was picking up the tricks of the trade.

During the next few months Allison lunched regularly with Wordsworth. Jenna's name usually came up on a more personal level, and Allison reported what little she knew to him. It seemed very odd to her that he never again brought up the subject of meeting Jenna.

Allison hired Harry Tomes as Wordsworth had suggested. She found him to be a funny little man. He dressed haphazardly and always looked disheveled when they met. He was short, grey-haired, in his late fifties, a contemporary of Wordsworth. Allison could never get a word in edgewise when they were together. He'd burst into her office, pick up the telephone, make at least fifteen calls, then go on to the matter at hand—Jenna. During their meetings, Allison would watch him pop at least ten antacid tablets into his mouth in between cigarettes. Within a ten minute period he'd issue a hundred orders: Jenna must be seen here, go there. He'd set up interviews for her with the editor of this magazine, that newspaper. It took all of Allison's concentration to write down what the man was saying as fast as he was saying it, then another half an hour to decipher her notes.

Jenna was so busy getting her name in print that she put more of a workload on Catherine. With Allison's new social calendar, and Michael starting his own law practice, they hardly saw one another. No one was complaining. They were starting to see the fruits of their labor paying off, even though the company itself wasn't seeing a profit as yet. Jenna had to hire an assistant for

Catherine, a secretary for herself, and two other salesmen for the West Coast and Mid-West. The money was going out as fast as it was coming in. Toward the anniversary of their first year in business, Harry advised them to throw a party. He made all the arrangements. He rented a suite at the Pierre Hotel, ordered all the wine, food and music. He invited the press and then presented Jenna with the bill. She couldn't believe her eyes.

"You have to spend money to make it," he told her.

"Not this much. Harry, we can't afford anything this luxurious."

"I know. But you have to put up a front. You can't let the others think you're working so close to the margin. It's the old saying: If you're successful people will buy from you. So put up a front," he tried to explain.

"And meanwhile, we'll be in the poor house," Jenna stated. "Let's face it, Harry, this is still a very small company. Sales have been good this year, but not good enough to warrant this kind of celebration."

"You won't turn back now. I know you. You'll figure out a way to pay for everything. And the night of the party, bring your checkbook."

"You mean all this is due next week?" she screeched.

"Yeah, and it wouldn't be bad if someone accidently saw you write out the check. You know, caught the amount. It will be all over town in no time. It's the best kind of publicity you can get."

"Is the press going to follow me to the debtors' prison? That would make a good piece also."

"Don't be so petty. I can tell you everyone's in hock. They all borrow from one to pay the other. This business is all front."

"Not for us. The invitations are out, so I can't get out

of this party, but it will be our last until I give the word. I won't put up a front for anyone."

"I'd say you're being foolish," he sighed.

"I'd say I was being wise," Jenna said, turning her back on him and leaving. "I won't let anyone stand in the way of my original goal. I need to make as much money as I can to go back into fashion. No more crazy unneeded expenditures."

The evening of the party, Jenna looked radiant. She was wearing one of her own creations—a black silk full-length gown, one shoulder bare and the lines cut to accent her tiny waist. The dress fell snug on the hips and flared toward the bottom. A simple single-strand pearl choker was the only jewelry she wore. She carried a large evening bag made of the same material as the dress. Jenna made her entrance like a queen. Everyone got up and applauded her. From the sideline, Wordsworth watched her every movement with pride. She turned out to be much more beautiful than he had imagined. Pictures hadn't done her any justice. Satisfied with what he saw, he put down his drink and left the party.

Allison and Catherine were already mixing when Jenna arrived. "Everyone seems to be having a good time," Allison said, moving toward Jenna.

"I think we did the right thing. It's a fabulous party. And everyone can't keep their eyes off of you."

"You look sensational yourself," Jenna said, changing the subject. "So when are you going to introduce me to our benefactor of sorts."

"Oh, Wordsworth. I saw him standing over there a minute ago," Allison said, searching through the crowd trying to locate him. "I don't see him now, but as soon as I do, I'll bring him over."

"Fine. Now let me go talk to the people I'm feeding and fueling with alcohol."

"Cheer up. Things could be worse. We could be celebrating our first real year in business, packing up our belongings and locking the door."

"I'm not complaining. It's the first step."

"Jenna, aren't you ever satisfied? We're doing all right now," Allison sighed.

"Maybe, but I'm not satisfied with what I'm doing. I'd be happier watching my own creations waltzing down the runway. Someday," she said, smiling at someone across the room and walking toward him.

*She's going to be the death of me yet*, Allison thought. Seeing Michael coming through the door, she ran to him. "I'm so glad you were able to make it."

"Would I miss my wife's first big party? I mean I've been curious about what you really do for a living," he said, gazing around the room. "No. I don't see one good-looking man in the bunch. I don't have to worry."

"Michael. You're not jealous," she played with him.

"Me? Never. Not anymore," he grinned, grabbing her around the waist, walking toward the bar. "When do you think you'll be ready to retire from the party scene and be happy just being Mrs. Fenway."

"I *am* happy being Mrs. Fenway. But I hate to quit just as things are beginning to happen," she told him.

"I have a feeling, Allison, that if you don't get out now, you never will. This business is beginning to take hold of you, pull you in. And we're six months behind schedule at this point."

"What schedule?" Allison was goading him.

"We made a promise that after I passed the bar and was established in my own firm, we'd wait six more months and then start having a family. It's been a year."

"We're not behind schedule at all. Well, maybe only four months," she told him, walking away. He followed.

"Allison, if we're only four months off . . . then that means you're pregnant," he whispered.

"I am," she whispered back. "See, I didn't forget." Michael stood there for a moment stunned. Then he grabbed her arm and pulled her outside the suite into the hallway.

"I can't believe it. Why didn't you tell me before?"

"I was waiting for the right moment. I can't say that this is it, but it will do," she said, hugging him. "Would you do me a favor?"

"Anything?"

"Don't say a word to anyone . . . not just yet."

"Why not? You don't intend to keep on working now."

"I do for a little while."

"You can't. It isn't good for you to push yourself this way."

"Michael, you're being very old-fashioned. I talked to the doctor, and he said I was in very good health and could keep on working for months yet. Besides, I'd go crazy sitting around the house all day."

"I'd have thought you'd be looking forward to finally taking a rest. Allison, you've been working since you entered school. You haven't had any time off."

"I know, and I've enjoyed every minute of it. Even the bad times. Michael, I promise to be careful. Don't fight me on this. Don't spoil the evening," she begged, and Michael gave in. He'd have given in to any request of hers. They went back to the party, staying with Jenna until the last guest left.

"Do you know, I never did meet Wordsworth?" Jenna said.

"I was so preoccupied with other people, I forgot all about him. But to tell you the truth, I didn't see him either," Allison said.

"I think it's strange. The man does so much for us and yet disappears. Well, if that's the way he wants to be, it's his problem," Jenna said, but Allison was a bit more intrigued. She made a mental note to call him in the morning.

Allison was exhausted when she and Michael got home. She fell into bed, leaving her clothes on the floor where she dropped them. Michael lay beside her, caressing her cheeks, then kissing her as if she were going to break. He made love to her gently, both of them falling asleep in each others arms, satisfied.

Jenna was in bed reading, feeling restless, when she heard her doorbell ring. She got up wondering who could be visiting . . . She should have known better. Catherine was leaning on the bell, drunk.

"I thought you might like a little company tonight. After all . . ." she started, letting herself in. "How can you celebrate your victory alone?"

"I'm tired and would like nothing more than to go to sleep. I think you'd be better off doing the same."

"Me? I'm not tired. I was sitting alone in my apartment thinking about the good old days. Remembering when we all used to live together. It used to be nice coming home and knowing there would be someone there. Now I come home and wander around three empty rooms," she went on.

"Why don't you get yourself a pet?" Jenna snapped.

"I thought I had one," Catherine came back like a shot.

"Very good. I see you're becoming very sure of yourself," Jenna said, walking over to the bar to fix herself a drink. She wondered how she was going to get rid of Catherine.

"I'd like a drink too."

"I think you've had too many already. Coffee might be better."

"No, a drink. I'd like to drink myself into oblivion," she said feeling dejected.

"Fine by me. You're over twenty-one. I won't baby you forever."

"Baby me! When did you ever baby me? I've been the one who's babied you," Catherine said, gulping down her drink.

"Okay, I can see we're going to have one of those nights. Do you want to tell me what's upsetting you?" Jenna asked, starting to lose her patience.

"It's you. Ever since we've started to make money, you've been running around to one party after another, seeing one man after another, or should I say, sleeping with one man after another? I mean, are we going to have to go through another marriage, another divorce and maybe another abortion?"

"I don't see what business it is of yours. You don't own me," she glared at Catherine.

"I own you more than you think. I know all your secrets. I know what makes you tick. I know you better than anyone else. And I also know that frightens you," Catherine went on. "Jenna, don't be afraid of me. I know the rules of the game. But give me some of your time now and again. It helps me get through the days and all the lonely nights when I know you're in bed with one of those men you don't give a damn about," she told Jenna, moving closer. Jenna knew Catherine was telling the truth. She was right about everything. She was only fulfilled when they were together.

Catherine stood behind Jenna, touching her shoulders, moving her hands down past her hips to her thighs. Catherine had learned swiftly and learned well how to please Jenna, and tonight Jenna needed her. She always needed her after coming down from a high. Jenna wanted her, now!


Allison didn't wait long to tell Jenna about the baby. Jenna looked at her half in surprise, half in disgust.

"Are you happy about it?"

"Very, and Michael is flying on cloud nine. I don't want you to worry about my working. I'll stay around until the both of you have to roll me home," she giggled.

"Well, I'm glad for you," Catherine said. "And in Jenna's half-baked way, she is too!"

"I don't know how I'll ever replace you. I never thought of us breaking up. We're like a team."

"Jenna, I think you'll be able to keep the company together without me for a few months. I'll be back."

"Not if Michael has anything to say about it. The father would like the mother to stay home with the baby," she mimicked.

"I make my own decisions. Let me handle Michael," Allison said. "Enough of sentimentality. How badly were we hurt financially with the party?"

"We're dead broke. I'm expecting some money in, but you can never count on bills being paid on time. God! We need a bigger cash flow."

"I had a conversation with Wordsworth a long time ago. I'd forgotten all about it until now," Allison started. "Wordsworth said that what you needed was to tie up with a big textile mill. Your label, name, clout—their money. He's heard that many of the big designers have done that in the past."

"Why would someone want to invest millions in this company?" Jenna asked. "I don't want to sell us lock, stock and barrel."

"I don't think you have to. I'm sure it's a fifty-fifty deal. It makes sense. You use only their fabrics and, as you know, the textile mills are the least publicized; in return, you'd bring glamor and style to them. The tag would read something like *Jenna Jones by . . .* whoever."

"So where do we start looking?" Jenna asked.

"I don't know but I can give Wordsworth a call, have lunch with him and ask. It can't hurt."

"Right now, nothing can hurt. I can't believe we're in a worse mess now than a year ago," Jenna stated.

"What does your accountant say?" Allison asked.

"It doesn't look good. And I didn't have to be a C.P.A. to figure that one out. We either need more orders, a backer, or I have to take a loan which I've been trying to avoid. There are people in the trade who factor against receivables. I don't see us getting by. Thank God Michael is representing us so I don't have lawyer's fees."

"I'll talk to him tonight, too. Maybe he has some ideas. Anyway, let me call Wordsworth. I wanted to anyway."

Allison dialed his number immediately. She spoke to his secretary and was told Wordsworth was out of town for a few weeks. Allison didn't remember his saying anything to her about going away. She sensed that something was wrong. Very wrong. It was as if he was trying to avoid her. She looked up. Jenna was standing in the doorway.

"I have another favor to ask. If we're going to cut corners, we'll have to get rid of Harry. Can you take over?"

"I think so. Do you want me to call him and tell him?"

"Would you? I think it wouldn't sound so harsh coming from you. And for appearances, don't tell him it's from lack of money. I think I overemphasized the party to him. I know when he's no longer employed by us, he'll blab his big mouth around town."

"I'll do what I can," Allison said, feeling the new pressure. Maybe Michael was right, it was time to leave. Keeping Jenna in the media wouldn't be easy. And now to add to everything else, she was feeling tired all the time.

Allison called Michael at the office before she made the call to Harry. She told him about her idea for financing. Michael said nothing at first, then told her he'd think about it, make some calls. He had an idea but he didn't want to get her hopes up. He'd call her as soon as he had any news. She hung up. Allison thought about making the call to Harry and decided against it for the time being. If Michael could get them out of their financial bind, then it would be better to leave Harry on the payroll. After all, if the buyers didn't want to take a chance on someone new, then they'd definitely never touch anyone who was having financial problems. No, she'd talk to Jenna again before letting Harry go.

The three sat in Jenna's office having lunch together. Jenna agreed with Allison. With the disastrous start they had had with the fashion line, and the slow start on the linens, she didn't need any more trouble. If she could find a backer, she thought she'd let Catherine design the linens, and she'd design the new line totally. With Wordsworth's guarantee, Bergdorf would have the first crack at the line.

"If Michael finds someone for us, there's a lot of preparation we'll have to make. It will be the hardest sell of our career, but imagine the results. We could grow by leaps and bounds. There's no limit," Jenna said, watching Catherine's expression change.

"I don't think we should move too quickly. Remember what happened last time," Catherine said.

"I remember. But we've all learned so much since then. We're not green kids anymore. I do have a name now, and we're here to stay whether anyone likes it or not. I know exactly how to get our new line off the ground. And it won't fail!"

"Let's not jump the gun. We have to find a mill first. . . ," Allison said.

"David White!" Jenna jumped. "Why didn't I think of him before? He knows everyone. He's got to know someone who's trying to buy into a business."

"He was very helpful to us in the beginning. Try everything," Allison said, beginning to sense Jenna's wheels turning and feeling much better.

The phone rang and Allison answered. It was Michael.

"I think I found your man."

"What!" she screamed. Jenna and Catherine were startled.

"Remember Raymond Bertinelli?" he started. "We went to school together. I was very close to him for a while, but then he dropped out and joined the army."

"I think so," Allison said, trying to place him.

"His father owns Bertinelli fabrics. Does it ring a

bell?'' Allison cupped her hand over the mouthpiece and asked Jenna. She thought for a moment, and then it dawned on her. She whistled, her way of expressing big money.

"I don't know the name, but it seems Jenna does," Allison told him.

"I looked Raymond up in the phone book. He's living here in Manhattan. I told him about you, Jenna and Catherine, and it seems he's read some of the press on you. He said he'd talk to his father right away. I'm waiting for him to call me back."

"Oh Michael, did he sound interested?"

"Very. It seems his father is a celebrity buff. He loves linking his name up with the beautiful people. And believe me, Allison, from what I hear, he's loaded. But he's a sharp business man. We'll have to do a great selling job on him. Jenna doesn't have a long record. I think if we get together and work out some numbers, we'll be able to sell him. The potential is impressive," Michael went on as excited as the rest.

"If this works, we'll be on easy street," Allison said.

"Don't start counting the money. Deals like this take months to put together. Can you girls stick it out?"

"Yes," Jenna screamed, by now listening in on the extension. "Michael, I'll take a loan if I have to, or borrow against my stocks. We'll make it."

"Good. I'll call you back as soon as I hear from Bertinelli," he said, hanging up.

"I'm madly in love with your husband," Jenna joked. "If he pulls this off the commission alone will set you up for life."

"Don't make us too independently wealthy," Allison said. "I may not have to work any longer."

"You'll work. I'll write it into the contract," Jenna

said. "'Now if we can only get through the day without staring at the telephone."

Raymond didn't call Michael back that afternoon or the next day. Everyone was on edge. Jenna decided to go to the bank and talk about a loan—just in case. They needed money to operate until the receivables came in. She took out a short-term loan due in ninety days, hoping by then something would come up.

Michael repeatedly tried to reach Raymond, but there was never any answer. He wondered if the guy was putting him on or didn't know how to politely say his father wasn't interested.

Raymond called Michael a few days later. It was close to midnight and Michael, half-asleep, answered the phone. His expression changed as soon as he picked up the receiver. Allison sat up in bed trying to listen to the conversation.

"Sorry I've taken so long to get back to you," Raymond said, "but my father can be very hard to reach, even for me. I had to track him down."

"Where'd you find him?" Michael asked, trying not to show his relief.

"Italy. He was yachting with some friends off Capri."

"Did you talk to him about Jenna?"

"Yes, and he was very interested. He was wondering whether she could fly over and meet him. They could, as my father puts it, sit around, relax, get to know one another and talk business," he said. "My father loves playing his role up to the hilt."

"I don't know if Jenna can pick up and leave. I'll ask her," Mike said, while Allison stamped her feet on the bed in excitement.

"I think she'd be a fool if she didn't go. Dad will pay

all her expenses . . . and yours too. I don't think she should go alone. You're her lawyer."

"Ray, I'll talk to her. Where can I reach you?"

"I'll be home in the morning. Call me as soon as you know. He'd like her to leave tomorrow if she can. Don't worry about waking me up."

"Thanks. I'll hang up and call right away," Michael said, putting down the phone and looking at Allison.

"What do you think?" he asked.

"I think she'd better start packing. We can cover for her. But I'm not so sure I want you to go. Yachting on the Mediterranean can be very romantic, and Italian women are *very* sexy," she kidded, kissing him.

"Maybe, just maybe, Jenna should go first. I'd follow in a few days. If anyone can charm the pants off the old man, she can."

"I don't want her to charm his pants off. Just the checkbook," Allison laughed. "I'm afraid to ask this question, but is there a Mrs. Bertinelli?"

"You know, I don't know. I don't remember Raymond ever talking about his mother. Why?"

"If I know Jenna, she'll marry him for his money if she has to," Allison said, while Michael dialed Jenna's number.

"It might not be a bad idea," he whispered, as Jenna picked up her phone. "Hello, Jenna, sorry to wake you, but I heard from Bertinelli. He'd like you to fly to Italy tomorrow if you can."

"What! Just like that!" she yelled.

"It's the way the man does business, I'm told. He's on his yacht off Capri. If anything, you'll have a nice vacation."

"What do you think?" she asked Michael.

"I think you should go. Ray advised me to go, too. I

can't leave as fast but I can meet you in a few days. When you arrive give me a call, let me know how things are going, and we'll take it from there."

"But Michael, I don't have anything to show him. We haven't worked up any figures. What will I say to him?"

"Jenna, be yourself. I've heard you talk for hours on the future of your business. Sell him the way you've sold everyone else. Let him see that you're a woman with ideas, a future. Bring him all the figures on the linen designs and the sketches on the last designs you did. Bring him your publicity folder. I don't have to tell you."

"I hope this works," Jenna said.

"It has to. He's buying you, your name, the future. He's a smart man. He'll know you failed the first time because you were under-capitalized and new in the business. Except you did more . . . Instead of quitting, you started again and the first year you made money. That, in itself, is impressive. The stores you're linked with are the best in the country. I'll see what I can do about putting together some rough numbers to show him. I'll bring them with me."

"Thanks, Michael. I don't know what I'd do without you. I don't know if Allison told you, but if we pull this off, there's a great deal of money in it for you . . . a finder's fee."

"I should say no, Jenn, I won't take it, but I've learned better. Let me get off the phone and call Ray back to tell him it's all set. Check with the airlines and see what flights leave for Rome tomorrow. Book yourself on the fastest one."

"I will. I'm not going to be able to go back to sleep. I have a million things to do," she said, hanging up.

Michael called Ray immediately. No one slept that night. Michael had a lot to gain if this deal went through, not only in money, but he'd be Jenna's attorney in a multi-million dollar company and he couldn't stop thinking about it. Allison lay awake too. She had them moving into a two-bedroom apartment uptown or maybe one of the lovely brownstones off Fifth Avenue. It seemed from day to day their lives were changing, moving up and down. If this came through, there was only one way to go—up.

All the next morning Allison and Catherine were gathering up material for Jenna to take with her. She was home trying to pack and take care of last minute business. It was hard to figure out what to take when she didn't know how long she'd be gone.

Catherine and Allison rushed over to her apartment to help her organize and finish packing. She was taking a five o'clock flight. A car would be picking her up. It was like a fairy tale. Michael came over to the apartment to give her last minute instructions. Everyone wished her the best of luck as they put her in a taxi for the airport. They watched as it pulled away.

"First, I want a very large steak, then I want to go to sleep," Allison said.

"It's been some day," Catherine agreed.

"Well, I'm buying. Catherine join us," Michael asked.

"I'd like that. Does anyone know how long she'll be away?"

"Not a clue. I'll know something more when she calls me," Michael said.

"It's frightening, isn't it? Three and a half lives are in Mr. Bertinelli's hands. I wonder what will happen," Catherine said.

# 3.

Jenna's flight took off on time. She looked at the material that Michael had asked her to read on the plane—articles on Milton Bertinelli. She was glad Michael had kept his head. When did he have time to gather this material? What would she have done without him? She never thought to read up on the man; she didn't have the time. She sat back in her seat and read everything twice. Bertinelli was in his early sixties. His grandfather had started the business, and his father took over after his death. Milton Bertinelli had other plans for his life. He didn't want to go into the textile business. He wanted to become a concert pianist. His father was against it, but, with the help of his mother, he took lessons and became a brilliant pianist by the age of fifteen. Milton studied with some of the finest men in Europe and the United States. He went back to Europe when he was nineteen and lived there most of his young life. During his stay, he mastered three languages, married Martha Younger, a violinist, when he was twenty-one. His marriage ended tragically when Martha died in a boating accident off the coast of France. Five years later, he married Dorothy Sloan, the daughter of an American industrialist. They had met while she was vacationing in France with her family. She was instrumental in having him come back to the United States and work in the family business. They had one son, Raymond, and their marriage ended in divorce nearly fifteen years ago. Upon his father's death, Milton inherited *Bertinelli Fabrics*. He stayed with the company as President. Milton surrounded himself with experts in the textile business, to lessen the burden of his running the company full time. He was now in semi-retirement.

Jenna studied the pictures of Milton. He was very handsome when he was young and, from what she could see, he still was a very distinguished-looking man— five ten, lean, thick grey hair, Roman nose, wide brown eyes, deep set lines around his eyes, and beautiful hands. Jenna was more anxious to meet this man than she had anticipated. He was a ladies' man, no doubt. In every photograph she studied, he was with a woman at least half his age. He was a casual dresser, seemed very relaxed, and made a success out of everything he touched. He gained much respect and admiration from the dubious-minded executives of his company, surprising them with his talent for seeing a good business move and taking advantage of every opportunity. He was personally responsible for more than quadrupling the Bertinelli mills, buying over a thousand acres of land in Georgia and North Carolina. He did have the reputation of taking advantage of his factory workers; they were underpaid and overworked. He had no guilt feelings about this, according to one article. He gave them jobs where once there were none. He expanded the family businss in Europe, building a factory in Italy, and then another in Hong Kong. He owned homes near all his factories, but lived mostly on his yacht. Liked to fish, play tennis, water ski and race cars. His close friends mostly consisted of artists and musicians, and he played the piano for relaxation.

*Phew* . . . Jenna thought, *What a man.* All she wanted was a simple man who would want to buy into her business. She never bargained for what she was getting. If Jenna was in awe of anyone in her life, it was Bertinelli. The flight was ready to land. Jenna couldn't believe she was already there. She was so engrossed in her reading material, she hadn't even asked the stewardess for dinner. She was starved.

As Jenna came through Customs in the Rome airport, she saw a small man in a chaffeur's uniform standing by the gate. He spotted her immediately.

"Miss Jones? I'm Andre. Mr. Bertinelli sent me to pick you up."

"Yes, good to meet you," Jenna said for lack of anything else.

"I'll get your luggage. Are you ready to go or is there something you'd like to do first?"

"I'd really like to eat something. I didn't eat on the plane."

"I've taken care of that for you. Mr. Bertinelli thought you might not like the airline food, so I have breakfast waiting for you in the car."

Jenna looked up in disbelief. Mr. Bertinelli thought of everything! The breakfast was remarkable. Hidden in one of the panels of the limousine was a hot plate; on it were eggs, bacon, cereal, fruit, juice, a pot of coffee and croissants. A feast for four people. Jenna ate heartily and exhaustion quickly overtook her. She fell asleep. When she awoke, they were driving through the crowded streets of Naples. The merchants were standing next to their carts, the smell of fish, and bakery goods in the air. The streets were dirty but still had a charm all their own. Small children ran around half-naked, approaching the car for money. Andre shooed them away, but Jenna felt sorry for them. The large black car slowed down while driving through town, the narrow streets too crowded to make any headway. Andre cursed in Italian and backed the car up to try another route. Jenna gazed at the run-down buildings, the wash hanging out on the lines, and the barefoot women in their cheap house dresses. She didn't mind the delay; she was busy soaking up the atmosphere as if she was seeing it for the first time.

Andre finally was able to get through and drove to the pier, got out of the car and opened the door for Jenna.

"Mr. Bertinelli is waiting for you on the yacht." Andre turned her over to the old man on the launch, put her bags on the small boat and said good-bye. They took off as soon as she sat down. The launch slowed as it neared the one hundred twenty foot cabin cruiser complete with crew, two master suits, three guest bedrooms, a large living room, dining room, library, three bathrooms, game room and its own swimming pool. If she hadn't known she was on a ship, she'd have thought she was in a hotel. The furnishings were all antiques. Jenna recognized some of the familiar paintings hanging on the walls. She was to wait for Bertinelli in the library. Her things were quickly taken from her and brought to her room. She wondered where her host was. Her question was answered promptly when she saw him enter the room.

"Miss Jones, so nice of you to come. Can I get you something? I know it's been a very long trip."

"No, thank you, and it was nice of you to see me," she said, shaking hands with the face she had studied in the photographs on the plane. He was much better looking in person.

"Sit down, please. I'm sorry I couldn't meet your plane. I have to confess, I'm a late riser these days."

"No. I didn't expect you to. I had a very pleasant trip. And thank you for breakfast."

"You're very young," he said, throwing her off balance.

"Does that make a difference?"

"Oh, no. I was thinking about myself at your age. I had no head for business, wanted to have a good time instead," he told her, not taking his eyes off her for one instant. "Have you come alone? Raymond told me you might bring your attorney."

"Yes. He'll be joining us in a few days. This trip was quite sudden."

"I know. I've been known for being impulsive. Why put off what you may have an interest in? Someone else might have stolen you away in the meantime."

"I have to be honest. No one was pounding at the door," she said. "Mr. Bertinelli . . ."

"Milton," he corrected.

"Milton. Why in semi-retirement would you consider taking a chance on a new company? You don't need the money."

"No, but every now and again, I feel the urge to try something new. I admire ambitious people, young people. I feel they deserve all the chances they can get. Enough of business for the moment. You must want to change, or take a nap," he said.

"Yes, I would like to freshen up. The pool looks inviting. I think I'd like to take a dip if you don't mind."

"Not at all. You have the run of the ship. One more thing. I do have other guests aboard. Would you like to dine this evening with them, or would you feel more comfortable dining alone with me in my private dining room?"

"It might be nice to dine with the others," Jenna told him.

"Do you have special requests for the chef?"

"No. I don't think so. Whatever the others are having will be fine," she said, not wanting to be too standoffish.

"Fine. We'll dine at eight. See you then." He rang for the maid who entered almost immediately. "Miss Jones would like to go to her room now. Please make her comfortable."

"Yes, sir," the petite dark-haired girl said, leading the way for Jenna. The two passed the other guests on the way. Jenna smiled and continued on. The maid took her to her suite. The room was magnificent, done completely in white. The large bed was set in the center of one wall. Two antique mahogany tables on each side of the bed had white marble lamps on top of them. Large windows overlooked the coast of Naples. The white silk sheets and floor-length bedspread, accented with lace, matched the chaise lounge set in the corner. The maid opened the double doors to the private dressing room and bath. Nina introduced herself, telling Jenna that she was assigned exclusively to her for the length of her stay. Nina had already unpacked all of Jenna's clothes, placing them neatly in the closet. A bath was drawn, and Jenna sat in the warm water, feeling the exhaustion setting in. She decided to lie down after her bath for a few minutes. She didn't know what time it was when the phone rang in her room. Looking at the clock, it was almost ten. She jumped up to answer the phone.

"Sorry to have awakened you, Jenna," Milton said.

"I know how the time change can upset the system."

"Oh, that's perfectly all right. I'm sorry. I must have slept through dinner."

"You did. Would you like me to send a tray to your room?"

"I'd much prefer to come up on deck and eat. I'll never be able to fall back to sleep if I don't get some exercise."

"Fine, I'll have everything ready for you when you come up," he said, hanging up.

Jenna dressed quickly, wishing she didn't look so tired. She thought a few days like this one would do wonders. Put a little color in her face.

Milton was sitting at the table by himself when Jenna found her way up top. He watched her walk toward him. She was dressed in a pale blue silk skirt and matching blouse, a single gold chain around her throat.

"You look lovely," Milton told her, holding out her hair.

"You're very kind, but I don't. I'd like to thank you for waiting dinner for me. You should have eaten with the others . . . It seems all I've done since I've come on board is thank you."

"Then, no more thanks. How did you sleep?" he asked, pouring wine into her crystal goblet.

"Very well. I guess I didn't know how tired I was. Oh . . . it's so beautiful here. The stars are bright, the sky is so clear. The moon is the only light we need. I feel like I'm on a movie set. Everything is so perfect."

"Yes, I know. I hate leaving here and going back to the real world," he sighed, breathing in the fresh air.

"I see what you mean. But I haven't earned the right to return yet," Jenna told him. "I have many things to accomplish. I only hope I can," she said, pushing him back into reality.

"Yes. One of the reasons you're here."

"The only reason I'm here," Jenna corrected.

"Why don't we enjoy the evening and talk business tomorrow. Deal?"

"Deal," she smiled. "And for the record, how long do you think I'll be here?"

"If it were up to me, as long as you want. But I'm sure you're anxious to get back, so I'd say three or four days . . . with an option."

"An option?"

"To stay longer if you want," he smiled.

"Your offer's very tempting," Jenna said, finishing her soup and starting on the main course.

Milton and Jenna talked through the night. He was honest, telling her all about himself, his business, his pleasures. She didn't stop him. She enjoyed listening. He was a fascinating story teller. Kept her interested, with a humor all his own. She hadn't felt so relaxed in years. They walked around the deck, sipping their brandy, and then returned to the library. Milton turned on Chopin, softly as background music. Jenna was tempted to ask him to play for her but thought against it. It was four in the morning when he walked her to her door.

"I had a very nice evening. I'm sorry I didn't get the chance to meet your other guests. On second thought, I had a much better time listening to you," Jenna told him.

"I did do a great deal of talking. I had a good time myself. After all, everyone else has heard my old stories," Milton said, turning to go. "Sleep well. See you in the morning."

"What time is breakfast?"

"I usually eat around nine. Will you join me?"

"I'd love to. And this time I won't sleep through the alarm," she smiled, closing the door to her suite.

Jenna fell asleep immediately, contented and relieved that her business would be saved by Milton Bertinelli. They hadn't talked about the future, but something inside her kept saying this man will go along with you. He'll invest the money needed. All fear and anxiety drained from her body.

Milton didn't sleep as well. His mind raced a million miles an hour. He thought about his new venture. He was very impressed with Miss Jenna Jones. She commanded his respect and was full of determination. He knew any money he invested in her could only make him more. Aside from the obvious—her beauty and sophistication—she was quick-witted, sincere, and wise beyond her years. All the ingredients added up to success. She was not one of those bored heiresses filling her idle time with a hobby. He knew, moments after meeting Jenna, that this was her life. And to have talent on top of all this was much too good to be true. He decided to call his lawyer in the morning and ask him to fly over. There were many papers to draw up, terms to meet, stocks to divide, a corporation to form, plus assets to make liquid to put into the account. He'd never had a partner as young as Jenna or as beautiful. He was confident he could keep the relationship a business one. Had she been here for any other reason, he would not be sleeping alone tonight. She was everything he loved in a woman. He kept reminding himself all evening, *hands off, never mix business with pleasure*, but it had never worked in the past and it certainly wouldn't work now. Besides, he was old enough to be her father. He tried to push Jenna out of his mind and let sleep overcome his tired body. When he finally fell asleep, he dreamed of her. She was in his bedroom, wearing a long white chiffon robe, nothing underneath. She stood at the edge of the bed waiting for him to awaken, and, as he did, she smiled, her shoulder length auburn hair brushing against the robe, silhouetting her face, her lovely complexion setting off the emerald green eyes. She said nothing. He sat up and extended his hand out to her. She touched his fingers, setting off a shock through his body. She slid her hand into his and moved closer to him. He reached toward her, unfastened her robe, letting it slide to the floor. He pulled her down to him, kissing her breasts, working his way down her stomach and the softness of her firm thighs. He woke with a start. The dream was still vivid in his memory and in his body. He jumped into the cool shower, the thoughts of Jenna still very much alive.

Jenna was waiting for him when he came on deck. Her long white terry cloth robe covering her bathing suit brought a twinge of excitement back to Milton. He tried to make idle conversation.

'How are you this morning?''

"Rested, contented, and ready to talk business. You did say we would talk today?'' she asked.

"Yes. I thought I'd give my attorney a call and have him fly down as soon as possible,'' he began.

"Don't you think we're jumping the gun a bit? We haven't decided to make any kind of a deal yet,'' Jenna was coy.

"I think you know how I feel. It's a matter of money and stock that's at stake. The little details which always seem to get in the way,'' he smiled.

"Then, am I to assume you're going to back me?'' she gasped, trying to hide her feelings.

"Yes, I'd like to very much, if we all can agree on the terms."

"Then I'd better call Michael, and tell him to come also," she began.

"Sit down. Eat your breakfast. I'll have someone take care of that for you. We have much to talk about," he began. "By the way I had a chance to look over your sketches. You're very talented."

"I'm sorry I didn't have the time to do up new ones, but . . ."

"No. Don't worry. It's the quality I'm concerned with, and your quality is the utmost in originality. Tell me, what type of clothing are you most interested in?"

"You mean, which season?"

"No . . . sportswear, evening clothes, daywear?"

"I have to admit that I love evening-wear. I adore getting dressed up myself, but, in these times, it wouldn't be wise. We are dressing down. The casual look is sweeping the country."

"Then you wouldn't consider doing up the evening-wear?"

"Maybe some, but I wouldn't emphasize it in the line. I think the trend is heading toward slacks . . . pants suits. You see more women are working and, unfortunately, they feel that they need to emulate the male dress code," Jenna stated.

"You don't feel as they do?" he asked.

"No. I love feminine clothes, soft material against my body—dresses, skirts. I think a woman should always look like a woman. But I'm not one of the masses."

"Very smart. You wish to leave your personal feelings out of the market, and give the people what they want."

"I have to. If I thought for one minute that I could be

a trend-setter, I'd try, but I'm only one person. That's not saying that in time, when I'm more established, I couldn't have more of a hold on my followers. But not now."

"I see you've been studying the trend closely. I like that."

"I can't take all the credit. I have a very competent team. Allison Fenway is the one who keeps her finger on the pulse of what's happening. And then there's Catherine Markham, one of the best new designers in town. She's extraordinary. It's almost as if she can read my mind. Our sketches are so alike," Jenna said, moving over to his side of the table.

"Do you know what happens to you when you talk about your work?" Milton asked, grinning.

"No, what?"

"You light up like a Christmas tree. Your eyes dance, and your whole mood changes. You do love what you're doing."

"More than anything else. And I know I'm right. I *can* make a success of the business."

"Oh, I have no doubt. What is it exactly you want from me?"

Jenna looked up at him, surprised. If he didn't know then what was all that talk about their lawyers meeting? "I need money to make my business grow."

"But Jenna, don't you think you could do that in time, all by yourself?"

"Maybe . . . Yes, but it would take so long. And the world is changing so fast. If we could ride the crest now, we'd have no problems. I know what's going to happen for at least the next ten years."

"How? No one really knows," Milton was taken back.

"I do. First, we'll go into the pants suits, as I said before. Coordinates, matching jackets and skirts—the tailored look. I won't tell you how I know, you'll have to take my word for it. The hemlines are going to set people off in two directions, for example . . ." Jenna stopped, taking another sip of her coffee. "The kids today are protesting, living together, trying to put aside all the values they once believed or, more importantly, their parents believed. They are wearing jeans, workshirts, overblouses, long dresses—everything out of the ordinary. So the establishment will try to adapt to their dress code; the skirts will be long, maybe mid-calf, worn with sweaters, belts, boots," Jenna said, making rough sketches as she talked. "Then there will be those who'll try to overcompensate for the new trend; they will wear their skirts very high, showing off the leg, not trying to hide their sex, the hemline approximately five or six inches above the knee."

"I think I like those women better," Milton interrupted, thoroughly absorbed in what she was saying. "Go on."

"As a consequence, there will be a complete shifting around in the fashion world. Women will begin to wear what they like, not what's in. No one set of Seventh Avenue designers are going to tell them which length is in. So we'll wind up in a three hundred and sixty degree turn. Femininity will be back in full gear with dresses and evening clothes. Ironically, all or most of the kids will be in their late twenties, working within the very establishment they had supposedly rejected. But they'll want to wear something to remind them of the freedom they experienced when they were young. Do you know what that will be?"

"No." Milton was mystified.

"Jeans. Expensive jeans. Designer jeans. Status. But not in the ordinary sense of the word. They will wear them with silk blouses, jewelry, high boots or heels. Jeans will be perfectly acceptable to wear in any restaurant."

"It's hard to believe, but you do look as though you've done your homework. When did you start?"

"Years ago, when I was in school. I'd watch, listen, research the field. I know I'm right. And with this information we'll be the leaders. With all the money we'll make on the other clothes, it won't be anywhere near the money that we'll make on the jeans. It will be a phenomenon like you've never seen before. And every designer will come out with them."

"Well, we had World War I and World War II, now we're getting ready for Jean War," Milton quipped.

"Get ready, because it's coming, but not for a long time yet. But long enough for me to make my mark as a designer, a trend setter, and allow me to accumulate enough money to finance one of the biggest campaigns that will keep me on top."

"Jenna Jones by Bertinelli," he said.

"Exactly," Jenna said.

"If you're right, then we'd better start researching a denim that's durable, fine quality and . . ."

"Will keep its hold. Jeans have a way of pulling out of shape, stretching. You have to find a denim that will hug the figure and keep its shape."

"What we're talking about is millions of dollars for promotion, publicity, research, merchandising, factories . . . It's a mighty tall order."

"Yes, but you will be starting another empire," Jenna said.

"At my age, I'm getting ready to retire and live

without all the deadlines and pressures. But I have to admit, I'm intrigued."

"Milton, you don't strike me as a man who wants to stay out of the stream of things. Really, how much involvement do you have to have?" Jenna went on. "My people will be doing most of the work; your company has to meet the fabric orders and produce the quantity. It doesn't have to be on your shoulders."

"No, not down the road, but I'd want to be involved in every aspect in the early stages. Then Raymond will take over at some point. When were you thinking of starting?"

"Not before next year. I need time to prepare, find a larger space, hire more staff, and, of course, create the new line. I'd say . . . next year at this time, we'll be having our first show. Michael will have all the necessary numbers with him."

"I'd like to take a look at them. I think we'll work very well together. It will be a very interesting year, Miss Jones, and I like the sound of our label—Jenna Jones by Bertinelli."

"It will bring Europe and America together. I like the sound of the label myself. It's better than I imagined. Milton, the New York designers still have stiff competition with the old established European designers. If there could be the best of two worlds, this is it," Jenna told him, leaning back in her chair.

"Jenna, enough business for one day. As it stands we can't go any further without figures and attorneys, so how would you like to accompany me to Capri?"

"I'd love it. I'm not dressed. I was ready for a swim, but it will only take me a moment to change."

"Fine, I have a few calls to make, and I'll meet you here in, let's say, half an hour."

"Good. I'm looking forward to it...," Jenna started to leave, turned around, looked at Milton. "I hope it all works out. Anyone other than you would be a compromise for me, and I don't like to compromise." She was out of sight before Milton had a chance to respond. *She is a remarkable woman. Jenna Jones is an original*, he thought.

Michael received his call and, already packed, caught the same plane Jenna had taken two days earlier. Catherine and Allison took him to the airport, fingers crossed, and hopes high. Allison stayed with him until the last possible minute.

"I'm going to miss you," she told him.

"I'm going to miss you, too. I really would rather be home," Michael said. "Please take care of yourself and the baby. I don't know if all this excitement is good for you."

"I'll be fine. Do you know what I'm going to do while you're gone?" she teased.

"No, what?"

"I'm going to look around for a bigger apartment, one with a second bedroom that I can fix into a nursery."

"Good. No matter what happens we have to move."

"You're going to think I'm silly, but I'm feeling maternal already. I can't wait to start making plans for the baby."

"Didn't I tell you, you were better off not working," Michael said, giving her another kiss.

"I know, but I can't leave now. I'll have time to do both. Besides, it will keep my mind off the long wait. I don't think it's fair. You find out you're pregnant so early then have to sit for months wondering if it's a boy or girl, if it will be healthy. It's agonizing," Allison went on. "I don't even show yet."

"Allison, the time will fly by. Sometimes I sit in my office and wonder where all the years went. I can remember entering college, and in a flash it was over. Do you realize we met seven years ago?"

"What's so amazing is that I still love you," Allison smiled. "I haven't gotten bored with you yet."

"You'd better not. You've put many long hard hours into my education. It's time you sat back and let me do all the providing. I love you so much and want you to have everything."

"I do have everything, Michael," Allison told him. "I have you. If you don't let go of me and board the plane, you'll miss it," she kissed him one more time.

"I love you," he said, as he walked through the door. "I'll call you tomorrow." He waved and she waved back until she couldn't see him any longer. Catherine joined her and they both sat there watching the plane take off. Both their loves were across the ocean. And they both felt the loneliness.

"Have you ever been to the Blue Grotto before?" Milton yelled, as they skimmed the water in the speed boat.

"Years ago when I was in high school. I remember it was spectacular. Are we heading toward it now?"

"Yes, if you'd like."

"I'd like to very much," she said. "Can we swim inside?"

"Yes, we'll leave our clothes in the boat. Instead of taking a rowboat to get into the cave opening, we'll swim." Milton slowed the boat down as they approached the mountainous area, and threw down the anchor.

"Are you a good swimmer?"

"Good enough," she said.

"Then let's take it from here," Milton told her, diving off the boat. Jenna dived in after him. The water felt cool and refreshing after the hot sun. She could feel her skin reddening from its rays. Jenna swam toward Milton and together they let the swell of the water push them into the cave. The water was as clear as Jenna had remembered. She could see all the way down to the bottom. It was a rare moment—no boats were inside the cave which was usually filled with tourists. They felt as though they were alone in a peaceful world.

"Oh, I love it here," Jenna said, holding onto a protruding rock for balance, tired from the long swim. She could hear her echo.

"It's my favorite place," Milton said. "I'm falling in love with Italy again."

"Have you lived here long?"

"A few years. I used to spend most of my time in France. But the Italians are in a class all their own—free, loving, warm, strong-minded people. They adhere to their customs and everyone else can drop dead. But, unlike the French, the Italians are warm, friendly, hospitable people. Money, of course, is the key, but it's always that way in poor countries. I met my first wife here many years ago," he felt himself tighten.

"You loved her very much."

"Very much. I couldn't come back here for a long time. The streets, the people . . . everything reminded me of her. It became too painful."

"And your second wife?" Jenna asked.

"I met her in France. I can go to that country anytime. The only memory I have is the money it cost to divorce her. We really were never in love. I do have to thank her for my son though. He's all I have."

"Is he much like you?"

"Nothing like me . . . maybe in a way that's good. I was always an idealist. Raymond is a realist. . . ," he stopped. "Do you want to go back to the boat?"

"Yes. I'll race you," Jenna said, catching him by surprise and getting a head start. Milton beat her. His speed and endurance were remarkable for a man his age. He looked no older than forty and in many ways he was younger in spirit than herself.

"I'll beat you at something someday," Jenna laughed, her hair and face still dripping from the water.

"I bet you will," Milton smiled, throwing her a towel. "We have today and the rest of the night to enjoy ourselves before the business part of our team show up. What would you like to do?"

"This is your home. You make the plans. I'm sure I'll love anything you choose," she said, knowing it was true.

"Okay, then we'll dock on the south side of the island, have lunch at my favorite restaurant, and play the rest by ear."

"Lead the way," Jenna told him, feeling high in spirit. She laid down, feeling the sun warm her body, and watched Milton out of the corner of her eye. He was carefully steering the boat in the right direction, but glancing over at her now and again.

They docked the boat and walked through the tiny village to the restaurant. Jenna could see in an instant why it was Milton's favorite place. The hotel sat on the base of a hill surrounded by trees and flowers. The curved walkways through the garden led to the small intimate dining room whose large-paned windows overlooked the sea.

"Ah, Mr. Bertinelli, it's so good to see you again," the waiter said, shaking Milton's hand. "And such a beautiful lady."

"Carmen, I'd like you to meet Jenna Jones, a business associate."

Carmen looked her up and down. "Ah, too beautiful to have a head for business."

"That's why she's so exciting," Milton winked, seating himself, while Carmen held Jenna's chair. "We are totally at your disposal. You make all the decisions for lunch. This way, I can concentrate on my guest."

"Ah, very good. You'll be very happy with my choice. Don't worry," Carmen rambled on, then leaving the two alone.

"He's a funny little man," Jenna said, sitting next to Milton instead of across from him. "I thought we weren't going to talk business anymore today."

"We're not, but I'd like to concentrate on you anyway. Remember I did all the talking last night. And this morning, we talked about the future. I'd like to know more about the Jenna Jones before fashion came into her life."

Jenna glanced away in thought, then faced him. "Milton, almost anything that happened to me was in one gossip column or another. My life wasn't all that interesting."

"I can't believe that. Moreover, I don't read the gossip columns. They dig their claws into people leaving them little or no privacy, taking every chance to crucify those they don't like, and building up with sheer nonsense those they do."

"I don't know if I was liked or disliked. I just wanted to be left alone. All anyone wanted to talk about was the trial. Did I miss my father? Did I ever see him again? What did I want to do with my life when I grew up? All the questions an adolescent wasn't prepared to answer."

"It's still painful for you to talk about your father, isn't it?"

"I don't know. I used to think about him all the time, now he's slipped away into my memory bank. I hardly think about him at all. I can't even remember what he looked like."

"Have you ever tired to find him?"

"No, there was no sense in trying when I was younger. My grandmother controlled my movements, and now I think it might be a mistake. It might be too painful for him. Besides, I wouldn't know where to look."

"I guess the important question is, do you want to see him or find him?"

"Sometimes . . . When things seem hopeless I wish I had a strong shoulder to cry on, a shoulder which supported me, someone who wanted nothing in return but my love . . . To fight for me the way he did, he had to have loved me more than anything in the world," she said, meeting his gaze. "What I wish I could do is see him from a distance . . . observe him. Know what he's like. What he's doing. I wouldn't want to intrude. I don't even know if he's still alive," Jenna said, tears welling up in her eyes. Milton patted her hand, wishing he hadn't brought up the painful subject.

"It's okay. I've never done this before. I must be becoming sentimental in my old age."

"Old age," Milton laughed. "You're twenty-five."

"Well, I feel fifty sometimes. But not today. Today I feel...," Jenna thought a minute. "Twenty-one."

"Big difference."

"If I were any younger, people would sit up and take notice of the two of us."

"Do you think we look odd together?"

"I guess not. I never really thought about it. And this is Italy where love rules at any age," Jenna told him, not knowing why she was opening up to him.

"Jenna, I must be frank. If we weren't talking about a business venture, I would definitely want to make love to you. You are a desirable woman in all ways. But I have to keep my love life separate from my business life. I've never learned how to mix the two."

"Neither have I. But our needs and our desires are so similar, and you are very attractive. It would be very hard for me to ever say no to you," Jenna told him, meaning every word.

Milton took her hand and kissed the palm, and she clasped her hand around his. They sat for a moment looking at one another, both feeling desire seeping through their bodies and the tension building. Jenna hadn't felt this way since the disastrous night in France. She thought she'd never desire a man the way she desired Milton. She picked up his hand and kissed it.

"I'm thirty-five years older than you," Milton said, breaking the silence.

"Should that make a difference? I don't feel thirty-five years younger."

"Jenna, you should be dating my son, but in so many ways you're much older than he is." He leaned over and kissed her. Carmen placed their lunch on the table, breaking the spell for the moment. He poured the wine, and the two sat back and ate their lunch.

Jenna ate heartily, enjoying the pasta, salad, veal, finishing off with expresso and fruit. Milton laughed in disbelief. "How do you stay so thin?"

"I don't know. I just do. Put it another way . . . I don't ask questions. I'm very lucky because I won't give up food."

"I can see why. You eat but with such gusto, such enjoyment. I love it. Every woman I go out with picks at her food as if I wouldn't like her any longer if she had a healthy appetite," he laughed. "Jenna, you definitely are your own woman. No one could ever change you. As if anyone would want to."

"I don't necessarily agree with you there. Many people have tried to . . ."

"And failed. . . ," he finished her sentence.

"Milton, when I flew over here, I had no idea what you were like, and what I would say to you. But now, I find you to be one of the easiest people to talk to. Although I'm in awe of your accomplishments and you as a man, I feel very comfortable around you. I know I can say anything, and be myself. I'm glad . . ." Jenna sighed. "And even if things don't work out, I'm not sorry I came."

"Jenna, everything will work out," he moved closer, taking her hand. "And I'm glad you're here," he said. "Excuse me for a moment," he left the table. When he returned, he helped Jenna out of her chair. "Had to take care of the bill, and . . ." he stopped, "Come with me." Jenna said nothing, he took her hand and she followed. They climbed the winding staircase to the second floor. Milton took the key to the room out of his pocket and opened the door. He held the door open, Jenna went in first. Milton closed and locked the door behind him.

"I hope you're not offended," he said, standing behind her, both looking out at the sparkling blue sea. She turned to him.

"I would have been offended if you hadn't taken me here." She looked up at him, reaching for his lips. As if he were dreaming again, he held her tightly. His tongue reached deep into her mouth, hers sought his. Jenna could feel herself melting into him, her knees weakening, not being able to stand if he wasn't holding her. She felt his strength. He moved away from her, unbuttoning her blouse, removing it, his hands moving over her shoulders, her back, and cupping her breasts, then kissing them. Jenna felt her flesh burning. He unzipped her skirt, letting it drop to the floor, she stepped out of it, her hands fumbling with the belt buckle of his pants. He helped her, and both stood there holding one another, flesh against flesh, savoring the moment, taking their time as if it were the last time they would be together. Milton led Jenna to the bed, —moving together, kissing, touching one another until Jenna couldn't wait, she wanted to feel him inside her. She slipped on top of him. Milton held her so tight she felt he could crush her. She kissed his eyes, his nose, his cheeks, and then reached long and hard into his mouth. Milton rolled over and entered her, moving gently with her. He could feel her peaking. He held back until she was satisfied, then he let himself go in a series of rythmic movements. He moved, taking some of his weight off her. "I'm still not full yet. I want more." Milton smiled, kissed her, and Jenna returned his passion.

# 4.

The guests sat quietly, eagerly awaiting the arrival of the bride. Eighty of Milton's and Jenna's nearest friends from around the world had come to congratulate them. The marriage was the talk of the industry. The news of their engagement shocked most of Milton's friends. They never thought he'd ever marry again. Young, prominent, society girl marries older millionaire and partner. Jenna glowed in the waiting room, Allison fixing the last-minute details on her dress and veil.

"You look breath-taking today," Allison told her.

"I feel glorious. I don't ever remember feeling so happy. I can't believe it's all happening."

"For every woman," Allison began, "there's a perfect man if she waits long enough. And, believe me, Jenna, you found him."

"I know. He's not only good to me, but I can talk to him. We have common interests. He makes me feel like his equal. I'm just not a pretty woman on a pedestal." Jenna looked at herself one more time in the floor-length mirror. Her wedding gown was a masterpiece of design. She fashioned it after the Southern Belles—high collar, fitted bodice and full skirt. The sleeves puffed at the shoulders and tapered to the wrists. The antique green satin and lace brought out the color of her eyes.

For one brief moment she was reminded of Scarlet O'Hara. The large wide-brimmed hat gave the final touch. She wore her hair pulled back at the neck, braided in a chignon. The emerald and diamond earrings she wore were a gift from Milton. The only other jewelry she had on was the six carat emerald-shaped diamond ring which she changed from her left hand to the right, to enable him to put on the diamond wedding band.

"I'm ready if you are?" Allison said. "I'm sorry Catherine couldn't be here today."

"So am I," Jenna smiled. "She loves all this pomp and circumstance. I think they're playing our song. Let's get out of here. I'm so nervous." Allison took her place in front of Jenna and proceeded down the aisle, unescorted, as Jenna had requested. She smiled at Michael and her daughter as she passed them. She turned and watched Jenna come down the aisle—confident, poised and radiant. Jenna took her place next to Milton as the Judge asked them to repeat their vows. The ceremony was short. In less than ten minutes Jenna Jones became Mrs. Milton Bertinelli. Allison followed the couple down the aisle, escorted by Raymond Bertinelli.

The guests moved into the Baroque Room at the Plaza Hotel and feasted on caviar, hors d'oeuvres, champagne, and laughter. Milton watched with pride as his new bride mingled with the guests. He loved her more than he ever thought he could ever love another woman.

"Congratulations, gorgeous," Michael said, kissing Jenna.

"Where have you been hiding?"

"No where. This was the first chance I got to come

over to you. You've been a very busy lady," he went on.

"I'm a very happy lady," Jenna corrected him.

"I'm glad. You deserve it."

"You mean after three disastrous marriages."

"Even so. You've worked hard. Done us all proud. I'm very happy for you."

"Thanks, Michael. For some reason your approval has always meant a lot to me," she told him, meaning every word. Jenna moved over to Milton, taking his arm, trying to follow the conversation he was already in the middle of. Her mind drifted off to two years ago when they first met. Even after the terms of the deal were agreed upon, and they had spent five glorious days together, she never thought she'd become Milton's wife. Jenna took a plane home with Michael, talking the whole way about a larger office, hiring staff, and the promotion of her new line. She had a hectic eight months in front of her but was basking in her own glory. Milton stayed on in Italy to complete his business and a month later returned to the States.

Jenna was busy the entire time with real estate brokers on the phone and meetings with Harry to decide how and when to break the news of the new company to the public. Catherine worked day and night on rough sketches for the new line, as well as hiring two other assistants. The small space was cramped, and Jenna was working them so hard that they didn't have time to breath. Catherine knew better than to ask Jenna any intimate details about the trip, and yet she knew Jenna was different, changed in some way. She hoped it was all because of the merger. Jenna sat behind closed doors most of the day with Michael and executives from the Bertinelli mills. Milton had given his research department the okay to start developing data on denim. Jenna made two trips to North Carolina to see the Bertinelli mill and talk to the team of salespeople assigned to her. The ball was rolling. It didn't matter how hard she worked, she never felt so energetic in her life. She lived on two hours of sleep a night and looked none the worse for it.

Jenna was beginning to feel the tension mount between Catherine and herself but she didn't have time or the inclination to start anything with her. If Catherine felt put aside when Milton was in Europe, she had no idea of things to come. As soon as Milton got to New York, all his free time was spent with Jenna; he was interested in all aspects of her business. He didn't care about the cost of having someone come in and decorate the new offices with the most expensive furnishings, paintings, leaving Jenna free to supervise the final sketches. Jenna left her private office for last. She wanted to give it her personal touch. With meetings every night, Jenna slowly moved into Milton's apartment. They enjoyed one another's company in as well as out of bed.

As the months passed, so did Allison's term; she was beginning to waddle to and from the office. Michael tried to get her to stay home, but Allison wouldn't hear of it. There was so much going on, she thought she'd never catch up if she stayed away any length of time. Michael knew better than to try to convince her to do less and threw up his hands in disgust. She stayed at work and moved into the new offices.

*Jenna Jones, Inc.* had rented the entire fourteenth floor of 2500 Broadway. The office was complete with its own showroom, dressing room, cutting room, public relations department, design studio and executive offices. Jenna made it a point to go into the lobby of the building and watch the manager place her name on the information board. *Jenna Jones, Inc. Fourteenth Floor. Very impressive,* Jenna thought, and returned upstairs.

She was having her first staff meeting. By the end of the week the sportswear line would be finished, and they were ready to talk about the new winter line. Allison had hired two in-house models for Jenna and her assistants to work with. Harry made sure Jenna's name hit every newspaper and magazine in the country. The Fashion section of the Times had done a spread on the *Bertinelli-Jones team*. For those in the industry who thought Jenna could be stopped, now it was impossible. She had unlimited capital, enough to surpass even the old established firms. Jenna talked and women around the country listened. Not only was she a woman, but she was young, pretty and feminine. The hardest competition to beat. A woman being dressed by a woman. What's more she seemed to know exactly what the women wanted to wear. The manufacturers on Seventh Avenue had to take a long hard look at themselves. They were now fighting a new breed of designer, and they'd have to change in order to keep up with the new competition.

Jenna was pleased with the new line. She watched her clothes being worn by her two models. Much to her own surprise, the changes she asked Catherine to make were only slight. Her sales force sat behind her. They were getting ready for the first big fashion show in the morning—Jenna meeting the public, and the press seeing the first Jenna Jones line.

Allison sat backstage, her feet hurting from the extra weight. She peeked out on the crowd applauding, taking pictures of the girls as they paraded down the runway. Pants, blouses, jackets, vests, coordinates, the skirts mid-calf, high boots worn with the skirts and pants, the material soft, hugging the body, showing its natural curves. Mixtures of burgandy and pink, brown and light blue, each elegant, and every piece of clothing well received. Her daytime dresses were made of the same fabric, simple, cut for the woman's body, and sensuous. Jenna chose to keep all her lengths consistently mid-calf. Jenna had done her homework. She was dressing the women of America, not the models, and she knew the problems, the flaws of the average woman's body, rich or poor. Most every woman could wear her clothes and look good. The higher heel of the boot or shoe and the longer length of the skirt would make all women look thinner and taller . . . *The American Dream*.

The lights dimmed, the music more sensuous, and the evening line made its grand entrance. Silks and satins. Black and white. Lounging pajamas with tapered legs, white three-quarter jackets tied with a wide belt. Comfortable and elegant. They could be worn anywhere —at home for a romantic evening or out to the finest restaurant. Jenna's evening clothes were all female— backless, high slits to the thigh, and low-cut in the front. The line reminded Allison of pictures of the starlets from the thirties. As soon as the last model left the runway, Jenna came out to the audience. It took almost ten minutes before she could say anything. Everyone was standing and applauding. Milton Bertinelli sat in the last row, observing. He was very happy that he let his instincts make the decision for him again. So far he was batting a thousand. He was never wrong.

"Thank you for coming," Jenna started. "I don't know what to say, except, it's very different from my first fashion show a few short years ago. And as I stand here now, I must admit all of you were right. I was not ready. But as most of you know, young people are impatient. And I was the most impatient person around," she paused as everyone laughed. "I thought that by sitting at my drawing table I could solve the fashion problems of the world. I know today it's not true. I had to take my time, stop, look around and listen to what women had to say. The people who wear my clothes are important to me. What they feel and what they want is what I intend to give them." Jenna paused, trying not to sound too humble or contrite. "I hope you enjoyed the new line and will not hesitate to tell our research department what you liked or didn't like about the designs. And, in turn, we can advise you what would look best on you. For you see, we may all be women, some of us taller, some of us shorter, but in essence we all want to look our best, feel our best, and wear the clothes in which we feel good and look good. Thank you." Jenna smiled at the applauding audience and left the stage.

"You were wonderful," Allison said, hugging her.

"I hope so. I really didn't know what I was going to say. I was so nervous. Did I make any sense?"

"Yes, and I'm sure you'll see your name in bold print next to a quote from your speech in *Womens Wear Daily* in the morning."

"Thanks, you've made me feel so much better," Jenna said, looking up and seeing Milton coming toward her.

"The fashion show was spectacular. Everyone is so excited. They loved everything," Milton said, giving her a kiss on the cheek.

"More important, did *you* like everything?" Jenna

said, searching for his approval.

"I loved everything. I know we're going to have a good season," he said, turning around to Allison. "We're having a small party at my apartment. Do you want to drive up there with me?"

"I don't think so, Milton, thank you. Would you do me a favor though?" she asked.

"Anything."

"Could you take me to Memorial Hospital?"

"Allison, you're not having your baby now, are you?" Jenna gasped.

"Jenna, I tried. I told the baby to wait as long as I could, but it's three weeks late and fed up already," Allison laughed, and Jenna joined her.

"My favorite partner. Worked right to the end, literally," Jenna told Milton who was escorting Allison out the back door. "Do you want me to do anything?"

"Yes, try to find Michael. If you can't within fifteen minutes, tell him to meet me at the hospital."

"I will," Jenna shouted, panicking for the first time. Exhaustion was setting in. Her first show, Allison's baby, it was all too much for one day.

Milton sat in the back seat of the limousine, holding Allison's hand. "Are you sure you can wait until Jenna finds Michael?"

"I think so. From what I'm told, first babies take a long time to be born."

"Have you been timing the contractions?"

"No. I've only had about five . . . six," Allison gasped.

"It's five ten. We'll see what time the next one comes," Milton told her softly. No panic in his voice. Allison thought he was so soothing. She felt no embarrassment about being with this man she hardly knew, in his car, about to deliver her first child. She was glad she had someone like him with her. She was becoming frightened. The pain she felt was unlike any she'd ever had. She knew the next few hours would be rough.

"I have to admit, you couldn't have picked a better time," Milton smiled, trying to take her mind off herself.

"I know. I wouldn't have wanted to miss the show for anything. Catherine and Jenna did a great job," Allison said.

"By the way where was Catherine?"

"On the other side, helping the models. I wish Jenna would find Michael."

"She will. I'm only giving her a few more minutes, after that, we're leaving," Milton said firmly.


Jenna ran back into the hotel. She had a hard time getting through the crowd of people, each one wanting to talk to her or congratulate her. She didn't want to be rude but she had to find Michael. She finally spotted his tall lean frame across the room. She tried shouting his name, but he couldn't hear her.

She pushed and shoved herself in his direction, yelling his name the whole time. Catherine caught her.

"What's wrong?"

"Allison's in the car. She's in labor! I have to get Michael."

Catherine darted toward him, moving faster than Jenna. She grabbed his arm as Jenna told him the news. Jenna watched his face turn white, and he darted through the crowd. Jenna worked her way back toward the exit, Michael a few feet behind her. She ran out the door.

"Catherine has him. He'll be here in a minute,"

Jenna said out of breath.

"Fine. Sorry to put you through this today. Get right back inside to your guests," Allison ordered.

"Have Michael call me the minute the baby comes."

"I will," Michael said, reaching the car.

"Now I don't want you young people to be nervous. Women have been having babies for centuries. You'll be fine. The contractions are only eight minutes apart. You have plenty of time," Milton reassured them, as Michael climbed into the car and sat next to his wife.

"Hold down the fort until I get back," Milton told Jenna.

"Really Milton, you don't have to come," Allison said. "You have guests coming tonight."

"So? Our first show and our first baby all in the same day. I wouldn't miss it for the world," he said, winking at Jenna. She smiled back at him, feeling his warmth.

"Enough thank you's and I'm sorry's. Get going," Jenna ordered. "Call me later," she yelled as the car pulled away.


Jenna went back inside, posed for pictures with Catherine at her side. She talked to reporters and left the hotel as soon as she could get away.

Milton's apartment was quiet. She sat down, put her feet up on the couch, and tried to collect her thoughts before his guests arrived. Catherine took a taxi up to the hospital, wanting to keep Michael company while he waited. Jenna was glad. The two hadn't spent much time alone lately, and she didn't want to answer any of Catherine's questions. It disturbed her somewhat that Catherine hadn't bothered her sexually in months. She wondered if Catherine was seeing someone else.

Another woman, or maybe a man. Jenna felt a twinge of jealousy set in, and quickly shook it off. If Catherine was enjoying someone else's company, Jenna was happy. She was very content with Milton. In seven months, she hadn't tired of being with him, she was still anxious to see him each day. At times she felt like a school girl with her first crush on her teacher. Jenna laid back and closed her eyes, falling right to sleep.

Allison had a baby girl at eleven fifty-eight. It was a memorable day for everyone.

Michael and Catherine went to the coffee shop to pass the half hour until he could see his wife and daughter. Michael was all smiles, his legs like rubber under him. He sighed in relief that both were fine and in good health.

"Did I thank you for staying with me?" he asked absent-mindedly.

"Oh, about a thousand times," she smiled. "But I forgive you."

"I've been acting like a crazy man. I can't believe it. I mean, during the whole pregnancy I was as calm as a cucumber. Tonight I fell apart."

"It's okay, Michael, really. I think all men feel the way you do, the first time that they become a father."

"I wonder how Allison is doing. She was in the labor room so long."

"I've heard worse. For the first baby, she made record time."

"Do you think we should go up yet?"

"No, the doctor said to wait a half an hour. It's only been fifteen minutes. Relax, drink your coffee. Why don't you try to eat something?"

"I couldn't. I'm too excited. I wonder what she looks like."

"Beautiful, I'm sure. She couldn't help but be," Catherine told him.

"I'd like to call her Ali. Short for Allison. I don't know if my wife will go for it though. You know her. She has a mind of her own."

"I think it's a lovely name. Hold your ground," Catherine said.

"I'm going upstairs. I can't sit here any longer," Michael said, getting up. Catherine followed him, shaking her head and smiling. This is what life was really all about. Bringing a new life into the world. She was envious of what Allison and Michael had together at that moment. She felt she had missed so much, wondering if she had been too hard on herself. She had never tried to pursue a relationship with a man. Catherine had thrown in the towel too soon. There had to be someone out there for her. A man who would love and understand her fears and try to help her get over them. Catherine decided to give it a try—maybe see a psychiatrist and work out her fears. Jenna would never be the answer to her problems. Jenna would never be the key to her happiness. She'd fight like hell to try to lead a normal life. Other people had problems, traumas, and they'd lived through them, gotten over them and went on. It was as if her meeting Jenna put an end to any happiness she might have had with a male. Jenna was the easy way out. Catherine remained loyal, and the dear girl went off and got married, had one affair after another. She gave Catherine nothing but her first orgasm. No, it was time Catherine became selfish for once, thought only about what was going to make her happy in the long-range, not just for the moment. She was still young enough to change, and now she had the determination to try. Catherine for the first time in years walked through the hospital corridors, feeling better about herself. She felt a sense of hope that life didn't deal her a dirty hand. She realized that she had dealt it to herself by giving up. She'd have to face one more problem—she'd have to go home. Catherine would have to stop blaming her mother for her life too. Before she could build a new life, she had to go back, make peace with herself, get rid of the old fears, put them out of her mind for good.

Catherine found Michael at the nursery window. The nurse was holding up his daughter. Tears started welling up in Catherine's eyes. The baby was so tiny and beautiful. His daughter had her whole life in front of her. A life with two understanding loving people. How lucky their little girl was. *If I had a daughter*, Catherine thought. *I'd hold her so close to me, love her with all my heart, and never let anyone hurt her.*

Michael knocked at the window. He asked the nurse if he could hold his daughter for one minute. It was against the rules, but the nurse was willing to break them for him. Michael went around to the side of the nursery, put on a gown and mask, and took his daughter into his large arms. The child looked lost.

"May I?" Catherine said, holding out her arms.

"I've stretched the rules letting the father hold her," the young nurse said.

"But she's waited with me all night," Michael said, his eyes beseeching her, then handing the baby to Catherine.

"She's like a bundle of warmth," Catherine smiled, the tears now running down her face.

"Are you okay?" Michael asked, never having seen

Catherine cry before.

"I'm just happy for you . . . It's nothing. I'm being silly."

"I think you're being sweet," he told her, knowing there was more in the tears than Catherine was willing to tell.

"She has to go back to the Nursery," the nurse said.

"Just one more minute," Michael asked.

"No. Mr. Fenway, you'll have the rest of her life to be with her. I'll tell you what. Why don't you get up for the two o'clock feedings and let your wife sleep," she winked. Michael laughed and handed his daughter back to her.

The doctor came out into the hall, and told Michael he could go in to see his wife. "Don't stay too long. She's tired and it's late."

Allison's eyes were closed when he quietly entered the room. He stood for a moment staring at her. He loved her more each day, now he was ready to burst.

"How long are you going to stand there before you kiss me?" Allison smiled.

"I didn't want to wake you. How do you feel?" he said, bending down and kissing her.

"Tired, sore, empty, happy. A mixture of a lot of things. But mostly anxious. Have you seen her yet?"

"Yes, she looks just like you."

"Of course," Allison said, taking his hand.

"I'd like to name her Ali."

"Only if her middle name is Michelle. It's only fair."

"You've got a deal," Michael said. "Do you think it's too late to call the folks?"

"You mean you haven't?" Allison was surprised.

"I was so worried about you. I didn't think about it until now. Catherine's been with me the whole time holding my hand."

"Then you'd better go call. They are going to be mad. You know how late this baby is. My mother's been phoning three times a day."

"I think I've made a serious error," he made fun of her. "But they love me and I'm sure I'll be forgiven. After all, this is our first child and I don't know the protocol yet."

"Go. Make the calls, get some rest and let me get some too," Allison ordered.

"I think we should have another baby right away," Michael said, caught up in the beauty of the moment. Allison said nothing, but the dagger stare she threw his way told the story. He picked the wrong time to tell his wife he wanted another baby.

Michael left the room, went to the first available phone booth and called Allison's family first, then his own. Both were excited, and both were coming up to see her the next day.

He decided to walk home from the hospital instead of taking a taxi. Catherine walked part of the way with him. The two were deep in their own thoughts, both thinking of the future. He was glad with all the heavy schedules, they were able to find the time to get another apartment. They were lucky their first day out. They found what they wanted. A two-bedroom apartment in an older, fashionable building. The rooms were large with high ceilings. The living room had a fireplace, and there was room for a maid off the kitchen, as well as a large den where Michael could work. A perfect home if only Allison would stay in it long enough to finish decorating. She was consumed by the business, and, much to his surprise, so was he. Now that he represented Jenna Jones, Inc., he spent more time with her than any of his other clients. He had no complaints—the finder's fee he received was sizable, and his monthly retainer was enough for the three of them to live on comfortably. Jenna had definitely changed the lives of everyone she came in contact with. Except for Catherine. She wasn't any happier or more settled now than she had been the first time Michael met her. He often wondered about the little girl lost. He looked over at her, walking quietly beside him. "Do you want me to take you home?"

"No. I'll be fine. I'll walk another block or two. The fresh air feels good. Then I'll hail a taxi."

"It's funny how everything turns out," Michael started, trying to get Catherine into conversation. "Our lives are settled. We've all gone our separate ways, yet we're all so close. Playing out the dreams we had in college. Time is passing quickly and I really don't feel any older."

"I do. I feel as though I've lived three lifetimes since school," Catherine said. "You were different. You had your feet on the ground. You knew what you wanted. Allison and Jenna did too. I never did. And I still don't."

"Don't you ever want to get married?" Michael asked for the first time.

"I never gave it a thought. I wanted to put all my energy into my art work. Before I met Jenna, I knew it would take me a long time to prove myself in the art world. It seems I was led down another road. Now I have to make other plans."

"You didn't answer my question."

"Find me a carbon copy of you and I'll marry him tomorrow," Catherine said, being very honest.

"I'll look, but I'm not that special."

"Yes you are. In more ways than you'll ever know.

Now that Jenna is on her way, I think I'll sit back a while, and take another look at my life. I'd like to have a child before it's too late."

"Catherine, you're still very young."

"Nearing thirty."

"Well, let me call the old-age home for you in the morning," he laughed. "Really, more women are getting married later in life these days. They're smart."

"Oh, why do you say that—Mr. 'Let's get married quick'?"

"It wasn't right for me, but it is for you. You had to prove yourself as many women today feel they have to. You have, and in the next few years you'll have gotten everything you've wanted to do out of your system. You'll be ready to settle down and have a family," he tried to make her feel comfortable.

"Could be. I'd like to think so. But something deep down inside me knows it will never happen. I get frightened sometimes. I feel so lonely," Catherine confided.

"I understand. Sometimes I look at Allison and wonder what life would be like without her. She fills my world with joy. I'd die without her. I'm a romantic. I want everyone to be as happy as I am."

"Face it, Michael, not everyone will be. As for me, it's in the stars," Catherine said, looking off into the distance. She turned and waved to a taxi. Michael knew he'd asked too many questions.

"I hope I haven't upset you," he said, touching her arm.

"On the contrary. Tonight I feel good, I feel as though my life will change somehow. But I have to be the one who changes it," she said, opening the taxi door.

Michael watched her drive away. "She's a strange

one," he thought. For as long as he had known her, he really didn't know her at all. Michael turned and walked the six blocks to his apartment. Thoughts of Allison and Ali filled his mind; nothing could spoil his mood. He was too happy and suddenly very tired. It was close to two in the morning when he finally hit the bed, feeling for Allison but she wasn't there. He fell asleep thinking how lucky he was.

The reviews on Jenna's new line made all the papers the next day. She had been a success. The orders and sales figures mounted. There wasn't a chain store in the country her clothes weren't in.

Wordsworth looked at the papers and the pictures of Jenna. He was happy. She was on her way, he thought. "No one can stop her now." He could rest easy. He felt a bit saddened by it too. He lived his entire life waiting for her to grow up. Waiting for her to need him, and when she did, he'd be there for her. He kept his promise, and now she didn't need his help anymore. He didn't want to fool himself either. Jenna was resourceful, and meeting Bertinelli was the best move for her career. He knew Allison was a smart girl. She picked up on everything he told her and followed through with it. He knew Allison had to be instrumental in Jenna's meeting Bertinelli. It was done. Over. There wasn't anymore he could do for Jenna.

Wordsworth sat alone in his darkened office. Everyone had gone home for the night. He stayed longer than usual. He didn't feel like going home tonight.

He reflected back on his life, or the only part of his life that ever mattered. He had lost everything—his money, pride, business—he had given it all up to finance the most sensational custody fight in history. FREDERICK SMYTH FIGHTS FOR DAUGHTER!

Wordsworth sat back in his chair, closed his eyes, the memory of his daughter still vivid in his mind. He recalled the same scene over again. If he had to do it again, what would he have done differently? He'd have run, run away with his daughter, so far that no one would ever have caught them.

Fred Smyth paced in front of the Jones' home in Palm Beach. Word had gotten to him that his wife was dying. He had to go in and see her one more time. Make some plans for their daughter. He stepped up to the door and rang the bell. Jensen's stern face greeted him. Without waiting for permission to enter the house, Fred pushed the butler to the side and ran up the large staircase to the second floor. He found Judith in her oversized, four-poster bed. She seemed to be asleep. She looked so pale and thin that she'd break if he touched her. Frederick tip-toed over and knelt down next to her bed. Judith's eyes opened slowly, a smile brightening her face when she recognized Frederick. He took her hand and kissed it.

"How did you get in?" she asked weakly.

"I pushed Jensen out of the way. I don't think we have very long though. I'm sure your mother will be up with the guards soon."

"I'm sorry, Frederick. I wish I hadn't brought such unhappiness to your life."

"Don't. It isn't my life I'm worried about, it's yours. You have to get well. Judith, please, for our daughter's sake. I love you."

"I don't think I will, darling. I'm too tired. I can't fight anymore," she sighed. "It's a losing battle," she closed her eyes again.

"Judith, please listen to me. I need you. Our daughter needs you. If you die, your mother will bring her up. She's already told me she wouldn't let me see her," he begged.

"Darling, promise me you'll take Jenna away from here. Take her as far as you can. Bring her up with love and understanding. Please," Judith said, her eyes searching his.

"I will, I promise. But there won't be any need. You're going to be fine," he said, tears rolling down his face. He knew she wouldn't.

"Mr. Smyth, Mrs. Jones wants to see you in the library. You only have a few minutes. Miss Judith is very tired," Jensen said.

Judith held her husband's hand tightly. "Remember what you promised me. You're the strong one. You can fight her. Take our daughter away," Judith said, falling back into a deep sleep. Frederick got up, took one last look at his wife and was ready to meet the enemy.

Mrs. Jones sat upright in her high back chair in the library. Her face was taut and her eyes, cold. In his heart, Frederick knew his mother-in-law blamed him for the fate of her daughter.

"Sit down, Frederick," she ordered in a hard voice. He did as he was told. "I'll come straight to the point. I want to raise Jenna . . ."

"Not as long as I'm alive," Frederick flared, cutting her short.

"Sit down. I will not stand for any outbursts in my home!" she told him. "You are not a rich man. You cannot offer your daughter anything. If I raise her, she'll have the best. She'll see the world, go to the finest schools, be introduced to the proper people and turn out as she should . . . A Jones." Frederick's jaw tightened, he clenched his fists, his knuckles becoming white. He knew if he got mad, his battle would be over before it started. He said nothing.

"You must agree. It's for your daughter's best interests. And Frederick, you've taken my daughter away from me. I won't let you take Jenna."

"I took Judith. Yes, I did. I loved her and she loved me. We didn't commit any crime. You'll be the cause of her death. You're the one who wouldn't give in. It was your way or no way. Judith is dying of a broken heart."

"Stop it this instant!" Mrs. Jones raised her voice.

"I won't. It's about time someone told you what you are. A sour, destructive, bitter old woman. You may have destroyed Judith, but you won't have Jenna. I made a promise to my wife just now. I told her our daughter would be coming with me."

"Never. I'll fight you. You don't have a chance, so don't waste what little money you have."

"No. I'll spend it all. Borrow money if I have to, but you won't get my daughter." Frederick jumped up, losing his temper. "I won't let you take her. There isn't a court in this country that would take a man's daughter away from him."

"You think not? Then Frederick we have nothing more to say to one another. For Judith's sake, I tried to save you as much suffering and expense. You were always stubborn. You'll have to learn the hard way," Mrs. Jones told him defiantly, getting up from her chair to leave the room. She turned to him. "Good night, Frederick," and she was gone. He sat for a moment, pulling his thoughts together. He knew he didn't have a chance against her in court, despite what he had said. She had the best lawyers, knew all the judges. It was all tied up and he was the loser.

Frederick's mind started racing. His only chance was to take Jenna away. After all, he couldn't get arrested for taking his own daughter. One afternoon, when he knew Mrs. Jones was out of the house, he'd come by and see his daughter. Mrs. Hart, her nanny, was fond of him. She'd sneak him in. He hated to hurt Mrs. Hart, he knew she'd get fired when his mother-in-law found out what she did, but then again, if Jenna wasn't there, there was no need for her.

It was all too crazy. He had to be out of his mind. He'd get caught before he had the chance to escape.

Frederick left the house, saddened by Judith, distraught over his daughter. He was a broken man. He didn't care what happened to him anymore. He'd lost the two people who meant the most to him.

Frederick paced up and down his living room floor for days after Judith's funeral. He couldn't think of anything but his daughter. The thought of stealing her away consumed him. He didn't have anything else to lose, why not give it a try?

Frederick sat down and mapped out his plan. He knew that on Wednesdays Mrs. Jones was always out for the day; even with her daughter's death, she'd be out. But for his own safety, he'd call Mrs. Hart to make sure. When Frederick called, Mrs. Hart was more cooperative than he expected. She was saddened by the loss of Judith and knew that his pain was overwhelming. She suggested they meet at the park where he'd be able to see his daughter without the watchful eyes of the other servants. Frederick was relieved. It was better than he expected. Frederick packed his clothes, cleaned out his savings account, sold what little he could, and made his plans to leave the state, and eventually the country. That evening Frederick went to bed but not to sleep. He was frightened. He even began to have second thoughts. What kind of life would his daughter have, running?

Frederick left his apartment early, drove to the park, patiently awaiting the arrival of his daughter. His fears and anxieties left him as soon as he saw her beautiful face as she ran toward him. He grabbed her, holding her so tight she screamed. "Daddy you're hurting me."

"Sorry, darling. Daddy's so glad to see you. Do you want to go for a walk with me?"

"Yes, where will we go?" Jenna asked eagerly.

"I don't know. Do you want to go somewhere special?"

"I want to go anywhere as long as I'm with you," she said, taking his hand. Mrs. Hart nodded in approval. She felt so sorry for both of them. Frederick walked around the park with his daughter, Mrs. Hart watching. When she felt everything was fine, she sat down on the park bench and took out her book. Frederick picked up his daughter and started to run toward the car.

"What are we doing, daddy?" Jenna asked excitedly.

"We're going for a ride. Wouldn't you like that?"

"Yes. Can we go for a ride on a pony?" the little girl giggled.

"Anything you want to do. We'll do it all," Frederick said, hugging her.

Their week's adventure started. Frederick drove one hundred miles on the back roads to a friend's cabin. He figured that they would be safe there until he could decide on their next move. He had to find another car; the police would be alerted and looking for his. His hands began to sweat on the steering wheel. Jenna sat quietly, loving their little adventure.

Frederick stopped for dinner a few miles away from the cabin. He bought a few things for Jenna to wear, and tried to hide his fear from her. Jenna was tired from the long trip. "Are we going to sleep here tonight?" she asked.

"We'll be here for a few days until we can take a boat to South America," he told her.

"Good, I love boats."

Frederick put her to bed in the small room next to his. She put her tiny arms around his neck when he bent down to kiss her goodnight. "Let's always be together, daddy," she said, her eyes heavy with sleep.

Frederick turned on the radio to listen to the news. As he suspected, the police were already on his trail. A wave of despair passed through him. He knew his happiness with his daughter was only temporary. As if he was resigned to his fate, Frederick decided to stay put in the cabin until they were found. He wanted to make the time they had together fun for his daughter. He had no other choice—he'd have to go into court and fight the old bitch.

The police and private detectives found the two playing in the back yard five days later. The scene remained in Frederick's memory for life. The young detective walked over to him, a look of remorse on his face. "You know we have to take your daughter with us," he said.

"Can I go with you? I don't want to alarm the child."

"You know we're going to have to take you in," the detective said, still solemn.

"I promise I won't give you any trouble. Can we drop my daughter off first, then I'll go with you," Frederick said, begging him.

"How do I know I can trust you?"

"Look, she's my daughter. I don't want her to see her father being taken away. I also don't want her to think I left her. I do intend to fight for custody in court. Please. She's only a little girl."

"Okay, I don't want to see the child upset. But don't try anything. You drive and I'll put one of my men in the car with you," the detective said. Frederick agreed. Jenna ran to her father. "I'm afraid, daddy. Why are all these men here?" she said holding Frederick around his neck.

"It's okay, baby. We have to take you back to your grandmother's house. Just for a little while."

"No! I don't want to go! I want to stay with you. I won't go!" Jenna screamed.

"Jenna, I'll be back to get you. I promise. I have to straighten a few things out first. It won't take long. Please be a good girl!" he said, crying.

"I'll wait for you, daddy. I'll wait for as long as it takes. Please come back and get me!"


Frederick sat up in his chair. He looked down at his watch. It was almost eleven o'clock. Time to go home. He wondered how his dear mother-in-law had explained the facts to Jenna. With all the years that passed, Frederick never lost his intense hatred for the old lady. His life was never the same. After he lost the court fight which cost him every cent he had and all the money he borrowed, he no longer wanted to live. The few years after the trial were still a blur to him. He drifted from one town to another, drinking too much, partying too much, fighting too much. Nothing worked. His features seemed to change overnight—his nose broken twice, his broad frame slimming, the deep lines in his face apearing as though overnight. He looked twenty years older. He followed every newspaper and magazine article on his daughter. It was a quote she made in one interview which changed his life. "I want to be a great lady of the fashion world," the ten-year-old said. He knew she meant it. Jenna didn't live in a fantasy world, changing her mind from day to day like other children. It was then that he knew he had to pull himself together, change his name, come back to New York and pick up the profession at which he was best. He'd work night and day to get into a position to help his daughter one day realize her own goal.

He had. His job was done. It was too late to go to her and say, "I've come back to get you like I promised."

Frederick shut off the light on his desk and left the office. He had a strange premonition he'd never step inside of it again. He tried to shake his fears, his own melancholy, but he couldn't.

*Womens Wear Daily* ran an article on Frederick Wordsworth a few days later.

*Frederick Wordsworth, Executive Vice President in charge of sales of Bergdorf Goodman dies in his sleep. Mr. Wordsworth was instrumental in launching the career of Jenna Jones . . .* Allison's eyes welled up with tears. She put down the paper without finishing the article.

"He was instrumental in launching Jenna, and he never had the chance to meet her," Allison thought. "He was such a good man . . ." Allison felt his loss more than she could have imagined. She had become very fond of him. They were good friends. She was saddened by the fact that she couldn't even pay her last respects to him. But Jenna should. Allison reached over and dialed the hospital phone. Jenna came on the line immediately.

"How's the new mother doing?" Jenna asked.

"Fine, but I called you for another reason. Frederick Wordsworth died of a heart attack the day before yesterday. His service is tomorrow at eleven. I can't be there; I think you should go."

"Allison, I never even met the man."

"Jenna," Allison shouted. "If it wasn't for him, you'd never be where you are today. Your name is mentioned in the article. I think if you didn't go it would be a mistake."

"I guess you're right. I'll go," Jenna sighed. She hung up, picked up the unread copy of *Women's Wear* and thumbed through it until she came to the article on Wordsworth. His picture gave her chills. There was something about his eyes that looked familiar. Jenna pushed the paper aside. She'd probably seen him at one of the press parties along the way. Jenna went back to work, trying to fight the eerie feeling she had deep inside. She picked up the paper again, taking another look at the picture. She couldn't figure out why she was drawn to the man she saw. She re-read the article. She suddenly felt cold. "Maybe I'm working too hard," she thought. "Allison spoke so much about this man, I feel as though I know him. That must be the reason I feel like this," Jenna told herself. More than ever she had to go to the funeral.

Jenna left the office early, visited Allison in the hospital, and went to Milton's apartment. He was away for a few days and, in some ways, she was glad. She needed some time to herself to sit back and collect her thoughts or think of nothing. The last year had been long and hard and she was feeling its effects. She climbed into bed exhausted and tried to fall asleep. At first no sleep would come and, when she finally drifted off, she had a dream long since wiped from her memory. A recurring dream she had had almost every night for years after her father left.

Jenna was five again. She was crying in her father's arms, her grandmother trying to take her away from him. "I don't want to go . . . I don't want to go," she screamed over and over again, until the black car her father had been in drove out of sight.

As she was screaming for her father, the article about Wordsworth crept into her dream, the man who gave Jenna Jones her start. Her grandmother was smiling, her father was crying . . . the man who launched Jenna Jones' career. Jenna jumped up, her body wet with perspiration. She got up, went over to the bar and fixed herself a drink. She reached into her briefcase and took out the paper, already folded to the Wordsworth article. She looked at the picture again. Jenna dressed quickly and took a taxi to her own apartment. She opened her closet, throwing everything on the floor that got in the way. In the back of the closet in a hat box, Jenna found what she was looking for—the small scrapbook with pictures of her mother. Years ago, she found a picture of her father in the back of one of her mother's drawers. She took it and hid it away so no one could find it. She was afraid her grandmother would destroy it. Jenna had long since forgotten about it. She searched through all the pictures until she came to the one she was looking for. The only picture taken of her mother and father together. Jenna looked at the photograph, realizing what her dream was trying to tell her. Wordsworth was her father! Now all the pieces fitted together. Why he never came to meet her. Why he was so eager to help. "Oh, daddy," Jenna sighed, as she slid to her bedroom floor, clutching his picture and shedding her first real tears since she was six years old. Jenna fell asleep on the floor, exhausted and heartbroken.

The following morning, Jenna tried to pull herself together. She had to go to the funeral. She had to pay her last respects to him. He had watched her from a distance, never interfering in her life, and was there to help her when she needed him. Now that he couldn't help her anymore, he died. It was no coincidence. Jenna understood, maybe for the first time, how powerful his love was for her. She suddenly knew she'd never be alone. He had watched over her all these years, and he was still very much with her.

Jenna stood alone at the cemetery. Everyone gone. Wordsworth had no family, many close friends, but no wife or children. Jenna threw a rose on top of the casket. "Thank you, father," she whispered. "I know you always loved me." She turned and walked to the car. She would tell no one. She would respect his privacy. She knew who he was and she was sure he was resting peacefully now. That was all that mattered.

Miton asked Jenna to marry him a few months later. She accepted his proposal immediately. It was something her father wished for her, and she knew she was making the right decision. Milton was her father, her lover, her friend. She had the best of all possible worlds and what's more, she idolized him. Although she heard the rumors about the May-December marriage, it didn't bother her. *Let them talk*, she thought. *Milton and I know the truth.*

"Jenna, I hate to leave the reception so early, but Ali is tired, and to tell you the truth, so am I," Allison admitted. "Have a good time in Hong Kong, and we'll see you in three weeks."

"I will. Take care of the office for me. You're the only one I trust," Jenna said, kissing her.

"Catherine's there," Allison said. "I know she'll make sure we meet the deadline," Allison said, shocked at Jenna's remark.

"Her mind is elsewhere these days. Keep an eye out."

"I will . . . Jenna, you're not upset about her not coming to the wedding."

"No. I realize it was Tom's one weekend off. They needed the time away. I just hope she knows what she's doing with him. I don't like him very much," Jenna went on.

"She's old enough to make her own decisions. And, to tell the truth, I haven't seen her this happy in years. The man must be doing something right," Allison defended him.

"I guess. See you in three weeks. Take that husband and child home," Jenna ordered. Jenna watched them leave. She had lied to Allison; she was upset with Catherine. She was making an absolute fool of herself with Tom and she was doing it for spite. The boy was ten years younger than she. He was living with Catherine because she was his meal ticket. This incensed Jenna. She knew that when it was all over and he had sucked Catherine dry, she'd come crawling back to Jenna, begging to see her again, have her again. Not this time. This time she was rid of her forever. She was married to Milton; Catherine couldn't threaten her any longer with telling him what they had together. Yet Jenna felt the same twinge of fear coming back. Milton was from the old school. He would never accept the relationship between the two girls. He'd be repulsed by it. *Let her make a fool of herself*, Jenna thought. For the present, at least, Tom was keeping Catherine out of her hair.

The Bertinellis left before all the guests did. They excused themselves because they had an early plane to catch. The chauffeur was waiting outside to take them back to Milton's apartment.


Catherine sat up in bed. Tom was sulking in the other room. They had decided to take this vacation for a change of scenery. Catherine hoped if she was away from her apartment, away from work and the frustrations, sex would be better. It wasn't. She couldn't help herself. Nothing Tom did could bring her to a climax. He was gentle, loving, and, in the beginning, tried for hours to please her. For his sake, she began faking it, and Tom pretended to believe her, both knowing it wasn't working. Catherine was incapable of being satisfied by him. They continually had the same argument: "It isn't important," Catherine would say. "I love making love to you. I love having you touch me."

"It isn't fulfilling to me. I feel insufficient. I must be doing something wrong. I'm not the type of man who can get his rocks off and not care what my partner is feeling."

"Tom, please. We're both so uptight about it . . . maybe if we didn't talk about it so much, I'd relax and sex would be better for me."

'How much time am I supposed to give you? I've been living here for three months. We've had sex every night. I don't see it getting any better," he told her.

"Please listen to me. What if we went away. What if we tried a secluded place away from telephones, work, tension . . . Please, let's give it a try," Catherine told him.

Tom looked down at the floor, he wondered if it would do any good, deciding to give it one more try. "I'll go, but I still think this whole thing stems from your being older than me. You're so afraid of what people will think, you can't relax and enjoy me."

"Maybe . . ." Catherine lied not wanting to tell him the truth. He was the first man she'd gone to bed with. "I'm willing to try if you are," she said, moving over closer to him in bed. She wanted this to work. She couldn't stand one more failure. Dr. Kaufman told her that she was ready to try new things, go out with men, have sex. After a year of therapy she was feeing better about herself, and she wasn't making love to Jenna. She'd have an orgasm as soon as Jenna touched her. Maybe in time she told herself, in time, Tom would have the same effect.

It didn't work. They were away, but the sex was no better. She got out of bed, wrapped the sheet around herself and went into the living room.

"I'm sorry, Tom. We still have the rest of the weekend. Let's try and salvage it," Catherine said, touching him.

"No! I've had it with you. Why can't you accept me for what I am? So I'm younger than you. I'm not as successful. There's no reason to be ashamed of our affair," he screamed at her.

"I told you, that isn't the reason," Catherine started to cry.

"Bullshit! You're worried about what your precious Jenna will think. She married an older man, a millionaire. You're going out with a lowly photographer who hasn't had a job for months. You're supporting me, Catherine," Tom yelled out. "You're making me feel cheap."

"Don't please. I wish I could tell you . . ." she stopped.

"Tell me what?"

"Nothing," Catherine said, getting up.

"You're seeing someone else," Tom guessed.

"Don't be ridiculous, you're acting like a child," Catherine blurted out.

"A child! I'll show you who's a child," he said, grabbing the sheet from her, pushing her on to the floor. Catherine was terrified.

Tom jumped on top of her, holding her hands over her head. She could feel him getting hard, excited, breathing heavy. He was going to take her against her will. Catherine struggled to get up but couldn't budge. Tom tried kissing her, but Catherine moved her head. She remembered her rape so many years ago—the boys pushing at her, pulling at her—and she screamed, the scream she couldn't release back then. Suddenly, Tom thrust into her. She stopped screaming. She felt aroused. Moaning and crying, she came with an intensity that left her trembling. When Tom came, he rolled off her, and smiled. "Now I know your secret. You want the man to be the aggressor, rape you, hurt you. It's kinky, but it's nothing to be ashamed of," he said, kissing her.

Catherine realized he was right. She enjoyed him. She loved the struggle. Maybe the only way she could relate to a man was to re-enact the rape. "Take me again," she said, rolling over. "Don't be gentle."

Tom smiled. He knew what he had to do.

# 5.

Jenna walked briskly down Fifth Avenue. The glances of recognition from the passers-by, which she had loathed as a child, now brought a feeling of self-accomplishment. Through the years her face had appeared on the covers of *Vogue, Harper's Bazaar*, and *Town and Country*. She posed for all of them wearing her own designs. In *Time, Newsweek, Life* and *Look* magazines, Jenna gave her philosophy of the clothing industry—where it was headed, where she was headed, what made her tick. She was described as one of the shrewdest business women of the decade. Her sales figures were in the high seven-digit range and still climbing. Allison, who now headed her promotion department, decided Jenna was her own best sales tool, and she was right on target.

"You've been photographed as a child, young adult, and gay divorcee. Now the woman everyone has read about will wear her own clothes," Allison told her.

"I think it's rather tacky," Jenna said, rejecting the idea.

"Think about it. Designers come and go in this business. They're looking to make a name from their designs. You . . . you're something special. You had the name . . . your name has made the designs. It's a perfect sales pitch. The country is watching the little-girl-lost who was the brunt of the most publicized custody battle in history," Allison went on, becoming more enthusiastic by the minute.

"I'd rather not remember . . . the publicity hounds. You can't imagine how awful it was," Jenna said. "I hated the questions, the flash bulbs, and all that print released so many years ago. I wanted to run and hide under a rock," Jenna told her. "I wanted to run away where no one knew me."

"You don't have to run anymore. Don't you see? You've grown up. You've become a strong, determined, creative woman. You beat them. Now turn around and *use* the press. You'll make more money than you inherited. See what I'm getting at?"

"Okay, it hits home," Jenna said, thinking of her father. "Not the money so much, but using the press the way they used me," Jenna was thinking out loud.

"Think of the respect people will have for you for going out and doing something with your talent . . . Jenna, do you realize that you are the epitome of what women want to look like, feel like, act like, and be like? The role model. The leader. When they see you wearing your clothes in a fashion spread, they'll want to try to look like you," Allison told her. "It will send the sales figures through the roof," Allison stopped, looked at Jenna and knew she had her. "You'll go out making across-the-counter public appearances at department stores, shopping malls . . . you'll pose for our ad campaign . . . You'll become larger than life."

"What do the Bertinelli people think about this plan of yours?"

"They love it. Your name adds class and prestige to their product. They realize your personal touch will do more for sales than anything they could come up with," Allison went on. "What's even more exciting is that the Bertinelli people want to spend up to ten percent of their investment yearly on publicity."

"If I do the campaign?" Jenna interrupted.

"Yes. They know as I do that you are a natural. You know what your family name means across this country and in Europe. I mean the Jones are as well known as the Rockefellers or the Carnegies. We couldn't ask for any more clout. Jenna Jones the trend setter," Allison finished her pitch, sitting down in her chair, out of breath.

"Well, it's hard to argue with your reasoning. But I wouldn't have time to do anything else. I'd have to turn over the design work to Catherine," Jenna said.

"True. But by now, Catherine knows exactly how you think and what you like. She'd be the natural successor. I don't think you should be out of designing totally. All sketches would have to be approved by you. You would be responsible for the final touch. The Jones' flavor. Of course, you'd remain the color coordinator. No one has the flair you do," Allison kept pitching.

"Okay . . . I get the point," Jenna smiled. "It's time for me to move on. It might be exciting, although I hate having my picture taken."

"Jenna, of all the women I know, you and only you are the quickest pose. One minute you're natural, talking in conversation, and out of the corner of your eye you see a lens and, poof, you're flashing that magnificent smile of yours," Allison laughed.

"No, I don't."

"It's so second nature to you, Jenna, I don't think you realize it. I think that's what gave me the idea to use you in the first place. Michael and I were looking at some old pictures of all of us the other night. In every one, you were posed. Beautiful, but posed," she laughed. "The rest of us looked awful."

"I guess it's because I spent so much of my life being hounded by the press. I had to look my best," Jenna told her. "Grandmother's orders."

"You always did. I remember looking at your pictures in some of the fashion magainzes when I was a teenager, wishing I were you. I don't know if I ever told you, but if I hadn't been talked into going to school, I would have pursued modeling," Allison blushed at the thought.

"You used to wish you were me? I never knew that," Jenna said, taking another look at Allison. "You would have made a good model. As they say in the trade, you have magnificent bone structure," Jenna mimicked. "So where and, more importantly, when do we start?"

"As soon as possible. I have another meeting with the Bertinelli people tomorrow to give them your answer. Then I'll talk to the editor of *Vogue*, I think she's a friend of yours," Allison looked at Jenna and she acknowledged her question. "You'll be on the cover. Then after a huge print campaign, we'll start off with about fifty spots a week on television. We'll grow until we reach the peak . . . about a hundred and twenty."

"Spots a week!" Jenna gasped. "That's some campaign you've been working on," Jenna was surprised. "It will cost a fortune."

"Yes. You have to spend money to make money. And didn't I hear you say you wanted to be on top? You can't do that without a saturation campaign like this one."

"Where do the personal appearances come in?"

Jenna asked.

"Your clothes are in about three thousand stores across the country. We'd like to double that figure. So when the print and television campaign hits, you will hit the stores around the country. Give seminars on how to stay beautiful, youthful, and, of course, answer questions about dress and the coming trends."

"This is more than a full-time job. I'll need to take my secretary with me . . . and a writer, a researcher . . . I have to be prepared. Each area of the country warrants different clothing and beauty hints. I'll have to know all there is about the people in the area before I get to the store," Jenna sighed.

"I figured on that. I have some of our people working on the information now," Allison told her. "Jenna, I'm more excited about this campaign than I can possibly tell you. No one has ever done it before."

"I know. It's the only reason I'm even considering it. I've said so much to the public about being interested in what they want, now I'm proving I'm sincere."

"Exactly . . . did anyone tell you you catch on quickly?" Allison laughed.

"Whatever you do, make sure I'm away a week at a time tops. Maybe one week on and one week home," Jenna suggested. "I can keep track of the office that way."

"I can work that out. For openers, we'll start off with the East Coast. Five cities in five days. If I can get everything ready on schedule, you'll start the print campaign next month. Then we'll shoot the television commercials. I'd say you'll be traveling within the next six months at the latest."

"I have time then to start coaching Catherine on the next few seasons. Clean off my desk and then I'm yours," Jenna said.

"Good, I'll call the Bertinelli people this afternoon and we'll get the ball rolling. Everywhere one looks they will see the name Jenna Jones," Allison said, envisioning the whole campaign. Jenna thought she looked as though she had seen a miracle.

Jenna went back into her office, trying to digest it all. The more she thought about it, the more she liked it. To have women want to wear what she did, follow her lead, would make her ultimate goal—her designer jeans—work even better than expected. The Bertinelli research team had come up with the right weight denim, and she had the design which would make its mark on the fashion trend of the country. Allison was way ahead of her these days. The whole campaign fit in with her plans. Jenna was eager to start.

A month later Jenna was sitting in Cal Sharman's studio. Conde Nast's latest find, the youngest photographer on their payroll, Cal had asked to meet with Jenna before he shot her. He wanted to study her hair coloring, skin type, stature, so he could do her justice with his lighting and choose the right stylists for her. Cal always took this liberty when shooting a new face, especially if it was for a cover. Cal breezed in the studio a half an hour late. Jenna was not pleased with his being late and he knew it. But having her pegged as a spoiled little rich girl, he wouldn't give into her mood.

"Sorry I've kept you waiting," he said nonchalantly. "I'm afraid I'm going to have to keep you waiting another few minutes," Cal stated, stretching out his hand. "I have to check on the lights in the next room," he told her and walked away. Jenna was incensed. She had a mind to leave the studio and tell *Vogue* to get her another photographer. After all, she was a busy lady and didn't have all day to sit around waiting for some arrogant photographer. She stopped herself. She didn't want to be called a *prima donna*—the name would stick. Jenna sat down again. Cal walked back to her, smiled, took her hand and led her to the studio. Jenna was put out by his familiarity. She stood defiantly, staring at him.

"Sorry, didn't know you didn't like being touched. It's my way," he explained.

"It isn't mine. I came here today to work, let's work," she snapped.

Cal, not wanting to give her the satisfaction that he thought she was even more beautiful in person than in her pictures, eyed her and grunted a few times, touched her hair, looked at her profile, and made a few mental notes.

"See you here tomorrow at ten," he said.

"Is that all?" Jenna asked.

"That's it. I know exactly what I'm going to do."

"I'd like to know. It is my photograph that will be on the cover," Jenna was angry.

"No, it's your face—*my* photograph," he corrected. "It's also my reputation. You'll look your best," he told her, pointing to enlargements of his photographs on the wall. Cal said nothing else. He walked out of the room.

Jenna looked up, studied his work, and, as much as she hated his attitude, she had to admit that his work was magnificent. The best she'd seen in years. He was a young Arthur Penn and he knew it. Jenna picked up her coat and left, deciding to give Cal a bit of his own treatment.

Jenna arrived at the studio after ten-thirty. Everyone was ready for her, and had been for more than a half an hour. Cal rushed over to Jenna and pulled her into the dressing room.

"When I say ten o'clock, I mean ten, sharp. You've kept a lot of people waiting and have thrown me off schedule completely," he screamed.

"I thought it would be better to stay in my own office a little longer than wait here for you. You've been known to be late," she came back.

"Very good," he started, knowing exactly why she was late. "You just don't come in and sit before the camera. I don't mind if you keep me waiting, but the others . . . " He ran on like a spoiled child. "You have to have your hair done, make-up, dress. I can't believe it," he threw his hands up in disgust and left her in the room.

A small timid girl came into the dressing room and smiled at Jenna. "I'm Dina. Cal hired me to do your hair," she said. "I wouldn't worry about what he just said, he goes off on tangents a lot," she whispered.

"It's all right. Why don't we start? I don't want to hold anyone up any longer," Jenna said.

Dina went right to work. Jenna's shoulder-length hair, styled in its own fashion, left little for the hairdresser to do. Jenna was herself, and to make her look unnatural wouldn't do. The make-up man sat on the counter watching until Dina was finished. Then it was his turn.

An hour later, Jenna was ready. Cal was a professional. He put his anger aside and worked his magic. Jenna was a natural before the camera. Her eyes sparkled and her face glowed. She could sense that the shooting was going well. Cal seemed to feel the same way. The tension between them broke half way through the shooting, putting everyone at ease.

As soon as Jenna saw the proofs, she hired Cal as her exclusive in-house photographer. She told Cal about the tour and said he had to be with her. She had enough to keep him busy for the next year. Cal was to travel with Jenna on her tours, supervise all photographs taken and printed of her, and shoot her whenever he was needed.

The newsstands were inundated with Jenna Jones. Jenna read the demographic charts. She never believed that she had the hold on the American public the way she did until she started going on tour.

It was December 3rd. Some of the stores requested that Jenna make a personal appearance to enhance their Christmas sales. Advance publicity was arranged, the papers were notified, and Jenna was on her way. Gloria, her secretary, was to arrive beforehand to get her rooms in order, check the store and see that everything was running on schedule. Jenna flew up to Boston with Cal, her data in hand. She was ready to meet the public, knew the questions and had the answers. But never in her wildest dreams did she ever anticipate the crowd of people waiting in line for the store to open. The attraction of the day—Jenna Jones. The store manager of Lord and Taylor's greeted her and brought her to the third floor. The doors opened and the crowds poured in. Teenagers, children, married women, single women, and, much to her surprise, men. The store's third floor was incapable of holding as many people as Jenna attracted. Their only hope was to split the group in thirds. Jenna couldn't believe it. Gloria spent the morning on the telephone making other arrangements, later departures, trying to get the feel of what the turnout would be at their next destination. It was more than any of them hoped for.

The store manager and the security guards were able to keep the people in line, but they also weren't prepared for the turnout. They had to add more security people to guard against looting and riots. Jenna had to compose herself, replan her speech, and go out and meet the masses. She was frightened, couldn't understand the reason anyone would come out to see her on a cold rainy day and stand in line for hours. For an instant, a riot flashed in front of her, the crowds in front of the court trying to sneak a peek at the little girl both father and grandmother were fighting for. She felt a cold chill. *Do they want blood?* she thought. Jenna went out, took her place on the podium and the crowd cheered.

She spoke into the microphone, trying to be heard above the cheers. "Thank you for coming." The noise died down to total silence. Jenna had a captivated audience. She looked around. "Im glad to see so many men in this group." She stopped, the men looked uneasy. "I think it is important for men to be interested in how their wives, girlfriends, or whatever . . ." they laughed, ". . . dress. Women through the years have been influenced by men. They were dressed by male designers. They wore what would please their fathers, husbands, boyfriends. Now it's time for both to meet and discuss what is practical and most comfortable for women to wear and yet pleasing to the male eye." Jenna stopped, looking around and then spoke again. "I am here today to listen as well as talk about fashion. I believe we all can help one another. Now, I would like to answer any of your questions. Please raise your hands and I'll call on as many of you as possible." Jenna waited for the first hand. "Yes?"

A woman in the back stood up. "I just wanted to come here today to say that I think you've done your family proud. You're a pretty girl and a hard worker. If I had your figure, I'd wear your clothes, too," she said.

"Thank you, I really can't see you back there. Can you step around to the front?" Jenna asked. The lady, small, overweight, struggled down to the front row.

"Come on up here," Jenna said. "Anyone who makes a statement about not being able to wear my designs, I want to see," she smiled, appraising the figure. The woman was very good-natured, and Jenna took the chance of being frank. The lady smiled, stood about a head shorter than Jenna.

"May I ask your name?"

"Sure, Mrs. Wendall."

"Well, Mrs. Wendall, first I think you could lose a few pounds," Jenna smiled, pointing to her hips.

"Are you crazy. I used to be thinner than you, but my husband likes 'um big," she laughed, and Jenna felt more at ease.

"Then, why don't you go with Gloria, my assistant. She'll put you into one of our suits, and I'll show you what the right clothes will do to make you look thinner —for yourself."

"I'd like that very much. Then I could have the best of both worlds," she giggled, and turned to go with Gloria.

"Questions?" Jenna asked the audience.

"I have one," another lady, younger and prettier, yelled out. Jenna acknowledged her.

"I'm a secretary and live on a budget. I love your clothes but can't afford them," she said.

"How much money do you spend a year on clothing?" Jenna asked.

"I guess between fifty and one hundred dollars a month," the girl answered.

"Can I then say you spend about eight hundred dollars a year?"

"Yes, that's right."

"Then think of buying your wardrobe yearly instead of monthly. What I'm trying to say is that clothes are an investment like a car or a house. Clothes make the woman as well as the woman making the clothes. Women should never be in a hurry to buy their wardrobes, nor should they invest too much money in faddish-type clothes. If you spent four hundred dollars a year, half your yearly budget, on very good clothes which will last, and the rest on coordinates to go with the better jackets, dresses, etc., in a few years time, your closet will be filled with fine clothing, clothing that you've chosen carefully and will want to keep. It isn't important to have a great many clothes if the ones you do have fit well and look well on you. Remember, if you feel good, you'll look good. Women need variety in men, not clothes." Jenna winked at the man in the front row, and everyone else laughed, liking her humor and frankness.

"Yes?" Jenna took the next question.

"I heard what you told the lady over there about choosing wisely. I have a lot of clothes in my closet, but I never seem to have anything to wear," she said.

"A very common problem. Like anyone else, a woman must plan her wardrobe like she plans a dinner party. Mixing and matching correctly. Do you buy your clothes as you see them? Not taking into account what you have in your closet."

"Yes, you're right," the lady admitted. "Nothing really goes together."

"I'll show you," Jenna said, as Gloria handed her the two suits. One solid grey, the other striped in burgandy and grey. "See? We have two suits here. One with pants, the other a skirt. See for yourself how interchangeable they are. In two suits we have six different outfits. Now you need blouses to bring out the colors, a few nice scarves and you can dress up or dress down your outfit," Jenna stated.

"Now I see what you mean about choosing wisely," the secretary yelled, excitedly. Everyone talked, shaking their heads in agreement. Jenna got her point across. At that moment, Mrs. Wendall came out, wearing a striped suit, high-heeled shoes and a pink blouse.

"How do you like the way you look, Mrs. Wendall?"

"I like it. This suit hides all the sins," she laughed.

"Do you see how the vest hides a bit of Mrs. Wendall's tummy; the jacket slightly longer and narrowed at the waist, gives her hips a slimmer look, and the verticle stripes make her look taller, especially when she wears higher heels; the pants legs can be cut longer, giving her the height and thinning the leg. It's magic."

"Sure is. I didn't lose no ten pounds in there," she said, everyone cracking up.

"I still say another five pounds and your husband will never miss it," Jenna whispered to her.

"You better believe it. I forgot how good I used to look. It don't matter. He won't talk to me for a week from the price of this suit," she laughed, stepping down.

"I got one for you," one of the gentlemen in the front yelled. "How come you don't design men's clothes?

Our women are getting all dolled up and we won't look as good. No one ever tells us how to dress," he said, surprising Jenna.

"I haven't thought about doing it myself," she said reflectively. "I will give it some thought. But for now, there are fine designers out there who are doing for men what I'm doing for women. Pierre Cardin, Calvin Klein and Bill Blass, to name three. I'm sure if you go down to the men's department here at Lord & Taylor, a salesman will be very glad to help you. You can, of course use the same advice for yourself that I gave to some of the ladies."

The questioning went on for another half an hour. Everyone seemed to like what she said, and Jenna herself was pleased, also exhausted. She wasn't looking forward to doing another session in less than an hour.

Jenna had another five cities on this tour—and then home. Gloria had transcribed the questions and answers and put them in Jenna's folder to read on the plane. The questions were basically the same. Jenna decided to turn over the report to the research department and see if they could come up with some answers to solve the problems. Basically, she was doing the important work herself—*showing* the women how to dress themselves better and more economically. She was satisfied with the results, and the press treated her very well.

"You were good out there," Cal said, his first words since they boarded the plane. "I mean, you are really trying to help them. It isn't just the old sales pitch . . . I heard you and I watched them. You were really good."

"Coming from you, Cal, that *is* a compliment!"

"I didn't know if I'd like working with you. I mean, it could have been boring shooting one subject, but it isn't. I have some great shots of the women who asked the questions. Especially the heavier ones. The looks on their faces when you redressed them are great. Even you, Jenna, looked radiant when you saw the results."

"It's a whole lot different than dressing the same size eight. I've learned a great deal this trip. My fabric can really do what I said it would do. It's very rewarding," she went on, "and exhausting. I'm happy Allison has me one week on and a week off. I couldn't go from city to city like this for very long."

"Neither could I," Cal said. "And I'm not up there on a podium like you are," he said, looking over and getting Gloria's attention. "What's next?"

"Day after tomorrow, Jenna has a thirty-second television spot to do. We have to cut a few radio spots on Friday, then the following week, we're back in the studio for a sixty-second spot . . . then nothing until after the holidays," Gloria told him.

"Good," Jenna said. "I'm going to stay home, relax and spend some time with my husband. What are you going to do for the holiday?"

"I'm going to the islands. Get some sun, do a little gambling, relax and prepare myself for a bitch of a tour after that," he said.

"I feel like taking a drive somewhere along a deserted beach, bringing my canvas and paints, and spending the day communicating with nature," Jenna said.

"I didn't know you could paint," Cal said.

"I don't know if I can anymore either. It's been years since I've even felt the need to paint. But I do now. And I'm going to do it," Jenna was definite.


"Okay, Jenna, hold it," the director yelled, Allison smiling with approval, not far behind him. The studio was more alive than a photography session, and much more detailed. Sound men, director's assistants, lighting crew, taping people, script girls, gofers, make-up people, set decorators, dressers, and other assorted hangers-on. Jenna was glad this spot was going to be shot indoors; the next few that Allison had planned were for outside where the crowds would gather, and Jenna was still self-conscious about acting in public. The whole ordeal took hours. Take and retake. Jenna was getting tired of saying the same sentence over and over again. Twenty times, thirty times, and when the commercial was shot, it would be over in a flash. No one ever realized how much time went into it. Jenna had a minute to look around her and watch the set decorators touching and retouching the sets. She had heard that commercials were more detailed than filming a movie, and now she realized why. These people had only thirty seconds to show what they could do. They all were perfectionists.

The background music started up again, then Jenna's large smile, white even teeth, and very *up* voice which was hard in itself to project because she was by nature very soft-spoken. She had to exude the excitement of the product—after thirty takes, it was hard to come up with all that sincerity. She watched Allison out of the corner of her eye and noticed how she lit up the set. She seemed to love the excitement, and, if Jenna hadn't known her better, she'd have thought that Allison was flirting with the director. The first time in more than fifteen years that she's looked at another man. She smiled to herself. *If Allison needs a little diversion after only one lover in her life and two children, more power to her. It isn't my business.* But there was a deeper happiness there. Jenna felt Allison was always superior to her morally and ethically. Now Allison was beginning to act human. After all, didn't Jenna marry Milton, yet have Catherine now and again for diversion? Everyone needs someone. Even that seemed to bother her somewhat. Catherine seemed to go through men more than Jenna ever had, although Catherine tormented herself with each affair's end. It wasn't natural. She wanted something out of the affairs she just wasn't getting. Except for this new one, Jon. *He seems to be keeping her happy. He is very sexy*, Jenna thought. Jenna found herself attracted to him in an earthy fashion. *He'd be good for a one-night fling.*

"We're ready for one last take, Jenna," the director called out.

"I hope this one will do it for you, Jack, I'm getting tired," Jenna said. The music faded in again, and the models started twirling down the steps around Jenna. She read her lines one more time.

"That's a wrap," the director yelled. "Good, I think you're going to like it, Jenna."

"I hope so. I couldn't go one more round. Between the lights and the continuous takes, I was melting."

"And this is only a short one. Next week, be prepared to go maybe two days," he told her.

"Two days . . . for sixty seconds!" she said, in disbelief.

"That's the way it is in this business. When you pay fifty or sixty thousand dollars for that sixty-second spot, you want it to be an attention-getter. In reality, you have to sell your product in one minute. Remember, one minute. So that minute must be the best that it can be."

"He's right, Jenna," Allison came toward them. "Jack's the best in the business. If he likes it, the public will like it. He has a very impressive track record," she said, looking at him.

"Thanks for the compliment. I love what I do and my work shows it. I'm one of those guys who'd rather lose some money and do it right. My name is attached to every spot. And in this business your name is all you have."

"In almost every business . . ." Jenna corrected. "I'm very impressed, Jack, and I am looking forward to working with you again."

"You are the best, Jenna. No compliments, you do what you're told. You should see some of the people I have to direct. I want to pull my hair out sometimes from the aggravation. What egos," he rambled on, Allison hanging on his every word. He was attractive, Jenna guessed his age to be around thirty, dark deep set eyes, dark wavy hair in desperate need of a cut, full beard, nice broad shoulders. She had to admit that he had a great deal of boyish charm. Yes, she approved, if that was what Allison wanted.

"Well, I'm going to call it a day. The car is outside waiting for me, I believe," Jenna said. "Can I drop you off, Allison?"

"Um . . . no, I think I'll stay around a bit longer. Finish up the preparations for next week."

"I'll make sure Allison gets home all right," Jack chimed in.

"I'm sure you will," Jenna thought.


The long black limousine crept down Fifth Avenue with the traffic. Jenna looked up and eyed the bus stopped on the opposite side of the car at the light. Her face was glued onto its side, with the slogan, *If it isn't quality, it isn't a Jenna Jones.* She smiled to herself. She no longer had to look into a mirror to see her own reflection. Everywhere she looked, everything she heard, was full of her. Jenna was seen coast-to-coast on The Johnny Carson Show, Merv Griffin, the Today Show and various syndicated talk shows.

Jenna wondered if she was flooding the market a bit too much. Would people tire of seeing her face? She made a mental note to talk to Allison about it. She'd like to cool it for about six months, then hit them bigger than ever with the jean campaign. She thought about taking a trip to Europe with Milton. Jenna realized he wouldn't be in New York too much longer. Raymond Bertinelli agreed to join the company, taking his father's place. Milton had had intentions of retiring years earlier before he met Jenna, and now he was beginning to become restless. Jenna knew he longed to be on the water, relaxing on his yacht. He looked tired, his age was catching up with him, although Milton would never admit it. Jenna acted as hostess at his dinner parties and company benefits, besides spending a great deal of time going to the theatre and the opera with mutual friends. They enjoyed their social life, but Milton seemed to be tiring of it now. There was a faraway look in his eyes. His mind was elsewhere and Jenna was frightened. Jenna knew he wanted to go back to Europe. She knew that she couldn't leave New York completely, nor did she want to. But, she didn't want to give up her husband. Milton would never ask her to make a decison like that, Jenna kept telling herself. If he did, she'd have to divide her time between New York and Italy.

Jenna's love for Milton changed with the years. Now she felt a deeper love, secure, comfortable, as though they were dear friends. He still made love to her and she adored him in bed, but Jenna found he was not enough. She sensed that Catherine also was feeling the same about her bed mates. As the years went by and they became more adult, both emotionally and physically, the two women felt more secure about their relationship; they found they were getting closer. Jenna and Catherine knew that they would always be there to help each other. In some ways, she was enjoying Catherine more now than she ever thought she could. Jenna was content in knowing that Catherine could now make the choice between the love of a man and the love of a woman. When she was younger, she didn't know the difference. Catherine's tantrums and demands had lessened with time.

The limousine stopped in front of the Bertinelli townhouse. Frank got out of the driver's seat and walked around to open the car door. "Good night, Mrs. Bertinelli," he smiled, and so did she. Frank was one of the few people who called her by her right name.

"Good night, Frank. See you in the morning," Jenna told him.

"Then I take it you don't need the car this evening?"

"I won't. I haven't talked to Mr. Bertinelli today. I'd better check," she said.

"Buzz me, if you need me," Frank told her.

"I will as soon as I can. No need for you to stay if we don't need you. I'm sure you'd like the free time," Jenna said, feeling generous.

Frank nodded and Jenna disappeared into the house. Milton was sitting in the library, holding a drink. Jenna walked in and kissed him.

"You seem to have something on your mind," she told her husband, throwing her sable coat on the sofa.

"I do. How about accompanying me to Italy for Christmas?" Milton looked up at his wife, searching for her true feelings.

"Milton, we made plans. We invited people over here for Christmas Eve dinner. I'd love to go, but do you think it would be fair to our guests to cancel out on such short notice?" she asked.

"I thought of that. Most of them are very good friends and they would understand."

"When were you thinking of leaving?"

"I thought about going right after you finish shooting that commercial of yours," he said, a bit bitter.

"Milton, are you sure that's all that's bothering you?" Jenna asked kneeling down in front of him, taking his hands.

"It's a great many things, Jenna. You're so young, so full of life, and exquisitely beautiful. I wake up each morning and stare at you until you awaken. With each year you grow more beautiful. Age doesn't seem to take hold of you . . . I'm feeling very old in this City. I want to go back to where age has no meaning."

"Milton, why now?"

"Everywhere I look, I see your face, and I'm reminded of the exceedingly great difference in our ages. I love you more today than when I married you. And I wonder how long you will be mine. I think, someday she'll come home and I'll know there's someone else in her life. Someone young, virile, stronger than I. I couldn't stand by and watch. It would destroy me. If I'm in Europe, I'll never know. I'll never see the betrayal in your eyes. Maybe I'll be able to keep you a little longer," he told her, and looked away. Jenna kissed his hands, said nothing for a moment, choosing her words wisely. "Milton, since I married you, I've never wanted any other man. I still don't. I adore you, I'm sure in your heart you believe me," Jenna told him softly. "I think Europe may be good for you. You'e always been happier there. But I'm frightened about not having you with me each night when I come home. You're my best friend, my lover, my father, and most of all, my husband. No man could ever replace you in my heart."

"I know you mean what you're saying at the moment. But . . . I feel I'm cheating you. Life is going by rapidly, and in one swift moment your youth will be gone. I'll be the man responsible for taking it from you. We've been together for ten years. I've been very happy . . . I've been selfish. It's time I let go of you. Gave you your freedom," he said sadly.

"Milton," Jenna started to cry. "I don't want you to go away. I've always felt free being married to you. I think that's why we've been so good together. You made no demands. You've never questioned me. I feel I could have an affair if I wanted, and that alone has made it impossible for me. I had the choice and I chose you. I'm not sorry. I love you. I would be lost without you," Jenna's head was on his lap.

"Jenna, I know but you must now learn to let go slowly. I wouldn't want you to have to deal with the total loss by death."

"Don't . . ." Jenna said. "Milton, you're in perfect health. You're going to be around for a long time . . . did something happen? Did you find out something and you're not telling me?" Jenna panicked.

"No, I'm not dying of a rare disease, my dear, just old age," he said.

"Then I think we'd better go to Europe this Christmas. It will be the best medicine for you. I know after one week you'll be back to your old self again," Jenna told him.

"Maybe you're right. Shall I make the preparations?" he asked.

"Okay, Milton, now I know what this was all about. You made this whole thing up just so you could get me out of here for the holidays," Jenna joked, trying to make him laugh. "What some men will do to get their wives to change their elaborate plans," Jenna said, getting up and smiling at him. Milton smiled back as if to pretend it was all a ploy, but both knew he was very serious.

Jenna spotted the red door a block away. She loved walking down Fifth Avenue after the Christmas shoppers had gone back to their suburban homes. She enjoyed window shopping, comparing her product with the other designers, and she discovered during her vacation that she enjoyed painting again the type of details she used to put into her wallpapers, sheets and quilts. She'd like to one day work on accessories again, maybe bring them into her line. She was feeling alone today, lonely but not miserable. Milton had stayed on in Europe and she had promised to join him as soon as she could. In just two short weeks, he had changed completely, feeling and looking better. Jenna was happy for him.

The doorman opened the red door to Arden's and she walked in. The sales girls recognized her and greeted her warmly. Jenna's eyes caught the familiar butterfly imprint on an evening dress hanging in full display on the first floor. She took the elevator to the fifth floor where Allison was waiting for her. The two decided to have a girls' day out, nails and hair done, facials and cocktails at the Plaza for toppers. They hadn't done anything together which didn't have business attached to it in years. Jenna was a few minutes late, and Allison was already in one of the private pink rooms having her facial. Jenna was escorted to another pink room across the hall. She knocked on the door, letting Allison know she had arrived.

"Always late," Allison shouted.

"At least I'm here. I'll meet you out front as soon as I'm finished," Jenna told her.

They both went upstairs after the facial, had their hair and nails done, and didn't utter a single word of business. They caught up on old news and some interesting new gossip of the day. Feeling ravishing, the two strolled up Fifth Avenue to the Plaza Hotel. They were seated at a table in the Oak Room.

"God, it's been a fun day. I feel like a woman for a change. I'm glad you could join me," Allison said.

"I'm glad you asked. Do you want to tell me why you're getting yourself all done up?" Jenna searched.

"No reason. I felt like it," she said, looking down at her drink.

"Say it again, this time looking me straight in the eye," Jenna teased.

"I'm having dinner with Jack this evening," Allison blurted out.

"Jack, our director?" Jenna made a pretense of surprise.

"I don't know . . . There's something about him that . . ."

"Turns you on," Jenna finished the sentence.

"I woke up one morning, looked over at Michael, and thought, what do I really know about life? I mean the kids today sleep around before they get married. I've only had one man, a good man, I love him, but, to be perfectly honest, I'm curious," Allison said, shyly.

"Curious about what it's like to have another man? Something to compare Michael to?"

"Yes, I have to try. Jack came along at the right moment. He made me feel . . . feel like a woman. He's attentive . . . the old feelings are back . . . the butterflies in the stomach. I sit by the phone and wait for it to ring. I guess my marriage isn't exciting anymore."

"No one's is, Allison. But let me ask you a question. Does Michael please you sexually?"

"Yes, he's considerate, loving, tender. He will never have an orgasm unless I do. He's the perfect mate. There's no question about it. But I would like the opportunity to have someone else," Allison said.

"And what if you like this someone new? Or you like the feeling of the affair? The next time your marriage is in a slump, are you going to go out and sleep with someone else?"

"I don't know. I hadn't thought about it," Allison said.

"And what about Michael? What if he found out? Is your curiosity for one quick roll in the hay worth destroying the years you two shared?"

"I don't know, Jenna, I wish you wouldn't be my conscience. I've gone through this over and over in my head. I've become so bitchy toward Michael as if I resent him for marrying me so young, for not letting me experience this before we got married."

"You wouldn't have. When we went to college, the girls weren't sleeping around as readily as they are today. And you were worse. How long were you and

Michael going out before you went to bed with him?"

"A long time," Allison smiled. "And I had to be in love with him. . . ," she paused in thought. "What else is there to do?"

"Allison, I'm glad you told me. At least I can cover for you. I wouldn't want to see anything happen to your marriage, the kids, and, least of all, the bitterness you'd go through yourself. Do what you have to do, this once, and I'll make sure you don't get caught," Jenna told her.

"Thanks, I was hoping you'd be my ally."

"I never will again," Jenna said. "I don't think you could handle running around the way other women do. You have a conscience and you wear it on your sleeve," Jenna said. "I'll help you, but don't blow it. And remember, don't ever tell Michael in a fit of honesty. You may be making a clean breast of things, but what you'll really be doing is putting the burden of guilt on him."

"I won't tell him. I promise," Allison told her.

"Where are you meeting Jack?"

"Here, in about an hour," Allison blushed.

"So you would have had to tell me," Jenna started. "I didn't have to pry it out of you."

"No," Allison blushed and rattled off the rest. "After we meet here, we'll be playing it by ear. Promise me you'll stay for one drink. This way if I decide to chicken out, I'll have an excuse."

"I'm in no hurry to leave. You give me the signal," Jenna said. "And where does Michael think you are tonight?"

"With you."

"So I've been part of this deal, hook, line and sinker, before I volunteered."

"Jenna, I knew you'd understand. You had three husbands before you got it right. You really couldn't disapprove."

"I do disapprove, but I understand," Jenna said, signaling the waiter to bring them another round of drinks.

"That's it, ply me with liquor. This way I can always say I was too drunk to know what I was doing," Allison said, gulping down the last of her drink.

"You are crazy. This affair is work to you, not pleasure," Jenna laughed.


Jenna sat in the screening room, waiting for the rough cut of her first Jenna Jones' Jean commercial. Allison and Jack were sitting to her right, both talking away excitedly about the biggest campaign in Jenna's career. Jenna wished she could be as optimistic as the two of them. They were caught up in their own world.

This morning she read the first draft of the report Mark had sent to her. It didn't look good. Three other designers were planning to come out with designer jeans within the next six months. Gloria Vanderbilt was among them. Jenna worried if the time gap would be sufficient for her to keep her hold on the market. Would it become flooded with so many designer labels that each and every one of them would only hold a small proportion of the market? And with the other newcomers, there would be an even larger dent in this hold. She hadn't anticipated the quickness of her competitors. They, too, had their spies out. She had been the leader for so long that it would only be natural for them to copy anything she did next.

"We're ready," the voice in the projection room shouted.

"Go ahead," Jack shouted back, and the film started to roll. The music was loud. Twelve girls, all perfectly proportioned, danced in front of her, their lovely asses to the camera, the name *Jenna Jones* on the right back pockets, and the familiar butterfly imprint on the front right pocket. The fifth jean pocket would be her trademark. Camera on Jenna, jeweled, smiling, wearing one of her own expensive blouses and a pair of her jeans, endorsing the new look and the new fit. The commercial was over.

"How do you like it?" Jack asked.

"It looks good, but I think we need to shoot a few more. I want to saturate the country. We don't have much time," Jenna told him.

"Jenna, I don't care how many designers come out with jeans. Yours are different, and you *are* the leader. Remember something. You've had years to develop your design, the others haven't . . ."

"Yeah, when it comes to the best fit and the finest quality, Jenna, we're on top," Allison chimed in.

"I know what you're saying, but I anticipated having a longer run. If the report I have is right, we have less than six months to get our message across—that is if they can afford to sit back that long!"

"According to my polls, the people still idolize you. They're still trying to be you. The others don't have a chance," Allison tried to convince her.

"I know, but their names are just as important as mine. Even Sassoon is coming out with his own line. I mean, too many people are jumping on the band wagon," Jenna said, feeling much too pessimistic for any sales jargon from Allison.

"What's the worst that can happen? We lose some of the market?" Jack asked.

"A large chunk of the market. That's why now is the

time to blow their minds, get as many commercials out—print, radio spots, the works. We'll be ahead of everyone in sales if we do. At least for this year," Jenna argued.

"Look, you're the boss. If you want more commercials, I'll shoot 'um," Jack said. "We may as well make our mark now while we can."

"And if our customers are satisfied, then they won't go over to the other side. We'll keep the repeat sales. Remember, Jenna, we have these jeans in a rainbow of color and different fabrics—velveteen, corduroy, all of them reasonably priced. A young girl can afford to buy three pairs at a time. The others don't have the time to be as elaborate in their planning," Allison pitched again.

"True, I hope we can count on word-of-mouth from our satisfied customers. Allison, check on the progress of the jeans for the fuller figure. I want to push them out sooner."

"I will. I'll put some fire under them." Allison made a note to herself.

"Yes, let's get them all while we have the chance. God. I had the feeling we should have come out last season," Jenna whined on.

"So your competitors would be coming out this season. What would you have gained?" Jack said, getting up. "Pretty lady, they're all following your lead."

Jenna also got up to leave. Nothing they said could stifle her anger. She made a promise to Milton years ago that the jean sales would far surpass any of the other designs she sold. She had to get a look at what her competitors were doing. And, as far as she was concerned, she wished Vanderbilt would stay home and paint. She didn't need her in the game at this late date, especially with the money she had in the till for advertising. Jenna would have to call Mark and find out what he could get on her.

"Allison," she shouted, catching up with her, "I want to push up the dates on the commercials as well as the delivery dates. I don't care how, just do it," Jenna demanded.

"Then you're giving the others time to look at what you've got."

"I'm not worried about that. They'll never be able to duplicate the jeans I've made. If that were the case, we'd be two years ahead of the market," she told her.

"I'll do my best. We're in 5,800 stores now. This isn't any easy assignment. Besides, we can give them early delivery but we have no guarantees they'll put them on the floor."

"They will if people start asking for them," Jenna said confidently. "And with 120 spots a week, they'll ask."

"You're right as usual. I'll get the entire crew on it this afternoon. They'll work late if they have to. With the time change around the country, we're at an advantage," Allison said, looking rather hassled.

"I'm sorry for the extra work. You and Jack have been . . . the best, superb, but this thing has me worried."

"I know I can't say anything that will make you feel better, so I'll do as you say. I still think you are over-reacting. Why don't we share a taxi and talk," Allison tried to comfort her friend.

"How are things at home?" Jenna asked, changing the subject.

"Same. Michael and I are growing further apart.

Especially since the girls are away at school. They used to keep us talking," Allison confided.

"You and Jack have been together a long time. Do you think you'll divorce Michael?" Jenna seemed concerned.

"I don't know. I really don't know how much Michael really knows about what I'm doing. He doesn't ask, and I don't volunteer the information. We're like two strangers sharing the same house. Last weekend we drove up to see the girls. During those three hours we spoke ten words to one another, and that was business," Allison sighed. "For all I know he's seeing someone else."

"How do you feel about that?" Jenna asked.

"I'd like to wring her neck, but I know I can't. If I'm not giving my husband what he needs, someone has to. I know I won't be the one who asks for the divorce. That will be entirely up to Michael," Allison stated. "In many ways I still love him, and, to be perfectly honest, there isn't another man I'd like to grow old with. We've grown up together, shared so much . . . Jack knows how I feel, and I'm lucky that so far he hasn't pressured me into making a decision. If it's at all possible to love two men at the same time, I do," Allison went on.

"It's very possible," Jenna said sadly. "Both men give you different parts of themselves. I hope the whole affair doesn't blow up in your face. I wouldn't want to be around to pick up the pieces."

"How's Milton?"

"Fine. I talked to him last night. He misses me and wishes I could fly over to be with him. Now is not the time. I wish I could convince him to come to New York for a visit."

"He won't?" Allison was surprised.

"Not anymore. He says it's too painful. He feels out of place. He's being childish, but there isn't anything I can do," Jenna said.

"As soon as the commercials are on the air, go see him. Take a week off. I'm sure everything will be fine."

"Allison, it's impossible. If I don't keep my finger on the pulse of this jean war, I could lose everything."

"You're really taking this very hard. I don't understand. You've come out on top all your life. Why not now?"

"Exactly. That's why I'm frightened. I'm reaching for the moon and may miss. I could be wrong and lose everything. How long do you think I can ride this winning streak?"

"As long as you want," Allison said, getting out of the taxi and paying the driver. "You're not slipping in the public's eye, not yet. If you were, I'd be the first to tell you. Believe me, with you, the product, and a six months lead, we won't have a bit of trouble," Allison said confidently.

"I hope you're right," Jenna said, resigned to the issue.

"Have I ever given you the wrong advice?"

"Don't let it go to your head," Jenna came back. "There are a lot of people who'd love to see us fall flat on our asses."

"They'll never see it. Remember when we started? You were the one with the drive. Now you have three times as much drive, and you have my support and Catherine's. We all have too much to lose," Allison smiled. "I wanted to retire a very rich lady, and you promised I would," she said, walking briskly toward her own office. Jenna smiled to herself. *I've created a monster!* Catherine was waiting in her own office when she walked in.

"How'd it go?"

"Good, we're pushing up the dates. Trying to get the most out of our lead."

"I hate to do this to you, but Mark called with another name. I've never heard of them before . . . Jordache?"

"Where the hell did they come from?" Jenna frowned, looking down at the notes Catherine had made.

"I don't know. As Mark said, they're small but they are planning a slam-bang campaign, the biggest he's ever heard of."

"Shit! Well I'm going to give them all I've got. It isn't going to be as easy as they thought," Jenna retaliated. "Catherine, get Mark on the phone. Tell him to dig deeper. I want design plans and advertising budgets," she said.

"Good. I'm glad to see the old wheels turning. I was skeptical for a minute whether what I had to tell you was going to be the straw the broke the camel's back or if it would make you mad enough to fight back. I'm glad you chose the latter."

"Catherine, one more thing. We can't be alone for awhile. I have a feeling this is going to be a dirty fight. I don't need anything being slung at me," she said.

"Like a scandal. Something to mar the great Jenna Jones' image. This is the seventies," Catherine said incredulously. "I mean, more of the designers are fags than straight."

"I don't care. My name will remain clean. And just for the record, I'm going to fly to Italy next week to be with Milton. I want everyone to think I'm unsuspecting of their plans. Let them have their laugh. Let them think they're going to catch me with my pants down. We'll show them!"

Catherine left the office. She hated Jenna's using their intimate relationship as a whipping post. With gay liberation, wife swapping, love-ins . . . why should anyone care if their favorite designer liked an occasional fling with a woman? She wasn't flaunting it in their faces. Her intercom was buzzing as she walked into her office.

"Catherine, scale down the jean design for children. I want to hit them at every end," Jenna said.

"What about jeans for men?"

"I don't know. I've been giving it some thought. I'll give you a decision in a day or two," she said.

Catherine went back to work and made her phone call to Mark. He agreed. He knew what he was supposed to do and he did it well. Jenna had put him on her payroll five years ago. Mark could easily make his way into the office of any designer and find out all the information that Jenna wanted. It didn't take long, and the results were remarkable. Catherine often wondered how Mark got his information. Did he pay for it, steal it or bargain for it? Jenna never cared what she had to pay as long as she got what she wanted. Often she'd beat her competitors to the punch and they wouldn't know how she did it. Now they were trying to get even.

Jenna was lucky. Aside from her, the only people who knew what was going on were Catherine and Allison, both of whom had too much at stake to be bought by a competitor. Jenna was always a smart girl. Giving her two key employees a piece of the action kept them hardworking, loyal, closed-mouthed slaves for as long as they wanted to stay on. The salary Jenna paid for the loyalty was too far out of reach for others to try and steal them away. And it would not cross their minds to leave her.

Catherine placed her head in her hands. She was so very tired and looked it. Whenever things seemed to be slowing down and becoming normal, they got worse—the calm before the storm, an old cliche, but nonetheless very true in this office.

Catherine wondered why she didn't up and quit after all these years. She didn't need the money any longer. She wasn't caught up in the razzle dazzle as Allison was. Nor did she have the drive Jenna had. She had accomplished all she'd ever set out to do. She'd far surpassed her expectations. The answer was simple—Jenna kept her there. Was it all worth it? Her life was a virtual mess. Yes, it was true that she was able to sleep with men. She *had* been for a long time, but not in the conventional way. Jon was the worst.

She had met her match this time. He didn't play hard because *she* wanted to. *He* loved it. He came up with tricks she'd never have thought up in her wildest imagination. And he was insatiable. He could go all day and all night. He loved humiliating her, watching her cower in the corner. The more she fought him, the more he enjoyed it and the more brutal he became. The frightening part was when he couldn't distinguish real fear from play-fear. Lately, Catherine was coming to work with bruises that she covered as best she could with her clothing. She couldn't give him up. He brought her to heights she had never dreamed possible. She was feeling sick inside. She felt like she was slipping away from reality, drifting into a realm of brutality where she punished herself, not even understanding why. Was she still feeling guilty for being in love with a woman and too ashamed to admit it? Why couldn't she openly admit, *I'm gay*, like so many others were doing. No, for the outside world she wanted to be as respectable as Jenna did. Catherine felt weak, defeated by her own insecurity. Even if Jenna said, "Let's move in together. Let the whole world know what we are," would she? She'd gone over it dozens of times with her therapist. Jon punished her for the sin of loving Jenna.

Now Jenna was playing her tricks again. No more evenings together because someone might see them. Someone might think they were playing dirty games. Jenna couldn't afford to dirty her spotlessly clean name. Catherine was discarded. Left to risk being half-beaten to death by Jon.

Catherine went back to work, there was no use dwelling on the inevitable. Jenna wouldn't change her mind. Mark would have to put a rush on the information they needed. Once Catherine could convince Jenna she wasn't in the line of fire, things might be different.

Allison was caught up in Jenna's fury. The sales staff started pushing for early delivery. Jack was arranging studio time for the taping of new, more extravagant commercials. Their ad agency was working overtime. The office was buzzing day and night.

Mark had a full file on her competition within the week. Catherine, Jenna, and Allison sat with him in Jenna's office the entire afternoon going over each detail.

Calvin Klein, as well as the others, were all copying Jenna, each with its own high advertising budget, and name stamped on the left pocket of the ass. Jenna sat back and laughed out loud. "This is ludicrous. I've never seen so many people vie for a market like this. Wouldn't it be funny if I was wrong? If they all followed the leader, and this time the leader was off the track?'' She continued laughing. "Do you know how many millions of dollars we're talking about losing in this industry? It's too funny for words," Jenna went on, everyone else laughing with her in sort of comic relief.

"The way I see it," Allison added, "is that everytime a television is turned on, all that will be heard is one jean commercial after another. It could work to our advantage. The public will be so confused, they'll go with the brand they've always done business with—us. We're beating them at their own game."

"I feel better," Jenna said. "We've got the lead and we'll stay on top. The others . . . Sure they'll make money, but they won't hurt us much. It's going to be too confusing. We'll hold our own, and in time the others will fall to the wayside. They won't be able to keep up with me. The air-time is too expensive."

"And Jenna will come out the victor," Allison shouted, waving her hands over her head. "I told you there wasn't anything to worry about."

"It sounds fine in theory, but I want to see it in black and white. I'm sure, from what Mark tells me, that we'll have over a dozen others trying to come in and grab what they can."

"Especially when they start seeing the numbers of jeans sold each season," Mark stated. "They'll continue to feel there's room for more and more labels. With everyone wearing designer jeans, it's too tempting not to want to jump in and grab a piece," Mark said, summarizing the others' thoughts.

"And we're not selling the jeans for ten or fifteen dollars a pair. They're thirty-five dollars. More than anyone has ever dared ask before," Catherine said.

"Except the French," Allison corrected.

"Even so. I think we've hit something here. When I started, I never knew this would happen. I knew we'd have people trying to compete as always, but never this way. We couldn't fail if we wanted. Everyone will have to own at least one pair of designer jeans."

"Look at all the fun I'll have watching girls' asses walking down the street. For the first time I can say I'm being paid to do it," Mark laughed.

"Well I think we've done all we can do for one day," Jenna said. "Keep on it, Mark. I want to know everything."

"I will . . . just a word of caution . . . People are buying your name and your image. They'll dig up anything they can to get people against you. They might bring up the old marriages, something in your father's deep dark past . . . I don't know. I've known you too long, and you've remained aboveboard as far as I'm concerned. But they may want to make something out of the men you see on a social basis, now that Milton lives in Europe," Mark said. Catherine felt a deep stabbing pain in her chest. Both Jenna and she knew what he was implying. And Catherine wondered how much he really knew about them. Mark was paid very well, but how much could they really trust him?

Jenna escorted Mark to the door. When she returned, Cathering was the only one left in her office.

"Do you think he suspects anything?" Catherine asked.

"I can't be sure. I'll have to watch him very carefully. It makes what I said to you the other day even more important."

"But, Jenna, don't you see? If Mark knows, it was from something we've done in the past. If we stop our regular routine, he'll know we're up to something,"

Catherine urged.

"You might be right. We may be able to trap him. Then I'll know for sure," Jenna stated.

"Do you think he might blackmail you and take the whole pot for himself?" Catherine asked, feeling sick.

"I can't be sure. We may be jumping the gun. He may know nothing or he may know everything. I do know if he gave the information to anyone he could ruin us. That would take him off our payroll. Even if he *is* careful and he can prove the information didn't come from him, I don't think he'd chance it. He'll come to me first," Jenna was sure. "If he does, I'll be ready for him. He was smart though, he planted the seed in my mind today. We'll have to wait it out," Jenna said, sitting back in her chair deep in thought. Catherine left the office. Maybe they were reading too much into what Mark had said. The guilty always seem to over-react.

Jenna picked up her private line. She dialed David White's number.

"Hello, David, Jenna, can we meet tonight for a drink? I have something important to discuss with you."

"I'll have to rearrange my schedule, but if you say it's important . . ."

"It is. Very important," Jenna urged.

"Then I'll be at the office around six."

"No, not here. Do you know where we can talk quietly where no one will bother us?"

"The only place would be my apartment," David said.

"No, I don't want to meet there either," Jenna went on. "I know, let's meet at Michael's office."

"Jenna is everything all right? Are you in trouble?"

"I don't know. I'll see you at Michael's at six,"

Jenna said, not wanting to say any more to him.

"I'll be there," David said, hanging up. Jenna wished she didn't have to be so mysterious over the phone. She might be pulling at nothing.

David was prompt. Michael had given them an office to talk in privately. Michael asked no questions as usual. Jenna was relieved.

"David, I'll get straight to the point. It may be nothing, mind you." Jenna began, while David sat uneasily in the chair across from her. "As you know, I've always used Mark Hammer to get information for me on the industry. I think he may be holding something back," Jenna said.

"He isn't giving you your money's worth?" David asked.

"On the industry, yes, but in a meeting today, he told me the others may be out for blood, trying to undercut my name."

"Was he hinting at blackmail?" David searched for answers.

"I'm not sure. As I said, it may be nothing. But this jean thing is getting too big. Billions of dollars invested. I'd take a bath if something comes out that shouldn't," Jenna stated.

"Jenna, is there something in your past no one knows?" David looked surprised.

"Oddly enough, yes. and I'm not about to tell you about it either. I trust you, David, and you're a good friend, a family friend, that's what makes you more vaulable to me than anyone. I want Mark's office searched and his apartment, too," Jenna told him.

"You want me to hire someone to break into a private

office?" David repeated.

"Yes," Jenna said firmly.

"Jenna, what are they supposed to be looking for?"

"I can't tell you," Jenna said.

"Oh, you're making my job a whole hell of a lot easier," David said impatiently.

"Just bring back anything that pertains to me. I don't care if it's bills, pictures, anything."

"And if there happens to be pictures, you want me to find you the negatives?"

"Yes, and I want you to hire someone you've used before. Someone you'd trust with your life," Jenna said, urging him.

"Jenna, if it's a man you're having an affair with and you don't want Milton to know . . ."

"No, it isn't that at all," Jenna said, nervously pacing her office. "David if I tell you, I don't know how you'll feel."

"Is it about you and Catherine?" he said, shocking Jenna.

"How do you know?"

"I've spent a great deal of time around the girl. I thought, until now, that it was she who loved you. I never saw anything in your eyes which hinted that you returned the affection. I took a wild guess," he said.

"Now you know why I can't let anyone know. If this should get into the wrong hands I'd be ruined," Jenna said.

"In today's society, Jenna, I don't think so; however, I can understand why you would feel uncomfortable. And if it is true about Mark, he wouldn't dare go to anyone else but you. He knows how much the name Jones means to you. You'd be putty in his hands," David said. "That's why I'll do what you want before he tries anything with you. It would only take one payment and you're hooked for life," David went on.

"Oh, thank you, David. I feel better already."

"I can't promise anything, Jenna. Mark is smart. If he does have pictures of you, they won't be easy to find."

"Maybe a month from now," Jenna started. "But I don't think he'd think I'd do something so fast. Time is of the essence."

"Tell you what. Keep up your regular routine. Don't let him know you're onto anything. And I'll do what I can," David said. "There's no reason why you and Catherine can't be together, as long as you don't get . . . personal." David avoided her eyes and looked down at the floor.

"Thank you," Jenna said, bending down and kissing him on his red cheeks.

Jenna met Catherine for dinner and explained what she had done. Catherine felt relieved and went along with the plan. They could see each other, but that was it. They returned to Jenna's apartment and slowly, methodically pulled the place apart for microphones or any bugging equipment. They found nothing in the dining room or living room. Jenna motioned for Catherine to follow her into the bedroom. It was the logical place for him to place the equipment. Jenna moved quietly around the large room, running her hands around the mantle of the fireplace. Catherine worked around the large brass headboard, pulling off the quilted bedspread and sheets. Catherine was remaking the bed when she ran her fingers against the wall and felt a bump. She caught Jenna's eye. Jenna helped her move the massive bed from the wall and saw the small, thin dime-shaped metal microphone glued below the box spring, mounted on the wall. Jenna ripped it off and flushed it down the toilet.

"Well that's one," she said.

"Do you think there's more?" Catherine stared at her.

"I'm sure. I wish I knew how long that thing was there. It gives me the creeps. Someone taping my most intimate thoughts," she shuddered. "God, how can people do it?"

"We've done it," Catherine told her.

"We're not interested in who anyone is screwing," Jenna came back, her eyes icy. "I just want to know what they're designing. We all do it in the business. It isn't a secret. I just do it better," she snapped. "No one is pulling the wool over anyone's eyes. But going into someone's home, taping their every word! That has nothing to do with business. When I get my hands on Mark, I'm going to wring his neck," Jenna shouted.

"Jenna, are you sure it's him? It could be someone else," Catherine said in Mark's defense. She always liked him.

"Who would do a thing like this? David was right. It's a long shot. With today's morality, anything goes. But Mark knows that if he came to me with this information, I'd pay to keep it quiet. It's pure blackmail," Jenna seethed.

"Is it all worth it, Jenna?" Catherine asked. "Is staying on top that important?"

"It is to me. I've worked too damn hard all my life to let some hustler take it away. Once you start paying these guys it never ends," she said. "Besides, Milton is getting much too old to be put in this position. He doesn't need trouble. It would kill him."

"I'm sorry. I was so wrapped up in what it would do

to us, I forgot about Milton. Why don't you come home with me tonight? This place is giving me the creeps," Catherine said. "You don't have to worry, Jon is there, and tomorrow you can call David and have him come here with someone and check the place out."

"Yes, you're right. Only the professionals would know exactly where these things are put," Jenna said, pointing to the toilet.

"Let's get out of here," Catherine said.

"Let me pack some clothes and we'll go. God, I don't know if I'll ever be able to live here anymore. I'd be so suspicious," Jenna said.

Jenna and Catherine arrived at Catherine's apartment a little after two. It had been a long exhausting night for both of them. Jenna slipped off to sleep immediately. Jon rolled over toward Catherine but she rebuffed his advances. He rolled back and went to sleep.


Jenna called David as soon as she got into the office. She told him what she found, and he advised her to stay out of her apartment a few more days. He had put someone on Mark already and should have some news in a day or two. The day crept by, and nothing more was heard from David. Catherine stopped to see Jenna before she left for the day.

"I have to see Dr. Galloway this evening. I should be home around eleven. Would you rather I went back to the apartment with you?"

"No, I'll be fine. I have the key," Jenna stated. "I asked Angenette to drop off more of my clothing at your apartment this afternoon. I'm all set. Go ahead," Jenna smiled. Catherine started down the hall. Jenna got up from the desk and looked out her door.

"Catherine, thanks, I'm glad I had someone to talk to," she smiled.

"Listen, we're in this together. David will make sure everything's back to normal in no time. He's a good man," Catherine said, leaving.

Jenna didn't feel like working any longer and left the office. She decided to walk to Catherine's apartment. There was a bitter chill in the air. She pulled the sable coat tighter around her chest to keep warm. She used her key to get into the apartment. Jon was home, sitting on the couch, wearing tight jeans and an open shirt, watching television when she walked in.

"Hi, Jenna. I just saw your jean commercial on television. It's great. You're going to sell a million pairs," the tall curly-headed man said.

"I hope so," Jenna answered, giving him the once-over.

"Dinner's ready. Nothing fancy," Jon told her.

"Didn't Catherine tell you she wasn't coming home this evening?"

"She never comes home on Wednesday nights, but I thought you'd be hungry. And I'm always hungry," he smiled his little boy smile.

"Can I do anything to help?" she asked.

"No, sit yourself down at the table and I'll serve," he said, jumping up and heading for the kitchen.

Jenna fixed herself a drink and walked slowly toward the kitchen. She stood in the doorway for a while, watching Jon. He didn't notice her. He was moving around like an expert, finishing the salad, putting the potatoes on the platter with the roast. She wondered why he was going to so much trouble for her. She felt herself becoming very attracted to the man in the kitchen. His shoulders were massive, his waist thin, and his legs were endless. She felt like a cat in heat.

"Are you ready to eat, your highness?" Jon joked.

"You really do think of me as an untouchable," Jenna asked.

"Sometimes, when I hear you talk. But as a woman, you're the same as all the rest. You have the same needs and the same wants," he said, eying her up and down.

"And you enjoy pleasing women," Jenna searched, digging into her salad, not realizing how hungry she really was.

"Sure, what man doesn't? It's my vocation. Women are my life."

"Then why live with one woman?" Jenna asked. "Don't you feel restricted?"

Jon smiled, "You're fishing, and you're not getting any answers from me. I like this set-up just the way it is."

"Then you've answered my question," Jenna smiled back.

"I've thought about getting you in bed," Jon said, getting straight to the point. Jenna felt uncomfortable, as if he could read her mind. She knew he was looking right through her clothes.

"I don't remember you ever making a pass at me," Jenna was cool.

"I don't know if I can trust you or not," Jon said.

"Now *you're* fishing," Jenna answered.

"Maybe, but about you and me, not about anyone else. Who you sleep with is none of my business."

"*Touché*," Jenna said.

"You haven't answered my question," Jon was persistent.

"Are you plying me with food in the hopes of a roll in the hay?" Jenna was straight too.

"Why not? You women have been using that technique for years and it works." He lifted his glass to her.

"What makes you think I'm turned on to you?" Jenna was coy.

"Lady, I just know it, and I know if I got you into bed, you'd scream for me. I'm going to prove it to you right now," he said, Jenna getting madder at his assurance. She was madder at herself for getting so turned on that she could hardly stand it.

Jon put down his steak knife and walked around the table. He looked down at her and took her hand. Like a little child she allowed him to lead her. They went into the guest room where Jenna was sleeping and Jon closed the door.

"Why would you take the chance on getting caught?" Jenna said.

"I know Catherine's patterns. She won't be home for hours. And believe me, lady, you couldn't take me for hours," Jon told her. Jenna said nothing more. She watched Jon undress, her eyes focusing in disbelief on his maleness. She sat down on the bed and started taking her own clothes off. Jon wasn't interested in slow, lingering foreplay. He had no desire to undress her. Jenna watched his eyes appraising her body. He nodded approvingly. She blushed. He somehow made her feel ashamed of what she was about to do. Just as she was about to get up and leave, his large hands started to outline her body. She felt a rise in excitement. He worked his way up toward her breasts. They got lost inside his massive hands. Jon bent down and sucked her nipples, biting them, using his teeth until Jenna screamed in pain and pleasure. He didn't stop, but the pain subsided. Abruptly he pushed her legs apart, forcing his finger inside her, then moving it with precision until she reached her climax. He pulled her closer to him, kissed her and flipped her over on her stomach, entering her from behind. Jenna felt a sharp stabbing pain. She relaxed, pushing her body up to him until she was on her knees. Jon's hands were all over her as if there were ten of them. She climaxed again. It was more intense this time. He brought her to her peak several more times. His strokes quickened, plunging deeper until she thought he was going to burst inside her. Suddenly he withdrew and pushed her over on her back, sliding on top of her. She hated the smirk of conquest on his face. Despite herself, she was enjoying him. He was insatiable, holding back longer than any man she had ever known. He had endless self-control. She understood that this was an assertion of mastery—an exquisitely painful game of domination. He had her where he wanted her. When she was ready to scream for him to stop, only then would he come. They made love for more than an hour, Jon thrusting into her, moving her into as many positions as he could think of. Some of them torturous, but she wouldn't scream for him to stop. She bit her lip and kept quiet. He came unexpectedly, his eyes watching her. She hurt, but she smiled at him. He left the bedroom and said nothing. Jenna took a hot bath. Jon's bedroom door was closed when she came out. She returned to her bedroom and closed the door.

She heard Catherine come home. Her bedroom door opened, but Jenna feigned sleep, and Catherine shut the door. Jenna felt relieved. She couldn't face her friend tonight. Her body still ached; Jon had drawn blood. She heard the muffled sounds of talking coming from Catherine's bedroom, then the familiar sounds of the bedsprings. *He's at it again*, Jenna thought. *Unbelievable!* Jenna tossed and turned, hoping to fall asleep. She looked at the clock—it was past midnight. For an instant, she thought she heard Catherine scream. She sat up, not hearing anymore, lay down again, hoping to fall asleep. They were still making love when her eyes closed and she finally drifted off.


Jenna left the apartment before Catherine and Jon woke up. She reached the office early, ordered up breakfast, and pulled herself together. She should be hearing from David today, then she could move back into her own house.

She heard voices out in the corridor, then the door to her office swung open. Cal had his hand on Mark's arm. "I want to talk to her," Mark screamed. "Let me go."

"Let him go," Jenna said coolly. "I'll be all right." Cal did what he was told.

"I'll be right outside if you need me," Cal told her.

"What do you want?" Jenna asked Mark coldly.

"I want to talk to you. I know a few of your goons were in my office last night. The tore the place apart," he said. "Lucky for me, I went back when I did. I wouldn't have known what went on until this morning otherwise."

"I don't know what you're talking about," Jenna told him.

"Cut the crap. Let's be straight for once. You think I'm the one, don't you?"

"What are you talking about?" Jenna looked at him blankly.

"Okay, if you want to play that game, I'll do all the

talking and you'll have to sit and listen. You took my advice the other day, but you picked on the wrong person. Think about it. Why would I want to bite the hand that feeds me? You've been fair with me, Jenna, and I think I've been straight with you. I don't have anything on you. I haven't even tried."

"Then why are you here?" Jenna asked, still not believing him.

"I'm here to get you to think. I want you to give me a chance to find out who is behind all this. I got a clue sometime a few months ago. I had been doing a little checking on my own. Free of charge. I have a lead, but I'd rather not say who it is until I'm sure," Mark went on. "You owe me that."

"I owe you nothing," Jenna told him.

"Listen, Jenna, for your own sake, if you don't let me follow my lead, you'll be the loser. They found nothing in my office. I don't know what they were looking for. I'm afraid if there is something, they'll try to pin it on me. Then you'll be wide open."

"Why do you want to protect me?" Jenna asked.

"Look, you gave me a chance. I'll be honest. I've made a good living working for you. You never questioned my ability, and you've left me to my own devices. I like things the way they are."

"So what do you plan to do?" Jenna asked.

"Give me twenty-four hours. I'll give you proof to knock your eyes out. Jenna, you're going to be hit hard. Your jeans will sell, you can be sure of that, but personally you'll be hit hard."

Jenna was listening to him now, on instinct. Something Milton had taught her: *Go with your instincts, you'll be the winner in the end.*

"I'll give you twenty-four hours. If you can come up

with proof, I'll listen," Jenna told him.

"You won't be sorry," Mark said, relieved. "I have a great deal of respect for you, Jenna. I wouldn't want anyone to hurt you. You're a lady. And no matter how this comes out, you will be hurt. I'm sorry," he said, leaving the office.

Jenna sat back trying to digest all he had said. If it wasn't Mark who had bugged her apartment, then who was it? She didn't have a clue, but maybe Catherine did . . . or Allison.

They all met that morning and discussed it. Allison didn't have a clue. Nothing. Jenna had no more insight into the situation than she did when Mark left. She was impatient. Jenna was tempted to call Mark back and ask him who he had in mind, who he thought it was, if it wasn't him? She thought again, remembering that he would be back in the office in the morning. It would be a long night, but she'd have to wait it out.


David called Jenna. He told her he found what he was looking for in Mark's office. He'd be by with the pictures in the morning. He still wanted to check the apartment. Jenna didn't tell him about Mark's visit. She didn't know what stopped her, she couldn't explain it.

David then told her it was safe to return home; if there were any more bugs in the apartment, they were taken out. She was safe. Jenna thought better about it. She'd stay with Catherine one more night until Mark told his side of the story.


Allison returned home to her apartment that evening. Michael was in the bedroom packing his clothes.

"Are you going on a trip?" she asked, fearing the worst.

"No, I'm leaving for a while . . . until we can sort things out," Michael told her.

"I don't understand. Sort what out?" Allison asked.

"Allison, I shouldn't have to tell you. You tell me!" Michael said.

"Michael, we've been married a long time. Our marriage was bound to go stale at least once. Everyone's does. That doesn't mean we have to separate," she said.

"It does until you can explain your behavior. I think I've been very patient, but my patience is wearing thin. Now I want to go out and experience a little action myself," Michael told her. Allison felt a lump in her throat. He *knew*, and he never said a word!

"Michael, I'm sorry. I didn't mean to hurt you. I don't know what I want right now. All I do know is that I don't want to lose you," she whispered, sitting down on the bed.

"Maybe you won't. I love you very much, Allison. I always have. I think we need breathing space," Michael said, tears welling up in his eyes, Allison had to turn away. She didn't want to cry in front of him.

"I understand. I'd ask you to stay if I thought it would do some good."

"Allison, if you asked me to stay I would. But I think it would be a mistake. Things wouldn't change. Give it a few weeks. We'll meet, talk, and maybe reopen the lines of communication."

"What will I tell the girls?" Allison asked.

"I don't think you have to tell them anything. They're not here. Why upset them?" Michael told her.

"You're right. They won't be home for a couple of months. Maybe we'll have things worked out by then," she told him.

"I hope so. I have one question," he said.

Allison feared the question; she knew what it was and didn't have the answer.

"Do you love him?" Michael asked. "From where I sit, it's the only important thing."

"I don't know. I never wanted to break up our marriage, if that means something to you," she was truthful.

"It does. I'll think about it," he said, picking up his suitcase and walking past her. He stopped at the bedroom door, put down his luggage, turned around and walked over to her. Michael placed his hand under her chin, pulling her face up to meet his. She remained seated. He looked into her eyes, bent down and kissed her on the lips. Allison kissed him back.

"I know some of this is my fault," he said. "I wanted you to know that," he turned and left. Allison heard the front door close and the house fill with loneliness. She ached inside, wanted to cry, but couldn't. She was numb, she couldn't believe he was gone. No scene, no accusations, he was sweet to her until the end. It wasn't his fault, none of it. It was all her fault. Her lust for pleasure, power and excitement. Maybe Michael was right. They needed some space to think about the future. She needed time to re-evaluate her life. She had spent so much time working to help Jenna build her business that she had lost touch with herself. Her girls were grown. They saw very little of her. Michael and she had become virtual strangers. In the beginning they used to spend hours talking, laughing and enjoying each another's company. *Where had the years gone?* Allison thought. The question Michael asked was *not* important. Not to her. If she had to choose, Michael would win. Her relationship with her daughters disturbed her. Could Allison fill the gap she had put between them? If she had another chance, she'd quit. Retire with Michael somewhere in the country and have one more child. A child she could watch grow, watch its first step, see its first tooth, be there for the first words, take it to its first day at school. She wasn't too old to begin again. Many women had children late in life. Michael would love it. He could open a small office in a town like the one they had fallen in love with in Vermont. Be near the girls' school. Was it all too much to hope for? Do people get a second chance? She was dreaming and it was keeping her from thinking about her husband's departure. For the first time in years, she was truthful with herself. She'd quit in a minute if Michael would agree to start again and leave the City. Allison undressed and climbed under the covers in the large empty bed. She thought more about the small town in Vermont. It would be a nice change. She could write part-time, take walks with Michael, have a garden, read. No more talk of fashion and advertising. Yes, it would be a nice way to spend the second half of her life. They could even take all the trips they dreamed about but never did because of conflicting schedules. Even if they had a baby, they could take it along, at least until it had to go to school. When Michael was ready to talk, she'd tell him what she wanted to do. Allison hoped it wasn't too late. She hoped he wasn't too tied into his business to escape. Allison wished that now the timing would be right for both of them. They could change their lives for the better. She never wanted to grow old with anyone except Michael. He was part of her past, part of her being. No one could ever take his place. Jack was a distraction. Although in many ways they shared the same interests, he could never take Michael's place. They'd been a team for more than twenty years. No one could really come between them. Allison felt better until she thought about Michael's feelings. What if he had found someone else? What if he left her to go and stay with another woman? Could she ever win him back? Allison was too tired to think about it tonight. She'd think about it in the morning. She took a sleeping pill and went to bed.

Everyone came to the office early. Catherine, Allison and Jenna sat nervously drinking their morning coffee and emptying a pack of cigarettes. Jenna was the first to speak.

"I wish he'd get here. I can't stand this waiting," she mumbled.

"I finished the sketches of the children's jeans, Jenna," Catherine said, changing the subject. "I like them. John said we could have them in the stores in less than three months. I think we'd better plan an ad campaign."

"So do I," Allison said. "Also, all the stores agreed to put out the merchandise as soon as they receive it. They're as anxious as you are to start the ball rolling. Oh, I saw the commercial last night and it looks good," Allison babbled on. "We're shooting two more next week."

"Let's make a few samples for the kids' line, and the jeans for the fuller figure and shoot them soon too," Catherine said.

Jenna nodded, not paying much attention to what they were saying. They understood and went on with their discussion.

"I heard from our sources that we'll have at least a year's jump on the kids and larger women. That should make you happy, Jenna," Allison said.

"It does. Where is he?" she asked.

"He'll be here and if he isn't, then we know he's guilty," Catherine told her. "It's simple."

"I don't think so. For some reason, I believed him yesterday. I think we're blaming the wrong man," Jenna told them.

Jenna jumped up. She heard Mark's voice out in the corridor. He was talking to her secretary. Jenna ran to the door. "Come in," she beckoned him. He had a large grin on his face. "You got what you were looking for," she said.

"Always. That's why you pay me. This, my lady, is on the house," Mark said, looking over at Allison and Catherine. "I don't want to appear rude, but I think I'd rather talk to you alone," he said.

"Oh, no. I own part of this business too," Allison said, demanding her rights.

"But this isn't really business. We're looking into the personal life of Jenna Jones," he told her. Jenna knew he was right. If he found what she feared, Allison had no right to know, and Catherine would be told later.

"He's right. I'll be fine. I'll tell you what I can later," she said, both Catherine and Allison getting up. Allison was very annoyed. Catherine understood.

When the door was closed, Mark walked across the room and sat down on her couch away from the door. He motioned for her to come and join him. Jenna walked over and sat down beside him.

"You're not going to like this. I hate to be the bearer of bad tidings."

"Get on with it. Nothing would surprise me at this moment," Jenna told him.

"I've got one thing to say. I've brought a lot of proof

because you're not going to believe it at first," he stated, Jenna becoming impatient.

"Who is it!" she shouted.

"David White," he blurted out much to Jenna's surprise.

"You're right, I don't believe you. The man has absolutely no reason to want to hurt me," she said. "I think you're trying to save your own skin."

"Listen to me. I'll start from the beginning," Mark said. Jenna sat patiently waiting to hear his tall story. "Months ago, when I was first told about the jean merchandising, I thought about the competition that was going to go on. I knew you were right and I thought I'd nip any of the competitors in the bud. I had a man stationed in front of your townhouse as a test . . . you know, to see if anyone was following you. Well, someone else was watching the townhouse, too. I went over myself for a few nights, waiting around to see if the guy was going to try something. He never did. I saw you come home late a few times. He never approached you. He watched . . ." Mark paused. Jenna was intrigued.

"I'd never seen the man before, didn't know where he came from, and then I did some checking. I found out that he had been hired by David White," he said.

"How?" Jenna interrupted.

"I have my sources. Believe me," Mark went on. "So I didn't think anything of it. I thought the old guy was trying to protect you or something." Mark stopped and poured himself a cup of coffee. Jenna knew he was stretching this out for all it was worth. She also realized that if Mark had been watching the house he knew about Catherine. "I was bothered about how quickly some of the designers found out about your plans. I started checking the usual sources and came up with nothing. Then I put it all together when my place was broken into. I threw you a fast ball the other night and you caught it. You ran right to David White. Of course, he wanted to cover his tracks and maybe plant something on me. He was never going to blackmail you. The pictures were to get you off the track. What he did do was sell your designs to three of your competitors. Got a pretty penny for them, too."

"I can't believe it," Jenna said. "Why? Why would he want to hurt me?"

"Money . . . He didn't think you'd lose too much by it," Mark went on.

"What makes you think he needs money?"

"He's hurting real bad, Jenna. He made some very bad investments in the market and he's been living above his means for years. The old guy is scared. He figured he could make a half a million on your designs. He knew, as we all do, that you're going to make a bundle on this jean thing no matter who had your secrets. He also know that he was above suspicion. He'd be the last person you'd think of. And when he discovered the pictures, he figured he'd become a hero in your eyes. No doubt you'd have fired me," Mark said. "And, if I read this guy right, he would have convinced you not to press charges. You'd be off the hook and so would he. Since you knew nothing of his financial difficulties, you'd be none the wiser," Mark said, handing over a manila folder.

"Are these the pictures?" Jenna asked, afraid to open the folder.

"And the negatives. They were in his office," Mark told her.

"How do I know they didn't come from your office?" Jenna asked.

"How could they? My office was cleaned out the other night," Mark said. "But anticipating the question, I have a copy of his bank deposits, dates for the last few months, and the sketches. It all fits together. The deposits were made three months ago. And here are the names. I found them in the back of his notebook. Jenna, look at them . . . the same three who came out with those huge ad campaigns."

"You also have a friend at the bank," Jenna said.

"Yes, I do other work. I only promised I wouldn't take any more garment accounts when I signed you on," Mark said.

Jenna opened the folder and looked at the pictures. They were of her and Catherine. The pictures repelled her. Jenna closed the folder.

"What about the tapes?"

"I have those, too," Mark said. "I didn't listen to them."

"What are you going to do with the information you discovered?" she asked.

"Me? Nothing. Frankly, Jenna, I don't care who you screw. It isn't any of my business. It didn't shock me, if that's what you mean. I've been in some kinky scenes myself," he said, trying to make her feel better.

"If David was in trouble, I can't believe he'd go to this length instead of asking me for a loan," Jenna said.

"He couldn't. He'd have no way of repaying you," Mark told her.

"I don't care. The man was good to me all my life. I would have given him the money," Jenna went on.

"He is proud. It seemed like a fool-proof plan. He never anticipated our moving so fast."

"I thought that about you the other night," Jenna said, looking at the bank sheets.

"It must be awful to work your whole life, get used to an expensive life-style, and then, when you need the money the most, in your old age, it's gone. What shall I do?"

"Don't do anything. I'm sure David will call you as soon as he realizes the pictures are missing."

"Are you sure you've got all of them?"

"No. How can I? But I think now that he knows the game is over, he'll destroy the rest," Mark said.

"I feel awful. All I want to do is burn these," Jenna said.

"Are you sure? If the jeans don't work, do you know how much you'd get for the nude pictures of you for some skin books?" he laughed.

"Don't be funny."

"I was just trying to throw a little levity your way," Mark said. Jenna's secretary buzzed her. Jenna answered.

"Yes, Gloria."

"Mr. White is here to see you," she said. Jenna looked at Mark.

"Do you want me to leave?" he asked.

"No, we'd better all sit and talk. It's the best thing. I'm not going to do anything to him."

"I didn't think so," Mark said.

"Send him in, Gloria," Jenna told her. David walked in, looking older than his sixty-five years. He glanced at Mark, then nervously sat down.

"You don't have to say anything, David. I know."

"I thought you did. I'm glad you have someone to look after your interests," he said in a low voice. "My mistake was breaking into Mark's office. He didn't give me time to finish my plan," David went on, Jenna listening.

"You were going to pin this on him?" Jenna asked.

"I didn't have a choice. When you came to me the other night, I was desperate. I kept the pictures in my vault for an emergency such as this, but Mark outsmarted me. I thought if I showed you the pictures, you'd be satisfied," David said. "I'm glad Mark cleared himself. I don't have any excuses for myself. What I did was despicable. I came here to ask for your forgiveness."

"David, I'm not going to press charges. Does Mark have all the pictures?" Jenna asked.

"Yes, they were all in my safe. You won't find any others floating around," David told her. Jenna was relieved. "I'll pay you back everything you might have lost because of what I did. I'll turn over all the money to you," David said.

"No, you need it. We'll survive. I don't think we'll be hit too badly," Jenna told him.

"I'm so ashamed," David said, turning away from them. Jenna walked over to him and placed her hand on his shoulder. What she went through this past week was nothing compared to what David was feeling. She couldn't hate him, she felt sorry for him. "No hard feelings," Mark said, holding out his hand to him. David slowly turned and faced them. His trembling hand reached toward Mark's. Jenna knew that this had been one of the most difficult moments of his life. And he had handled himself with dignity.

It was all over. Time to get back to work. No one knew about the children's jeans and the jeans for the larger women. More importantly, though her three competitors now had her basic design, they didn't know the type of denim she was using. Yes, she'd survive. Jenna called Allison and Catherine into her office. She told them what happened. They felt as she did. They couldn't hate David, they felt sorry for him.

"Do you think he'll try to do something foolish?" Catherine asked.

"I don't know," Jenna said thoughtfully. "Would you put someone on him, Mark? But, be very sure that it's handled discreetly."

"I'll see that he's all right," Mark assured her. "I'd like to sit here all day and chat with you ladies, but I have a very messy office to put in order."

"Send me the bill for the damages," Jenna said.

"No. I'll take care of it," Mark said.

"I feel responsible," Jenna said. "I can't thank you enough."

"For what? Breaking an old man into pieces? I almost wish I hadn't started this whole thing. The damage was already done, we can't rectify it," Mark said, feeling as badly as everyone else. He left.

"Well if everything is under control, I think I'm going to go to Europe as soon as possible to be with Milton. I shouldn't be gone for more than ten days . . . two weeks at the most," Jenna said.

"I think you need the rest," Allison told her. Catherine agreed. Jenna was free to go back to her own home, leaving David White and Jon behind her.


Allison sat at her desk and read the early sales reports on the newly-delivered jeans. It was less than a month and ninety percent of the stores were reordering. They couldn't get the jeans in fast enough to keep up with the demand. Allison was thrilled; they were making an impressive first start. The jean commercials were shown during prime time, as many as six or seven spots a day.

Jenna had a hold on the best spots for six months, renewable at that time. It was a hard contract to pull off but Allison could work miracles. Within the next few months, Jenna started seeing ads by her competitors. Sometimes the jean commercials appeared on television back to back, but the other labels were not selling enough to cut into her profits. Jenna was still the highest selling jean manufacturer in the country.

Jenna sat soaking in the sun on The Jenna II, Milton below, enjoying drinks with some of his Italian cronies. For a time Jenna felt at peace with herself and with her future. Yet the sight of those pictures still left a sour taste in her mouth. She hadn't been able to spend any time with Catherine since then. She had to go back and finish what she started so long ago. Jenna had to learn how to let go. *Let go of Catherine*, she told herself. Maybe then, Catherine would find some peace in her own life. She might even be able to find a man and have a normal relationship. Jenna had had a narrow escape from personal ruin. A horrifying fate. She had burned the pictures and the negatives in her fireplace the night Mark gave them to her. No one else had seen them. Yet they stayed indelibly printed on her mind. She couldn't stand the thought of anyone or anything being revolting in her life. Jenna's thoughts passed on to Michael and Allison. They, too, were having a difficult time. Jenna hoped that with time and effort they could put the marriage together. Start over and put the past behind them. It was a horrendous year for all of them.

Michael sat alone in the darkened restaurant sipping

his martini. Allison was late. Michael was getting impatient. This was supposed to be the new Allison. The girl who wanted to quit her job and start life anew. The woman who wanted to leave the glamor and excitement behind her. Michael decided to give his wife five more minutes, enough time for him to finish his drink. If she didn't arrive, he'd leave. He put his drink down on the table and started to light a cigarette, then he saw a familiar shape walking toward him. The same girl he met in college but more assured, more sophisticated, and if it was possible, more beautiful. She sat down at the table, breathless.

"I ran all the way. I'm sorry I'm late. Jenna called the office just as I was leaving. She sounded wonderful," Allison said. Michael signaled for the waiter to bring a drink for his wife.

"What is she up to?" Michael asked, half-interested.

"She wanted to tell me when she was flying back. Next Tuesday," Allison went on. "How was your day?"

"Same as usual. Thought about what you said the other night . . ."

"About giving up the business and moving away?" Allison sounded excited. "What do you think? Is it worth another try?" Allison went on.

"It sounds ideal. I don't know if I can drop everything and go on my merry way. My grandfather started the law firm. I'm too young to up and leave it," he said.

"But Michael, you have competent partners. I'm sure you can leave the business in their hands."

"I'll have to be on call. Stay on at the firm as a consultant."

"That sounds like a good idea. You wouldn't have to report to the office daily, and maybe you can handle most of the work from Vermont."

"I could," Michael said hesitantly. "I don't know. How long do you think it would be before you got bored?"

"Never. I've had enough excitement for one lifetime." Her voice was enthusiastic. "Michael, I know you think it's a good idea. I believe you're afraid more for me than for yourself!" she fished.

"Maybe you're right. I am afraid. I know I can be happy in Vermont," he said. "Then I think I'll wake up one morning and see the look of boredom on your face, and know it's all over. I couldn't stand it, Allison. I'd rather go on like we are here than live in false hope."

"You won't. I promise. I've given it a great deal of thought before I even talked it over with you. I know it's what I want," Allison pleaded.

"You think you can get everything cleared off your desk in six months?"

"Yes. I intend to tell Jenna when she returns. Then I'll look around for a replacement and spend the rest of the time training the new girl. I'm sure the company can go on without me," Allison said, feeling relieved.

"Allison, I like the idea very much. I hated living alone the past few months. I'm uncomfortable around any other woman but you."

"You didn't like the dating scene?" Allison kidded.

"No. I'm too old fashioned for today's women. What a difference. I think my head's been buried in the law books too long. You take a woman to dinner, and right away she invites you up to her apartment. What happened to the courting stage?" Michael asked, looking adorable.

"They don't believe in it any more. I've heard women say the same thing. One drink, and the man wants to get into my pants," she mimicked. "I don't think we fit out there," Allison said.

"But you did sleep with Jack?" Michael asked the question Allison hated.

"I don't want to talk about it. That was different. He really loved me," Allison told him, not able to look her husband in the eye.

"And he doesn't love you anymore?" he asked.

"I made my choice. I guess he knew he didn't stand a chance against you the whole time. Michael, let's not go through this anymore. It has to be painful for you."

"It is. I still can't picture my wife making love to another man . . . I don't know if I can ever forget."

"Then I don't see how we can plan for the future until you can put it out of your mind. I can't sit here . . . see the sadness in your eyes and feel the contempt you must have for me. I know you were hurt. I said I was sorry and want to go ahead with our lives, but you have to decide if you want to put the past behind you, too," she said, getting up and leaving. Allison stood outside the restaurant. She knew she had been hasty. She couldn't go on being accused, being browbeaten for the only mistake in her life. *Damn it, everyone is entitled to slip back once*, she thought. *How long was Michael going to stay bitter?*

The telephone was ringing when Allison walked into the apartment. She was too tired to answer it. If it was Michael, let him sit back and think about how he was ruining their last chance to be together.


The Bertinelli board members sat in the conference room looking over the latest figures. The first work-up since the other designers actively started selling jeans to all the stores. Their expressions were impassive, they turned the pages methodically, eyeballing each number. Jenna sat at the end of the table waiting for someone to say something. Raymond Bertinelli looked up first and flashed a large grin at Jenna. The others closed their files and looked up. Raymond was the first to speak. "You've done it. I can't say we all weren't apprehensive about the competition. Especially now when the ads are flying in between every television program from seven to midnight," he started. "We're way ahead, and it would take a miracle for any of the others to catch up."

Jenna nodded approval, remembering how much more nervous they all would have been had they known the plans were stolen. "I think it's time to start coming out with the coordinates . . . blouses, shoes, boots, scarves, jackets to go with the jeans," Jenna said. "They've hit bigger than I even expected. You walk down the street today and all you see are women, even men, wearing designer jeans. It's as if all other clothes have been abolished from their closets," Jenna went on.

"The sales from your other designs have not fallen though," Raymond said.

"I know. I don't understand it. I guess the women wearing dresses and skirts must be wearing them at home," Jenna laughed and they all laughed with her.

"You know, Jenna, anything you want to do is fine with us. Let us know when you have the report finished, time dates, quantity, the usual," Raymond said. "I've taken the liberty of sending a copy of this report to father. I know he's going to be thrilled."

"I'm glad you did," Jenna said, rising and the rest followed suit. One by one they walked over to her, shook her hand and filed out of the conference room. Raymond stayed. "How is he, Jenna?"

"He looks wonderful. He's very happy living on his

ship. You know your father; he'll live to be a hundred," she smiled.

"I was pessimistic about the marriage, and I know I haven't been too friendly toward you all these years, but you've shown me I was wrong. Dad was right again. You've been good to him, and you've certainly been kind to our mills. We've made a great deal of money on your name." Raymond stopped. What he was saying was harder than he thought it would be. "I want to apologize and I'd like to be your friend," Raymond went on. He searched Jenna'a eyes for the answer.

"Well. It's been a long time. I never felt uncomfortable around you, though I knew it must have been difficult for you to accept a stepmother younger than yourself. It wasn't bad enough that I was marrying into the family, you also had to put up with me in the business, too. You've been more than polite all these years. I would have wanted to slit your throat had the positions been reversed," Jenna smiled, and Raymond knew it was all up hill for them from that point.

"Well, the others are waiting. I'll be taking a more active interest in you, Jenna. I've pushed your account off on the others too long," Raymond said, Jenna walking with him to the door. "We'll talk soon," he said. Jenna nodded and thought how unlike Milton Raymond was. He had none of his father's instincts, none of his sensitivity, and none of his charm.

Jenna walked through the office looking for Catherine. She'd been acting strange lately. Although she hadn't mentioned it, Jenna was sure that she was having problems with Jon. Catherine was nowhere in sight. Both her partners were in emotional limbo, although the business was flourishing.

Jenna had kept her word—she was staying away from any personal contact with Catherine. It was getting to her designer. Catherine was feeling the loss and looking the worse for it each day. Jenna had explained to Catherine why they had to stop seeing one another, but Catherine was still hanging on. Now she had to get tough, maybe even cruel. Catherine had to let go. Jenna had to make Catherine believe that there would never be anything more between them, there was no hope. Jenna walked back to her office, sat down and went back to work, the work she once loved more than life itself. Now it had become a regular routine. She thought back on all the ups and downs they had had. The struggles, the fights, the near bankruptcy. Their climb to the top. Jenna wondered how different it would have been if her father didn't mysteriously come into her life. What would have happened to her if he hadn't been the first to take the chance on her? Would she have made it? Jenna felt it was time to take out the small picture of her mother and father and put it in the silver frame she bought in France and place it on her desk. She was no longer ashamed of what was once her childhood. She no longer feared the gossip and stories the media played up. Many articles were written recently, but she had no inclination to read them; if she happened across one, she read it as though it were a story about someone else—not her. The little girl they wrote about no longer existed, neither did the man. He was gone, loved by some of the people who still talked about him not knowing who he really was. How all his life he kept the deep secret to himself, was incredible to Jenna. Her father had a lot of guts, she thought. She must have inherited his srength and determination. She was more her father's daughter than her mother's.

Grandmother had retired to Palm Beach, wrote occasionally, but stayed out of her life completely. It was almost as if she had become jealous of her. When she married Milton, her grandmother was not at the wedding. Jenna couldn't remember the excuse she gave. But Jenna had turned out differently from what the old girl expected. She stuck to her designs, made more money than she inherited, and was now her own person.

Many things went through Jenna's mind that afternoon. She even thought about old Doctor Hernandez. The speech he gave her three lifetimes ago. *Are you ready to make an irreversible decision? Could you look back years later and say without a shadow of a doubt that you weren't sorry?* No, she couldn't. Jenna remembered sitting in bed with Milton one evening after they had made love. He had asked her if she wanted a baby. He knew he was old, but she was still in the prime of her life, and he would be happy to give her a child. Yes, she would have wanted *his* child. But she told him the only thing she could tell him—all that she needed in life was him. Was he hurt or contented with her response? She didn't know, and the question never arose again.

Jenna felt tired, drained, restless. Blouses next, shoes, maybe perfume, jewelry . . . her empire. Yet the thrill was gone. For a moment she wished that David had done a better job, hurt the business so that she could have the challenge of putting it together again. Jenna knew she wasn't the only one who felt this way. Allison was slowing down. Catherine was taking more time off. They were losing interest. How could she blame them? She was losing interest herself. She had nothing more to prove, and really nothing more to gain. The company was solid, it would go on forever. In time, someone would come to her and ask if they could buy her out; buy the name, use it and keep the company going. Jenna placed the picture frame on her desk. It gave her solace to look at it. There were her beginnings. And she had kept all her promises. Jenna heard a knock on her door. Allison walked in and sat down across from her.

"We've sent out the reorders," she said, but Jenna wasn't really listening. Allison caught it. "It's been one of those days. I don't feel like working either," she said.

"Thinking about Michael?" Jenna asked.

"Yes, and life in general. Oh shit! Why aren't we jumping around the office? We're number one. We made it despite the spies, the competition, the struggle. We made it and it looks like we're going to hold the position," she said. "So how come I feel lousy?"

"The challenge is gone. What we need is another challenge," Jenna started. "We need to tap a market we've never tried before," Jenna said. "And I think I've got it . . . men's clothes. Turn it around . . . instead of men looking at women dressed in our sexy line women will be chasing men wearing our designs." Her voice was becoming more enthusiastic. "I need something new, and we've got the best team around. It will take time, probably years, but what the hell, I'm sure we can do it," Jenna stated.

"I wondered how long it would take before you decided to tap that market. You can do it, I know you can, but not me. I'm going to quit. I'm going to try and get my marriage together again. Michael and I have been talking, not too successfully, but it's a start. We would like to start over again. Move away from the City. Retire to a small town near the girls' school," she said, watching Jenna's face, the smile wiped away with shock.

"Allison, you can't. I know you, you'd go crazy in less than three months. Your heart's in this industry. You thrive on the challenges. You'd never be happy."

"I don't think you're right this time. I want to give it a try. I'm going on my gut instinct. Jenna, I can leave this town tomorrow without a second thought. As usual, I'm doing everything backwards," she smiled. "Most women are supposed to raise their children, then, when they go off to school, return to work and pick up their career. At least it was that way when we were young," she said.

"Today, all women are working, trying to make ends meet," Jenna interrupted.

"I don't have that problem. Early on we could have lived comfortably on what Michael earned, especially after he started representing you. Now I don't feel I'm working for any gain. We have enough money to retire and live any way we want." Jenna's silence made her nervous. "I'm tired, worn out and, as the expression goes, burned out. I don't feel as though I have anymore to give," she said, pacing Jenna's office. "I hope you understand. The children's jeans will be my last campaign."

"What if Michael doesn't agree to your plan? What if he doesn't want to come back to you?" Jenna asked.

"Then I'll go without him. There are places I'd like to see, things I'd like to do; maybe write at my own leisure, take a good look at life, slow down. The years have gone by so fast. I feel as though I've been on a merry-go-round and now I'm too dizzy to stay on any longer."

"I know how you feel, but I'd feel much better if you would take a leave of absence . . . a year, two . . . as long as you want. Just so you know you can always come back." Jenna was taking her resignation much better than Allison had expected.

"I don't want you to have false hopes. Once I leave, I know it will be for good," she said.

"I remember, years ago, having to pitch you day and

night to come and work for me. You were just as stubborn then, and I got my way," Jenna smiled. "You'll be back."

Allison got up, took a long look at Jenna sitting on her throne, and felt a twinge of remorse. Jenna was lying to herself. She knew as well as Allison that it was over. She'd never be back. As she said, Allison had to be talked into coming to work. She never wanted to live her life the way she had. Allison had to be honest, she was seduced by the business, she had it in her blood for a time. She lusted for success as the rest of them had. She was guilty of the same needs, wants, and drives that kept them in business. There were times she coaxed Jenna to keep going when all seemed lost. But the glitter seemed tarnished to her now. Quiet and contentment was all she wanted. She had her girls, her husband. Jenna, in reality, had no one. *Jenna Jones, Inc.* was her child, lover and husband. It always had been and always would be. Allison knew in time that Jenna would see her dream for men's clothing come to be. She'd probably be very successful, using her charm and her sex appeal to lure the skeptics.

Allison passed Catherine's office on her way to her own. Catherine was hunched over the drawing board. Her eyes were red and swollen. Allison went in and shut the door.

"Do you want to talk about it?" she asked. Catherine jumped up as if she were caught in her own thoughts.

"It's nothing. I've had a bad day. Jon left me the other night and I'm feeling a bit blue. I'll get over it," she rambled nervously.

"We corporate women are having a fine time keeping our mates," Allison said.

"I didn't want to bother you with it," Catherine said. "You have your own problems. I can't even come close to the years you've spent with Michael."

"But the hurt's still the same," Allison soothed. "Is it permanent? Do you think you can patch things up?"

"I don't think so. He came by last night and took the rest of his belongings. I guess one would say it's final," Catherine broke down again.

Allison walked over to her and hugged her. "It will be okay. You'll live. It takes time for the hurt to leave, but they tell me it does," Allison consoled her friend.

"I know I'm acting like a fool. But Allison, it's so lonely. I hate going home at night. I hate having no one to talk to. I have no one to blame but myself. I should have straightened out my life a long time ago and found a nice man and married him. But I was grasping for something more," she said, meaning one thing, Allison taking it another way.

"We are all guilty of the same dream," Allison told her.

"What am I going to do?" Catherine sobbed. "I can't go on like this anymore." Allison held her but didn't know how to make the hurt disappear. Catherine was in real pain.

"Do you want to tell me what the fight was about?" Allison asked, for lack of anything else to say.

"It was silly," Catherine said.

"They usually are," Allison interrupted.

"It wasn't the one fight. It was a series of things. I don't know how to explain it. He wanted more from me than I could give. I don't want to talk about it. I have to get these sketches finished," Catherine moved away, and sat back down at the board. "Thanks for being here," she timidly smiled. Allison walked out. She knew Catherine was telling her something. There was much more than met the eye. But she couldn't pry it out of her. If Catherine wanted to talk about it, Allison would be willing to listen.

Catherine felt relieved when Allison left. She almost blurted out the whole story. She was tempted to tell her what really happened, and why she was so upset. But as always, she was sworn to secrecy. Now someone else shared her secret and she was scared. Jon had been in a foul mood for a long time; he had been out of work for over a month and the monotony was getting to him. Catherine was coming home later every night from the office, and Jon was jealous. She tried to ignore Jon's temper tantrums but found him impossible to reason with. He was in bad shape when she returned home after ten the other night. Catherine found him sitting on the couch, the television on, his clothes strewn all over the floor and the kitchen a total wreck. Catherine was too tired to clean up after him. She walked past Jon and straight to the bedroom. He stormed after her.

"No hello, no how was your day? What's the matter? The working girl too stuck up to talk to the unemployed slob?"

"I just didn't want to get into a fight tonight. I'm too tired."

"Being overwhelmed by madam highness," he mocked Jenna, "I mean, when she gives an order, my dear Catherine jumps. Why the hell can't you tell her to go shove it, that you want to come home early one night."

"God, Jon, you sound like a bored housewife on a sitcom. The woman is trying to run a business, meet her deadlines. I have an important job to do," Catherine went on, weary of his ridicule.

"Do you know you spend more time with her than in this house with me. If I didn't know better, I'd wonder if there was something going on between the two of you," Jon said sarcastically. Catherine clenched her fists, and said nothing. "But then again, I've had the lady in bed, and she doesn't seem like the type who would go for a weakling like you," he taunted her.

"I know what you're trying to do, and I'm not going to let you get to me. Jenna would never stoop to going to bed with you," she shouted, losing control.

"Oh, no? Don't you remember when she stayed with us, the night you didn't come home for dinner. We were here alone, and it didn't take much to get her into the bedroom. I fucked the living sense out of her," he went on enjoying Catherine's hurt.

"Stop it! I don't want to hear anymore! I don't care what you did," Catherine said, believing him.

"She's a much better lover than you. She likes a man to be gentle, caress her and kiss her body, smother her with affection," he smiled. "I love making love to her."

"So do I!" Catherine shouted before she knew what she was saying. Catherine watched his expression change, from victory to defeat. She had gotten to him.

"You're lying," he yelled.

"No, we've been lovers since college. I'm the only one in her life. She laughs at you men, you mean nothing to her," Catherine went back at him with full fire.

"You're sick, repulsive, I could never touch you again," he told her, picking up his jacket and leaving the apartment. Catherine collapsed on the sofa and broke down in tears. She not only lost him, but she broke her promise. Jon was devious, he might go to Jenna and confront her with the information she had given him. Jenna would be so furious she'd never talk to her again. God! What did she do? How could she have fallen into his trap?

Jon didn't come home that night, nor the next night. Catherine was frightened. She was walking on thin ice. She didn't tell Jenna what happened for fear she'd blame the entire incident on her, but she also was angry at Jenna for letting Jon make love to her, in her house, when she was trying to help her. It was the slap in the face Catherine hadn't expected.

Jon came by the apartment a few days later. He hadn't expected her to come home so early. He was hoping to slip out with his things without having to see Catherine. Catherine saw the suitcases neatly piled in the hallway, and she could hear him opening and closing the drawers in the bedroom, checking for a forgotten item. She heard him walking toward her, she stood firm, and met his glare. Jon didn't say anything. He placed the key to the apartment on the table and started to pick up his luggage.

"Jon, I wish you'd forget what was said the other night. I'm not asking you to stay, I'm asking you to keep my personal life secret," she asked humbly.

"I don't give a damn what you do. I'm not going to your precious lover to tell her anything," he said. "You can both rot in hell for all I care," he told her, still bitter. Jon walked past her and closed the door behind him. Catherine couldn't move. She hoped she could trust him to keep his word. She couldn't take much more.


Catherine ripped up the sketch she was working on. It wasn't right, nothing was right. Why was everything and everyone closing in her?

She couldn't go on like this anymore. She had to confront Jenna, talk to her about their future. The fear of getting caught had to stop.

Catherine, waiting until everyone had left the office, walked quietly into Jenna's inner sanctum. She watched her deep in concentration, working on another damned report. Jenna felt her presence. The cold green eyes pierced right through Catherine. How desperately she needed to feel Jenna's warm inviting body and hear her say that everything would be fine, they'd leave the craziness behind them and go away together. But it didn't happen. Jenna was cruel, cold, crushing every hope Catherine had. Later, alone in her bedroom, she tried to remember Jenna's exact words. All Catherine knew was that Jenna had been firm—no hope—nothing would change her mind. Catherine wasted her entire life on a dream she'd never see come true. All of them had dreams. Allison had hers and Jenna . . . Jenna's were the most spectacular. They had all come true. But Catherine's . . . her's were the least demanding . . . the least rewarding and would never come true.

*Why* Catherine screamed, hiding her head in the pillows on her bed. *Why was I the loser?* she thought. *Why did I have to be the one who got hurt? I'll fix her! I'll show her she can't get along without me! The precious company will fall on its ass without my talents. If I wasn't around what would she do? Who would design her clothes? Who else knew the way she thought—what she wanted besides me?* The pain subsided momentarily as she walked toward the medicine cabinet. Jenna would receive the ultimate punishment. With a steady hand, Catherine reached for the bottle of sleeping pills. Poured herself a glass of water and without hesitation swallowed a handful of pills. She walked to her bedroom, undressed and calmly got into bed, drawing the large-printed quilt over her body. Catherine was at peace.

## *EPILOGUE*

Jenna watched as the others left the cemetery and drove away. Michael and Allison were waiting for her in their car. Catherine was dead, Allison was preparing to go off and start a new life with her husband. The business was all hers. Her dream, her power and her name.

Jenna took one more look down at Catherine's mahogany casket. *What a waste*, she thought. *Why were the most sensitive, creative people the most self-destructive? Catherine, you really didn't hurt anyone but yourself by taking your life. I'm still here. I'm still breathing, living, working. Life will go on for me. I will miss you, now more than ever, but in time you will be a fond memory. I wasn't worth taking your life. No one is*, Jenna said softly, and walked toward her limousine.

Michael and Allison watched her get into the car. They started their motor when they saw her car take off. Michael followed behind. Jenna took a deep breath, and felt a weight lift from her shoulders. The past is past, it's as dead as Catherine. The future was all Jenna looked forward to. And from where she sat, it looked very bright.